THE PAINTED DRUM

THE PAINTED DRUM

LOUISE ERDRICH

■ HarperCollins*Publishers*

Grateful acknowledgment is made to the editors of *The New Yorker*, where the
chapters "Revival Road," "The Painted Drum," and "The Shawl" appeared in
slightly different form.

Nothing in this novel is true of anyone alive or dead.

Designed by Elliott Beard

ISBN 0-7394-6447-7

To my daughters

PART ONE

REVIVAL ROAD

1

Revival Road

Faye Travers

Leaving the child cemetery with its plain hand-lettered sign and stones carved into the weathered shapes of lambs and angels, I am lost in my thoughts and pause too long where the cemetery road meets the two-lane highway. This distraction seems partly age, but there is more too, I think. These days I consider and reconsider the slightest of choices, as if one might bring me happiness and the other despair. There is no right way. No true path. The more familiar the road, the easier I'm lost. Left and the highway snakes north, to our famous college town; but I turn right and am bound toward the poor and historical New England village of Stiles and Stokes with its great tender maples, its old radiating roads, a stern white belfry and utilitarian gas pump/grocery. Soon after the highway divides off. Uphill and left, a broad and well-kept piece of paving leads, as the trunk of a tree splits and diminishes, to ever narrower

3

outgrowths of Revival Road. This is where we live, my mother and I, just where the road begins to tangle.

From the air, our road must look like a ball of rope flung down haphazardly, a thing of inscrutable loops and half-finished question marks. But there is order in it to reward the patient watcher. In the beginning, the road is paved, although the material is of a grade inferior to the main highway's asphalt. When the town votes swing toward committing more money to road upkeep, it is coated with light gravel. Over the course of a summer's heat, the bits of stone are pressed into the softened tar, making a smooth surface for the cars to pick up speed. By midwinter, the frost creeps beneath the road and flexes, creating heaves that force the cars to slow again. I'm glad when that happens, for children walk this road to the bus stop below. They walk past with their dogs, wearing puffy jackets of saturated brilliance—hot pink, hot yellow, hot blue. They change shape and grow before my eyes, becoming the young drivers of fast cars who barely miss the smaller children, who, in their turn, grow up and drive away from here.

As I say, there is order, but the pattern is continually complicated by the wilds of occurrence. The story surfaces here, snarls there, as people live their disorder to its completion. My mother, Elsie, and I try to tack life down with observation. But if it takes a lifetime to see things clearly, and a lifetime beyond, even, perhaps only the religious dead have a true picture of our road. It is, after all, named for the flat field at its southern end that once hosted a yearly revival meeting. Those sweeping conversions resulted in the establishment of at least one or two churches that now seem before their time in charismatic zeal. Over the years they merged with newer denominations, but left their dead sharing earth with Universalists and Quakers and even utter nonbelievers. As for the living, we're trapped in scene after scene. We haven't the overview that the dead have attained. Still, I try to at least record connections. I try to find my way through our daily quarrels, surprises, and small events here on this road.

We were home doing pleasant domestic chores on a frozen Sunday in the dead of winter when there was a frantic beating at our door. In alarm, Elsie called me. I came rushing from the basement laundry to see a young man standing behind the glass of the back storm door, jacketless and shivering. I saw that he'd lost a finger from the hand he raised, and knew him as the Eyke boy, now grown, years past fooling with his father's chain saw. But not his father's new credit-bought car. Davan Eyke had sneaked his father's new automobile out for an illicit spin and lost control coming down off the hill beside our house. The car slid toward a steep gully lined with birch. By lucky chance, it came to rest pinned precisely between two trunks. The white birch trees now held the expensive and unpaid-for white car in a perfect vise. Not one dent. Not one silvery scratch. Not yet. It was Davan's hope that if I hooked a chain to my Subaru and backed up the hill I would be able to pull his car gently free.

My chain snapped, and the efforts of others only made things worse over the course of the afternoon. At the bottom of the road a collection of cars, trucks, equipment, and people gathered. As the car was unwedged, as it was rocked, yanked, pushed, and let go, as different ideas were tried and discarded, as the newness of the machine wore off, Davan saw his plan was lost and he began to despair. With empty eyes, he watched a dump truck winch his father's vehicle half free, then slam it flat on its side and drag it shrieking up a lick of gravel that the town road agent had laid down for traction.

*   *   *

Over the years our town, famous for the softness and drama of its natural light, has drawn to itself artists from the large cities of the eastern seaboard. They have usually had some success in the marketplace, and can now afford the luxury of becoming reclusive. Since New Hampshire does not tax income, preferring a thousand other less effective ways to raise revenue, wealthy artists find themselves wealthier, albeit slightly bored. Depending on their surroundings for at least some company, they are forced to rely on those such as myself—a former user of street drugs cured by hepatitis, a clothing store manager fired for lack of interest in clothes, a semi-educated art lover, writer of endless journals and tentative poetry, and, lastly, a partner in the estates business my mother started more than fifty years ago.

At any rate, one such artist lives down at the end of our road, in a large brick cape attached to a white clapboard carriage house (now studio). Kurt Krahe—last name correctly written with an umlaut, a vampire bite above the *a*—is a striking man. Formerly much celebrated for his work in assemblages of stone, he has fallen into what he calls the *Zwischenraum*, the space between things. Kurt has lost his umlaut to American usage, but he loves German portmanteau words. Sometimes I think he makes them up, but *Zwischenraum* is real. It is the way I see the world sometimes. Kurt has fallen into the space between his own works and is now mainly ignored. He hasn't done a major piece in years. Often, his sculptures incorporate native slate or granite and to help with the massive project of their execution he occasionally hires young local men. Krahe's assistants live upon the grounds—there is a small cottage sheltered by an old white pine—they are to be available for work at any time of day or night. There is no telling when the inspiration to fit one stone a certain way upon another may finally strike.

Kurt's hands are oddly, surprisingly, delicate and small; they remind me of a burly raccoon's hands, nimble and clever. His feet are almost girlish in their neatly tied boots, a contrast to the rest of him, so boldly cut. I'm always curious about the stones that Kurt chooses for possible use. I inspect the ones he's kept and I think I know, sometimes, what it is about them that draws him. He says that the Japanese have a word for the essence apparent in a rock. I ask him, why don't the Germans? He says he'll think one up. I suppose that I love Kurt for his ability to see that essence, the character of the rock. Only, I wish sometimes that I were stone. Then he would see me as I am. Peach-colored granite with flecks of angry mica. My balance is slightly off. I suspect there is another woman— maybe on his trips to New York City—but he has deflected and laughed off my questions. He has implicitly denied it, and I haven't the confidence, I cannot bring myself, to ask him point-blank. Still, in spite of my suspicions, I am leaning toward him, farther, farther. Do I right myself? This is not an aesthetic choice.

When Davan Eyke was forced to leave home, he did not go far, just up to Krahe's to inhabit the little cottage beneath the boughs of the beautiful, enfolding pine. It is a tree of an unusually powerful shape, and I have speculated often with the artist upon the year of its first growth. We are both quite certain it was small, a mere sapling, too tender to bother with, when the agents of the English king first marked the tallest and straightest trees in the forests of New England as off limits to colonists and destined for the shipyards of the Royal Navy, masts to hang great sails. A large pine growing now was a seedling when the climax growth, the pine canopy so huge and dense no light shone onto the centuries of bronze needles below, was axed down. This tree splits halfway up into three parts and forms an enormous crown. In that crotch, there is a raven's nest, which is unusual since ravens are shy of northeasterners, having a long race memory for the guns, nets, and poisons with which they were once eradicated.

When Davan Eyke moved in, the ravens watched, but they watch everything. They are a humorous, highly intelligent bird, and knew immediately that Davan Eyke would be trouble. Therefore they dropped sticks upon the boy's roof, shat on the lintel, stole small things he left in the yard, and hid them. Pencils, coins, and once his car keys. They also laughed. The laughter of a raven is a sound unendurably human. You may know it if you have heard it in your own throat as the noise of another of Krahe's favorites, *Schadenfreude*, the joy that rises as one witnesses the pain of others. Perhaps the raven's laughter, the low rasp, sounds cynical to our ears and reminds us of the depth of our own human darkness. Of course, there is nothing human in the least about it and its source is unknowable, as are the hearts of all things wild. Davan Eyke was bothered though, enough so that he complained to Krahe about the way the birds disturbed his sleep by dropping twigs and pinecones on his roof, which was of painted tin. End over end, the refuse clattered down.

"Get used to them" was all the artist said to Davan Eyke.

Krahe tells me this the day I bring the mail, a thing I do for him often, when he feels he is close to tossing himself into the throes of some ambitious piece. Then, he cannot or will not break the thread of his concentration by making a trip to the post office. There is too much at stake. This could be, I know although he will not admit it, the day his talent resurrects itself painfully from the grief where it has been plunged.

"I have in mind a perception of balance, although the whole thing must be brutally off the mark and highly dysphoric."

He speaks like this, pompous, amused at his own pronouncements, brightening his eyes beneath harsh brows.

"Awkward," I say, deflatingly. "Maybe even ugly."

In his self-satisfaction there is more than a hint of the repressed Kansas farm boy he was when he first left home for New York. That boy is covered by many layers now—there is faked European ennui, an aggressive macho crackle, an edge of Lutheran judgmentalness about, among many things, other people's religions. He says he has none. I can infuriate him easily by observing that, all the same, he is still Lutheran—a fire-breathing crank. Lapsed, maybe, but still tearing down hypocrisies. Still nailing his theses to the doors of cathedrals. He also descends at times to a strata of ongoing sadness over the not-so-recent loss of his second wife, who was killed on a road out west when her car ran over a large piece of stone. "Do you know," Krahe said once, "that a stone can be wedged just so into the undercarriage so that, when you press the gas pedal, the accelerator sticks and shoots the car forward at an amazing speed?" That was the gist of the fluke accident that killed his wife. A high school prank near Flathead Lake. Stones on the highway. Her speed increased, says Krahe, as she pressed on the brakes. Not a beautiful woman from her pictures, but forceful looking. Resembled by their daughter, Kendra, a girl evidently committed to dressing in nothing but black and purple since she's entered Sarah Lawrence.

"He's not working out," Krahe says now, of Eyke, who has moved just out of earshot. "I shouldn't hire locals."

I tell him that I resent his use of the word "local." After all, I am one, although I qualify in his mind as both local and of the larger world since I spent several years in London, living in fearful solitude on the edge of Soho, failing my degree, and also because he senses that I've had a life he knows nothing about, which is true, but I never talk about who I really am with him. The work I do with mother takes us into an extremity of places and lives, too, and I suppose this also exempts me from the "local" tag.

"You wouldn't have to hire anybody if you used smaller rocks," I answer, my voice falsely dismissive.

"This guy's a brainless punk," Krahe continues.

"I thought you knew that when you hired him."

"I suppose I could have told by looking at him, but I didn't really look."

"The only job he's ever had was cutting grass, and half the time he broke the lawn mower. He broke so many on this road that people knew enough not to hire him. Still," I tell Krahe, "he's not a bad person, not even close to bad. He's just . . ." I try to get at the thing about Eyke, but there just isn't much to get. ". . . he could learn a lot from you." My defense is lame and my lover does not buy it.

"I was desperate. I was working on *Construction Number Twenty*."

That is the working title of a piece commissioned many years ago by a large Minneapolis cereal company to rise on the corporate grounds. It is still not finished. Krahe slowly flips the mail along his arm, frowning at each envelope as though it holds a secret outrage. In contrast to those sprightly hands and feet, his body is thick, he favors the heavy plaid woolens sold by mail, and his movements are ponderous and considered. His black hair is cut in a brushy crew cut, the same hairdo Uncle Sam once gave him. At fifty-six, he hasn't lost his strength, and though he complains about his loss of energy, when I see him and my heart charges up, it is like being near a power source. When he speaks of Kendra coming home for a weekend, his voice is tender, almost dreamy. In those times there is a kind of yearning I'd do anything to hear directed toward me—I think I also love him because I want to know this side of him. Kendra doesn't seem to have a complicated view of her father. And he sees Kendra, I tell myself, partly as the incarnation of his lost wife and not as his actual self-absorbed and petulant daughter. I don't like her and she doesn't like me.

I stay and watch the two men wrestle steel and stone. Davan Eyke is slight by contrast. He doesn't look in fact as though he can lift as much weight as his boss. Together, though, they haul stones from the woods, drag and lever blocks of pale marble delivered from the Rutland quarries and farther away, too. His studio contains German Jurassic limestone, ammonite fossil-bearing rock, a granite shot with bits of hot blue. If Davan himself was artistic, this would be an ideal job, a chance to live close and learn from a master. As it is, Davan's enthusiasm dwindles in proportion to the resentment he quickly transfers from his father to his boss.

Elsie sighs and makes a face when I tell her Kendra Krahe is visiting her father, and that he has invited us to dinner. I laugh at her eye-rolling. Krahe often invites us to dinners that do not materialize once Kendra becomes involved. She rails against me; more than once I suspect she has prevailed upon her father to break off our friendship when it turned more serious. She would not tolerate my sleeping there while she was in high school, and the habit of Kurt's coming here has persisted. There is a low energy about Kendra, a fantastic drama, a way of doing ordinary things with immense conviction. Her father has never believed the dots splashed on the paper, the C+ science projects she displayed with such bravura, were only adequate. Seeing through the lens of her dead mother's image, Krahe firmly believes that Kendra is extraordinary.

I shouldn't be so hard on her, I suppose. But is it proper for the young to be so disappointing? And Krahe, why can't he see? I have wished she'd find a boyfriend for herself, wished dearly, and still, such is the engrained denial of class distinction in our country that neither of us thought it strange not to consider Davan Eyke, either to dismiss or encourage such a match. There he was, sullenly enduring his surroundings, winging pebbles at the tormenting birds, but since he was not of the intelligentsia, such as we are, who live on the road, he didn't occur to us.

This is the sort of family he is from: the Eykes, our closest neighbors. The father is a tinkering, sporadically employed mechanic. The local gas truck was driven by Davan's mother, until she took over the school bus route. They belong to an Assembly of God church, a scruffy-looking place with the same sort of plastic sign in front that gas stations use to display shifting prices. The two-word mottoes change weekly. God Loves. God Knows. God Sees. In the Eykes' packed-earth yard, a dog was tied for many years, a lovely creature part German shepherd and part husky; one eye brown and one blue. The dog was never taken off the short chain that bound it to the trunk of a tree. It lived in that tiny radius through all weathers, lived patiently, enduring each dull moment of its life, showing no hint of going mean.

I suppose I am no better than the Eykes. I called the Humane Society once, but when nothing happened and the dog still wound the chain one way and then the other, round and round the tree, I did nothing. Rather than confronting the Eykes, which seemed to me unthinkable since Mr. Eyke not only hauled away the trash but mowed our field, yanked out saplings to prevent the trees from closing in, and lived close enough to call in emergencies, I remained silent. From time to time, I brought the dog a bone as I passed on walks, and felt a certain degree of contempt for the Eykes, as one does for people who could mistreat an animal. Still, I did nothing.

That is one failure I regret, having to do with the Eykes, for all of us on the road were to pay for what was done to that creature. The other failure was the shortsightedness regarding Davan and Kendra.

A turbulence of hormones flows up and down this road. On my walks, I've seen the adolescence of each neighbor child hit like a small quake. Except in the wide loop sold off by a lumber company, divided into twelve five-acre parcels, and settled in development style, most of the houses on this road are surrounded by a depth of dark trees and a tangle of undergrowth. No two are within shouting distance. Yet you know, merely waving to the parents whose haunted eyes bore through the windshields of their car. You hear, as new trail bikes and motorbikes rip the quiet, as boom boxes blare from their perches on newly muscled shoulders. The family cars, once so predictable in their routes, buck and raise dust racing up and down the hills. It is a painful time, and one averts one's eyes from the houses containing it. The very foundations seem less secure. Love falters and blows. Steam rises from the ditches and sensible neighbors ask no questions.

Davan hit like that, a compact, freckled boy who suddenly grew long-jawed and reckless. Elsie says she knew it was the end once he started breaking lawn mowers, slamming them onto the grass and stones so savagely that the blades bent. She quietly got my mower fixed and did not ask him back to cut the grass. I took over that job. Davan's brown hair grew until it reached his shoulders, and a new beard came in across his chin like streaks of dirt. Frighteningly, Davan walked the road from time to time dressed in camouflage, hugging his father's crossbow and arrows, with which he transfixed woodchucks. That phase passed and he lapsed into a stupor of anger, which lasted for years and culminated in the damage he did to his father's new car. It was the most expensive thing his family ever bought, and since he left home soon after, it was clear he was not forgiven.

Kendra, on the other hand, had resolved her adolescence beautifully. After a few stormy junior high school years following her mother's death, she settled into a pattern of achieving small things with great flair, for as I mentioned she had no talents, and was at most a mediocre student. She gave the impression that she was going places, though, and so she did, though her acceptance into a prestigious college was a mystery to all who knew Kendra. Her teachers, including me, were stymied. Perhaps it was the interview, one woman told my mother. Another was convinced of a mistake in the college computer records.

At night, in raw blue winter darkness, Krahe enters our house via that back screened porch, a door to which he has the key. The back door inside the porch is the only one that unlocks with that key, and I keep things that way for the following reason: should I decide, should I tire, should I have the enlightenment or the self-discipline or the good sense to stop Krahe from coming to me in the night it will be a simple matter. One locksmith's fee, nothing more. One tossed key. No explanation owed. Though my mother must sense that Krahe's night visits occur, we do not and have never spoken of it. Her room is downstairs at the other end of the house. We live privately, in many respects, and although this is how we prefer to live, there are times I nearly spill over with my need and wish to confide my feelings.

For when he steps into my room it is to me as though I am waking on a strange and unlikely margin. As though the ocean is set suddenly before me. Landlocked, you forget. Then all of a sudden you are wading hip-high into the surge of waves. In the moment, there is so much meaning, so much hunger in our mouths and skin. I think every time is the last time I will be with him. I am physically amazed. What I like best is the curious, unfolding, confessional quality of sex. I seek it, demand it of him, and for a matter of hours he is bare to me, all candor and desire. How can he lie? He begs things of me. *Put your mouth here.* We are reversed from our day selves in nakedness. I gain assurance in some switch of roles I do not altogether understand but which I suspect is entirely due to my manufactured scorn. He believes I am invulnerable. I protect myself with every trick I know.

Ravens are the birds I'll miss most when I die. If only the darkness into which we must look were composed of the black light of their limber intelligence. If only we did not have to die at all. Instead, become ravens. I've watched these birds so hard I feel their black feathers split out of my skin. To fly from one tree to another, the raven hangs itself, hawklike, on the air. I hang myself that same way in sleep, between one day and the next. When we're young, we think we are the only species worth knowing. But the more I come to know people, the better I like ravens. If I have a religious practice, it is the watching of these birds. In this house, open to a wide back field and pond, I am living within their view and territory. Krahe's family group of birds divided up a few years ago. Once, they numbered eight or more. Now just three live within and around the pine, and six live somewhere in the heavy fringe of woods beyond my field. Two made their nest. Three hatchlings were reared. The other raven was killed by Davan Eyke.

You may wonder how on earth an undisciplined, highly unpleasant, not particularly coordinated youth could catch and kill a raven? They are infernally cautious birds. For instance, having long experience with poisoned carcasses, they do not taste first of dead food, but let the opportunistic blue jays eat their fill. The ravens watch, amused, to see if these bold greedy birds keel over in agony. Only when the jays are seen to survive do the ravens drive them off and settle in to feed. Davan had to use his father's crossbow to kill the raven. One day when Krahe was gone, Davan sat on the front stoop of his little cottage and waited for the birds to gather in their usual browbeating circle of derision. As they laughed at him, stepping through the branches, he slowly raised the crossbow. They would have vanished at the sight of a gun. But they were unfamiliar with other instruments. They did not know the purpose or the range of the bow. One strayed down too far and Davan's arrow pierced it completely through. Krahe drove into the yard and saw Davan standing over the bird. Amazingly, it wasn't dead. In some fascination, Davan was watching it struggle on the shaft of the arrow, the point driven into the earth.

Krahe walked over and bent to the bird. He snapped the arrow's point off and drew the shaft tenderly, terribly, from the bird's body. For a moment the raven sprawled, limp and addled, on the ground, and then it gathered itself. The two humans watched as the bird simply walked away from them and entered the woods to die.

All of this time, overhead and out of range, the other birds wheeled. For once, they were silent.

"Let me see the bow," said Krahe conversationally.

Davan handed it to him, prepared to point out its marvelous and lethal features.

"And the arrows."

Davan handed those over too.

"I'll be right back," said Krahe.

Davan waited. Krahe walked across the yard to his woodpile, turned, and fit an arrow into the groove. Then he raised the bow. Davan stepped aside, looked around for the target, looked uneasily back at Krahe, then touched his own breast as the sculptor lifted the shoulder piece. Shot. Davan leapt to the other side of the white pine and vaulted off into the brush. The arrow stuck just past his shoulder. Then Krahe walked over and removed the arrow and laid the bow on the block he used to split his firewood. He axed the weapon neatly in half. He laid the arrows down next like a bunch of scallions and chopped them into short lengths. He walked into his house and phoned me. "If you see that boy running past your house," he said, "here's why."

"You shot at him?"

"Not to hit him."

"But still, my God."

Krahe, embarrassed, would not speak of this again.

Davan had saved enough money from his pay (we thought) to buy himself a small old Toyota, dusty red with a splash of dark rust on the door where a dent had raised metal through the paint. The car now spewed grit and smoke on the road as he drove it back and forth to town. He'd returned to his room in his parents' house and he resumed, every day, his chore of feeding the dog, though he never untied it from the tree.

That dog's maple grew great patches of liver-colored moss and dropped dead limbs. The dog was killing it. Shit-poisoned, soaked with urine at the base, and nearly girdled by the continual sawing and wearing of the chain, the tree had for years yellowed and then blazed orange, unhealthily first of all the trees upon the road. Then one day it fell over and the dog walked off, calmly, like the raven, into the woods, a three-foot length of chain dragging. Only the dog didn't die. Perhaps it had been completely stark mad all along, or perhaps it happened that moment after the tree went down when, unwrapping itself nervously, the dog stepped one step beyond the radius of packed dirt within which it had lived since it was a fat puppy. Perhaps that step, the paw meeting grass, rang down the spine of the dog, fed such new light into its brain, that she could not contain the barrage of information. At any rate, the outcome of that moment wasn't to be seen for several weeks, within which time Davan had successfully raised dust near Kendra on illicit visits hidden from her father, and secretly taken her out with him to local parties, where at first she enjoyed her status as a college-goer and the small sensation caused by her New York clothing styles. Then, at some point, something awakened in her, some pity or con-science. Before that I'd seen nothing remarkable about Krahe's daughter, other than the clothing. Her lack of kindness, laziness, feelings of enormous self-worth, all typical of women her age. Then all of a sudden this urge to care for and rescue Davan Eyke, a sudden unblocking of compassion that made Kendra come clean with her father. Her humanity terrified Krahe more thoroughly than if they'd been trying to get pregnant.

I step out of the car with the mail and see Krahe standing square in front of Davan, who slouches before the older man with obdurate weariness. Locked in their man-space, they do not acknowledge me. Krahe is of course telling Davan Eyke that he doesn't wish for him to see his daughter Kendra, in the course of which he probably calls Davan some name, or makes some threat, for Davan steps back and stares at him alertly, hands up as though ready to throw off a punch, which never comes. Krahe kicks him over, instead, with a rageful ease that astonishes Davan Eyke. From the cold ground, there suddenly, he shakes his head in puzzlement at Krahe's feet. When Krahe draws his leg back to kick again I move forward. The kick stops midway. Davan rises. The two stare at each other in a spinning hatred—I can see the black web between them.

"You still owe me," says Davan, backing away.

"Say you won't see her first."

Davan just starts to laugh, raucous, cracking, a raven's laugh. I can still hear it through his car window as he revs and peels out.

I turn to Krahe.

"You should let Kendra see him," I say.

He is as astounded at my temerity as I am. Not only am I not the sort to get involved in other people's business, and this is definitely not mine, but he also knows that I'm not fond of Kendra.

"What's it to you?" he says, more amazed than defensive.

"She's got a right," I say. "And besides, she'll see him anyway."

"No, she won't," says Krahe.

We hold each other's gazes belligerently. "You're the dad," I finally shrug.

I suspect that he will learn soon enough just how much weight his objections carry with Kendra. Still, I don't understand why Krahe detests the boy so much—it is as though Davan has tapped some awful gusher in the artist. Is it partly the fear we nonbelievers have for what Krahe calls "the fundamentally insane"? He adds holy rolling to the list of Davan's undesirable Eyke-ish qualities when he sees the family truck pulled up at the unkempt church, which he calls a Quonset hut. Is he afraid that Davan Eyke will draw his daughter into the flock? Whatever else, his anxiety is also a productive, dark vein, for now in a welter of frustrated energy, Krahe starts working. He finishes *Twenty*. He produces, hardly sleeps. Hardly sees me.

It is difficult for a woman to admit that she gets along with her own mother—somehow it seems a form of betrayal, at least, it used to among other women in my generation. To join in the company of women, to be adults, we go through a period of proudly boasting of having survived our own mother's indifference, anger, overpowering love, the burden of her pain, her tendency to drink or teetotal, her warmth or coldness, praise or criticism, sexual confusions or embarrassing clarity. It isn't enough that she sweat, labored, bore her daughters howling or under total anesthesia or both. No. She must be responsible for our psychic weaknesses the rest of her life. It is all right to feel kinship with your father, to forgive. We all know that. But your mother is held to a standard so exacting that it has no principles. She simply must be to blame.

Elsie and I are past the blame, and as she sits before me now we are listening to a CD of Schubert's Piano Sonata in E-flat Major. It is a familiar piece, a thoughtful conversation between old friends. I am writing as usual in my daily journal, a red hardbound book that I order every year through the mail. This journal company has been in existence a long time and I have thirty-three of these books stacked among my other notebooks, shelved in my room. My mother's eyes are closed. It strikes me that there is something in the nakedness of her face and shut eyes like that of a newborn animal.

Her skin has always been extremely clean and fine. Always, she has smelled to me of soap, but now she's added a light perfume.

I think that she knows he has been here. Last night, he came down off the manic high in which he hung, raven- or hawklike, between one uninspired month and the next. It is morning. Even to me the house seems different, more alive, alert, and with a comforting maleness, after Krahe has made love to me in the night. Still, openly becoming Krahe's lover would upset the balance. As well, I believe my deadlocked secret love and unsecret contempt is the only hold I have over him, my only power. So things remain as they are. Elsie and I maintain a calm life together, the treasure of routine. I do not dread, as others might, her increasing dependence. It is only that I have the strange unadult wish that if she must pass into death, that rough mountain, she take me too. Not leave me scratching at the shut seam of stone.

Winter lets go of this road with a rush of dark rain. The snow and slush melt away, raising slick mud that freezes to a glassy tar. One day the weak sun heats the bark of young birch trees; the next, a sudden temperature drop ices the drawn sap and splits the trunks. All through the woods they gape like throats. New sounds are heard. The caterwauling of the barred owls startles me from sleep, raising bubbles of tension in my blood. I cannot imagine myself changing the locks. Without a word, without a sound, I circle Krahe, dragging my chain.

During these weeks, there is no sign of the dog that slipped free of the dead maple, and Elsie and I can only assume it has been taken in somewhere as a stray or, perhaps, shot from off a farmer's back porch for running deer. Indeed, that is how it probably survives, squeezing through a hole in the game-park fence, living off hand-raised pheasants and winter-killed carcasses.

The dog reappears during a false three-day warmth that doesn't fool a soul. My neighbors up the road, the ones who clear-cut fifty acres of standing timber in four shocking days, have their cocker spaniel eaten. They leave the dog out all night on its wire run and the next morning, calling in poochie from the back door, Ann Flaud in her nightgown pulls the dog's lead toward her. It rattles across the ground. At the end of it hangs an empty collar, half gnawed through. She stands with the collar in her hand, on her back steps, wondering.

There is little beyond that to find. Small evidence. Just a patch of blood and the two long, mitteny, brown ears. Coydogs are blamed—those mythical creatures invoked for every loss—then a bear, then Satanists. I know it is the dog. I have seen her at the edge of our frozen field, loping on long springy wolf-legs. She has no starved look. She is alive—fat, glossy, huge.

She takes a veal calf for supper one night, pulled from its stand-up torture pen at the one working farm on the road that survived the nineties. She steals suet out of people's bird feeders, eats garbage, meadow voles, and frogs. A few cats disappear. She is now blamed for everything. And seen every day, but never caught. The farm panics over missing chickens. One of my rougher-hewn neighbors misses a bear's hide and finds it chewed to yarny bits deep in the woods. It is not until the dog meets the school bus, though, mouth open, the sad eye of liquid brown and the hungry eye of crystal blue trained on the doors as they swish open, that the state police become involved.

*   *   *

A dragnet of shotgun-armed volunteers and local police fan through the woods. Parked on this road, an officer with a vague memory of a car theft in Concord runs a check on Davan Eyke's red car as it flashes past. Eyke is on his way up to Krahe's, where Kendra, less boldly attired than usual and biting black paint from her nails, waits to counsel him. Apparently, they go for a walk in the woods, leaving the car in the driveway in view of Krahe's studio. They return and then, against Krahe's express, explicit, uncompromising, direct orders, Kendra does exactly as she pleases. The human heart is every bit as tangled as our road. She gets into the car with Eyke.

On the computer check, the car turns up hot, stolen, and as it speeds back down from Krahe's an hour later, the police officer puts on his siren and spins out, giving chase. There ensues a dangerous game of tag. On our narrow roads filled with hairpin turns, sudden drops, and abrupt hills, speed is a harrowing prospect. Davan Eyke tears down the highway, past his family church and the week's wishful-thinking motto, God Cares, hangs a sharp left on Jackson Road, and jumps the car onto a narrow gravel path mainly used for walking horses. He winds up and down the hill like a slingshot, meets the wider road, then joins it and continues toward Windsor, over the world's longest covered bridge, into Vermont where, at the first stoplight, he screeches between two cars in a sudden left-hand turn against the red. Leaving town, he pops an old man walking the road—John Jewett Tatro—high into the air. The car has vanished before Tatro rolls to the bottom of the embankment. Tatro lies there, dying among the packed brown leaves, the snow crust, the first tough shoots of trillium. No doubt, the ravens are curious. On blacktop now, Davan's car is clocked at over a hundred miles per hour. There isn't much the police can do but radio ahead and follow as fast as they dare.

Another left, and it seems Davan is intent on fleeing back toward Claremont on the New Hampshire side. The police car slows as Eyke swings around a curve on two side wheels and makes for the bridge that crosses over the wide, calm Connecticut that serves as our boundary. The afternoon air is on the verge of freezing, the mud's a slick gloss. According to the sign that blurs in Davan's eyes, the bridge is liable to ice up before the pavement. It has. The car hits transparent black ice at perhaps 120 miles per hour and soars straight over the low guardrail. A woman in the oncoming lane says the red car travels at such a velocity it seems to gain purchase in the air and hang above the river. She also swears that she sees, before the car flies over, the white flower of a face pressing toward the back window. No one sees a thing after that, although there is a sort of witness near the scene. An early fisherman pulling his boat onto shore below the bridge is suddenly aware of a great shadow behind him, as though a cloud or bird has fallen out of the sky and touched his back lightly with its wing.

Within minutes of the radio call, all of the pickups and cars on our road gather their passengers and firearms and sweep away from the dog posse to the scene of greater drama at the bridge. Although the wreckage isn't found for days, and requires four wet-suited divers to locate and gather, the police make a visit to Krahe's on the strength of the woman witness's story. Fearing that Kendra has gone over the bridge as well, they take me along to question my friend.

I wait on the edge of the field for Krahe, my hand on the stump of an old pine's first limb. From deep in the brush, I hear the ravens, the grating *haw, haw*, of their announcement, and it occurs to me that he might just show up with Kendra. But he doesn't, only shambles toward me at my call. As I walk toward Kurt, I feel for the first time in our mutual life that I am invested with a startling height, even a power, perhaps more of an intelligence than I am used to admitting that I possess. I feel a sickening omnipotence.

He starts at my naked expression, asks, "What?"

"Davan's car," I report, "went over the bridge." I don't know what I expect from Krahe then. Anything but his offhand, strangely shuttered nonreaction close to relief. He has apparently no idea Kendra might have disobeyed him and gotten into the car. Unable to go on, I fall silent. For all of his sullen gravity, Davan had experienced and expressed only a shy love for Krahe's daughter. It was an emotion he was capable of feeling, as was the fear that made him press the gas pedal.

I stare at Kurt. My heart creaks shut. I turn away, leaving him to talk to the police, and walk directly into the woods. At first, I think I'm going off to suffer like the raven, but as I walk on and on, I know that I will be fine and I will be loyal, pathologically faithful. I will be there for him when he mourns. The knowledge grounds me. The grass cracks beneath each step I take and the cold dry dust of it stirs around my ankles. In a long, low swale of a field that runs into a dense pressure of trees, I stop and breathe carefully, standing there.

Whenever you leave cleared land, or a path, or a road, when you step from someplace carved out, plowed, or traced by a human and pass into the woods, you must leave something of yourself behind. It is that sudden loss, I think, even more than the difficulty of walking through undergrowth that keeps people firmly fixed to paths. In the woods, there is no right way to go, of course, no trail to follow but the law of growth. You must leave behind the notion that things are right. Just look around you. Here is the way things are.

Twisted, fallen, split at the root. What grows best does so at the expense of what's beneath. A white birch feeds on the pulp of an old hemlock and supports the grapevine that will slowly throttle it. In the deadwood of another tree, fungi black as devil's hooves. Over us the canopy, tall pines that whistle and shudder and choke off light from their own lower branches.

The dog is not seen and for a time, at least, she abandons Revival Road; there are no spaniel or chicken killings, she does not appear again near the house where her nature devolved, she doesn't howl in the game park or stalk the children's bus stop. Yet at night, in bed, my door unlocked, as I am waiting, I imagine that the dog pauses at the edge of my field, suspicious of the open space, then lopes off with its snapped length of chain striking sparks from the exposed ledge and boulders. I have the greatest wish to stare into her eyes, but if I should meet her face-to-face, breathless and heavy muzzled, shining with blood, would the sad eye see me or the hungry eye? Which one would set me free?

He has weakened, Kurt, he needs me these days. Elsie says, out of nowhere, *Don't let him use you.* I touch her shoulders, reassuringly. She shrugs me off. Perhaps because she senses, with disappointment, that I actually don't care. Shame, pleasure, ugliness, loss. They are the heat in the night that tempers the links. And then there is forgiveness when the person is unforgivable, and the man weeping like a child, and the dark house soaking up the hollow cries.

2

The Painted Drum

I am called upon to handle the estate of John Jewett Tatro just after his Presbyterian funeral. Elsie has her hands full rearranging the shop, so I drive to the Tatro house to make the appraisal of its contents. The morning is overcast, the sky threatful, an exciting dark gray. The Tatros have always been too cheap to properly keep up their road, and the final quarter mile is all frost heaves, partly crumbled away, the gnarled bedrock exposed. I bump along slowly so as not to slide into the frozen swamp grass and iced-over ponds at either side. I wish for thunder, then take back my wish. The wind is still brittle and icy. Any rain that falls will turn to slush and send us swerving back into the cold exhaustion that was February. We are over halfway done with March. April, though fickle, will inch us toward May's tender, budding, bug-hatching glory.

The Tatro house is not grand anymore. The original nineteenth-century homestead has been renovated and enlarged so many times that its style is entirely obscured. Here a cornice, there a ledge. The building is now a great clapboard mishmash, a warehouse with aluminum-clad storm windows bolted over the old rippled glass and a screen porch tacked darkly across its front. The siding is painted the brown-red color of old blood. The overall appearance is rattling and sad, but the woman who greets me is cheerful enough, and the inside of the house is comfortable, though dim. The rooms are filled with the odor I have grown used to in my work. It is a smell that alerts me, an indefinable scent, really, composed of mothballs and citrus oil, of long settled dust and cracked leather. The smell of old things is what it is. My pulse ticks as I note that even on the ground floor an inordinate number of closets have been added during some period of expansion. Some run the length of whole walls, I estimate, roughly noting the room's proportions.

The niece, whose name is Sarah, surname also Tatro, is an RN at the hospital just north of here. She is a pleasant, square-jawed woman, hair of light brown and eyes of blue, a woman in her midthirties, years younger than I am, the sort of mother who volunteers to supervise recess or construct grade school art projects. The sort of community citizen who campaigns for historical preservation and school bond votes. I know the type. I have attempted to be the type. So has my mother. But our fascination for the stuff of life, or more precisely, the afterlife of stuff, has always set us apart. Mother started the business and we have run it jointly now for nearly two decades. We are fair, discreet, honest, and knowledgeable. We are well-known in our part of New Hampshire, and well respected I think, although I've always known that we do not fit in. There is a certain advantage to our gender. More often than not, it is the women of the family who get stuck dealing with the physical estate, the stuff, the junk, the possessions, and we are also women.

We understand what it is like to face a mountain of petty decisions when in grief. As I sit down with Sarah, formalizing things over a cup of coffee, I feel that comfortable and immediate sense of connection that one can have with other women in this time—sympathy, of course, but also some relief. Finally, to get on with things! There is even some excitement at the idea of the task ahead. Cleaning out a house is bone-numbing work, but there are always discoveries along the way. Some are valuable—under a coat of milk paint an original Shaker table, Herter Brother chairs, a fabulous porcelain or saccharine but valuable old *Hummels* amid chipped salt and pepper shakers. Once, an old bucket forgotten in a pantry corner turned out to be a hand-painted Leder, worth thousands. First editions turn up, first printings, a signed Mark Twain, a Wharton, a pristine Salinger—you never know what will surface from even the most unpromising pile. And, too, some discoveries are revelatory—diaries, packets of love letters, a case of antique pornography featuring trained ponies, death certificates that list surprising causes, unknown births. The contents of a house can trigger all sorts of revisions to family history.

There is also, in my eagerness to take on the Tatro estate, a thread of personal connection that reaches back several generations. It is nothing my mother or I would have pursued while either of the Tatro brothers was alive, although it has to do with our specialty—Native American antiquities. In *The History of Stiles and Stokes*, a book published on subscription by our local historical society, there is an entire chapter devoted to the branch of the Tatro family that lives in Stiles, and within that chapter a paragraph about the grandfather of the most recently deceased Tatros. Jewett Parker Tatro was an Indian agent on the Ojibwe reservation where my grandmother was born and where she lived until the age of ten, at which time she was taken east and enrolled at Carlisle Indian School, in Pennsylvania. A young teacher from Stokes, only twenty years old, had written to Tatro and was even put up at Tatro's house on the North Dakota reservation while he recruited students there. He's the one who got my grandmother to come to Carlisle. There, she learned to sew intricately, to add and subtract, to do laundry, scrub a floor clean, read, write, and recite Bible passages, Shakespeare's sonnets, Keats's odes, and the Declaration of Independence and the Bill of Rights. Carlisle Institute was also where she fell in love, or came to know her husband, I should say. It is hard for me to imagine that the cold little woman I remember, the anti-Grandma, I used to call her, ever fell in love or felt much in the way of human emotion.

The young teacher whom she married kept her in the east, though she returned to the reservation for a while when she inherited land, and bore my mother on her own allotment. My grandfather lived there too and apparently was, in turn, educated by the Ojibwe in the arts of trapping and hunting, occupations he so thoroughly loved that he returned to Stokes and worked for the rest of his life in the rich people's game park that abuts Krahe's land. My grandparents lived in a little house just outside the game-park gate. Elsie and my father bought a new house and we kept living in it when he died—six months after my younger sister. So that's our little cat's cradle of connections. That is why we are not really Easterners and partly why, I suspect, Krahe finds me interesting—he can't quite place exactly who I am.

The connection between Tatro and the reservation is also of interest because it wasn't uncommon for Indian agents to amass extensive collections of artifacts, and of course mother and I have always wondered whether the Tatro house held such a trove. We have had little indication, beyond the odd reference here or there. The last two Tatros were a forbidding couple of fellows who lived meanly and died within two months of each other—the younger of natural causes and the older, of course, of the shock and injury he sustained when struck by that doomed Toyota. Although once in their house I see little that would lead me to think that their closets hold anything more exotic than magazines and clothing and phonograph records, there have been rumors. And to our knowledge, there has never been a large-scale Tatro collection donated to any local, state, or college museum. There are those many closets and the thick walls of the downstairs rooms. Also, there is or was the nature of the Tatros—oh, there is certainly that—to consider.

They were sharp, they were shrewd, they were flinty, unreasonable, calm cheaters and secret hoarders. They haunted tag sales. Bought food in bulk. Hitchhiked when gas was expensive, though they were not poor. Ate day-old rolls and bread and drank post-dated milk. Saved the rubber bands off broccoli and bananas, when they bought such luxuries. They boiled the sap from their trees and stole the corn from their neighbor's fields. They picked fiddleheads, tore fruit off stunted trees, shot and roasted raccoons. Each fall they bought and salted down or froze half a pig, devouring it from snout to hock over the course of a year. To my mind the Tatros were exactly the sort of cheap old Yankee bachelors who'd have kept a valuable collection of artifacts just because it never occurred to them to part with anything. They never would have thought of donating, or even selling; they would have simply hung on to their stuff—moldering, mothballed, packed away with cedar blocks—until Judgment Day. Or so I hoped.

Curiously, perhaps, as we are put in the way of many fine objects, the house I live in with my mother is not cluttered. It's not that our vocation has turned us snobbish. Rather, it is the constant reminder of our own mortality that reins us in. The useless vanity of holding on to anything too tightly is, of course, before us always. To strive to own anything of extraordinary value mostly strikes us as absurd, given our own biodegradability. Still, there are a few things we've come across and found irresistible. That they are in our line of specialty probably reveals that we are more captive to our background than we admit—a lustrous, black, double-throated Maria Martinez wedding vase; an Ojibwe cradle board, the wrap intricately beaded on velvet; three very fine Navajo rugs; a bandolier bag that was probably carried by the last Ojibwe war leader, Buganogiizhig; a few seed pots; several shaved-quill boxes; and some heavy old silver and turquoise that must be continually polished. Oh, we'd like to leave our path to heaven clear. Travel a spare, true road. Yet we're human enough.

Sarah Tatro did not intend to let the house and its contents trap her. Over the cup of coffee—one of those thick diner-style white mugs surely swiped from a local café by one of the uncles—she told me that she was anxious to clear the place out and put it on the market. I found her forthrightness appealing and yet, at the same time, that the Tatro house should pass from Tatro ownership after nearly two centuries infected me with a faint melancholy. It is unusual for one place to remain so long in a single family's hands—I was, surprisingly, tempted to try dissuading her from breaking with the past and carrying on with, of all things, her own life. I controlled myself. I took out my notebook and began to make a rough list of the contents of the house. Later on, I would be joined by two assistants, but I prefer to work alone at first, as does mother. I like to get a feel for the things in the house, a sense of the outlook or taste of the person who, though safely in the next world, still lingers in the arrangement and treatment of goods. I like to make peace with the dead.

Were I a traditional Ojibwe, I would have a special place in the community because of my line of work. According to a number of written sources from my collection, the objects left behind by a dead person were regarded with fearful emotion. They were never kept by family, but immediately gathered up by a person whose job it was to parcel the belongings of the deceased out to others. I assume things haven't changed much, at least among people who live the old way. Possessions are thought to attract the spirit back to their loved ones, and so only persons unrelated to the dead are considered safe to handle them. Those persons who distribute the objects should not wear the color red—it is the one color the dead are thought to see clearly. It attracts them. They wander toward it. I avoid wearing red in my work, for somehow I find that idea compelling.

I tell Sarah that I am ready to begin a preliminary tagging and cataloguing of the main portion of the house, and then I ask if her uncles had any particular interest, field of study, or collection that might require special handling or appraisal.

"Oh, I don't know, there's just so much of everything." She waves her hands. "So many old sets of dishes. Uncle John owned a number of guns. Some of *those* are old. And then the closets on the ground floor go way back behind the walls. They're stuffed. That's pretty much to say it's anybody's guess."

I am on my own, and very soon I am immersed in the pleasures of my job. The sorrows of strangers are part of my business, and were I to examine my motives in continuing this work, I might find that from their losses I extract some bit of comfort—as though my constant proximity to death protects me and those I love. The furniture in the first two rooms on the ground floor is in adequate repair and quite good, though there are no "finds." Predictably, the Tatros weren't bibliophiles, nor is there much in the way of decorative little touches—lamps, vases, figurines. Yet the walls are hung with six nicely done paintings by local artists and there is one oil sketch, a sort of pre-painting drawing, by Maxfield Parrish. I am pleased to see it and I wonder if the Tatros were acquainted with him. That particular discovery would have made my day at any other time. In this case it also indicates the Tatro tendency to hold on to things, as the Parrish was well-known to have value and could easily have been sold. I try not to get my hopes up, but when I open the door to the first closet my fingers are clumsy with excitement. Quickly, I go through what I can see—the usual boxes of magazines. Piles of curtains and old and faded linen. A great many boots of all styles, reaching back for decades. Mothballed coats of everything from wool to skunk skins. The closet goes on and on, but soon enough I decide to leave its contents to the patience of my assistants. The next closet, running between two parlorlike rooms, one of which probably at one time held a piano and other musical instruments, is stuffed with records. 78 rpm. Most swing or big band groups. I'm not an aficionado of the music of that era so I only make notes and leave the details. I am beginning to worry that the rumors were just that when, upon opening the first of a wide bank of drawers built into a wall, I find the first indication of, it seems curious to say, life.

Some estates come to life and others don't. Some holdings have little personality, others much. For instance, there is a moment I think of still, one I nearly missed. Years ago, I opened a small wooden chest containing what appeared to be handkerchiefs wrapped in tissue paper, only handkerchiefs, bearing the owner's initials, L.M.B. I was about to empty the box and stack its contents among the linens when I noticed a label. Pinned to each cotton, lawn, lace-trimmed, or embroidered handkerchief, I realized, was a carefully cut piece of paper. Of course, I examined the papers. Each bore a date inked in ladylike script. A name or names were written. And then occasions. Teddy's Christening. Venetta and John Howard's Wedding. And then, Teddy's Funeral. Brother Admantine's Wake. First Opera, La Traviata. Wedding. Broken Arm. And far down at the bottom, perhaps the first such kept handkerchief and the author of the collection, a child's small square of fabric clumsily sewn with the initials and labeled My Mother's Funeral. I remember sitting with the handkerchiefs belonging to L.M.B. as the rest of the work of pricing and sorting swirled around me. Here was a box containing a woman's lifetime of tears. I passed through several stages of emotion. The first was elation at the novelty of such an odd, Victorian idea, and the urge to show the box and its contents to my assistants. Next, I was swept through with such irritation for this evidence of outrageous thrift that I had a rare thought. I almost never think of non-Indians as white. After all, my own skin is pale. But I experienced a sudden bolt of prejudice that surprised me. *Just like a white lady, so stingy with her tears she kept them,* and then I recovered myself and sat further, still holding the box, which was very light, the wood dry old varnished pine, and turning over one and the next handkerchief. Theodor's Precious Birth. Aunt Lilac's Deathbed Supper. What was a deathbed supper? Cousin Franklin's Wedding to Mildred Vost. More funerals. As the other workers tackled the next room, I was left alone with the box in my lap and it was then, sitting with L.M.B.'s sorrows and joys, that my own eyes filled with tears. There weren't many. I am not the crying sort anymore. So when I did feel that swell of sadness I reached immediately for one of the handkerchiefs, dabbed my eyes dry, and added my own tears to the box. Then I closed the box. I knew what had happened was exactly right. Tears Shed for L.M.B., I might have written on a scrap of paper. I'd have to buy the box myself now, but that seemed the proper close to the collection.

Later, I heard that L.M.B. was a ferocious old bore in her age, critical, churchy, and prone to making complaint calls to the parents of young boys who cut across her front lawn or spoiled her tulips. But that's what I mean by coming to life.

The estate of John Jewett and Burden Tatro comes into a similar focus when I make the acquaintance of a doll with a face of fawn-skin and eyes of jet. I know that the doll is something special the moment I put my hands on it. She is wrapped in faded red trade cloth and placed inside a shoe box. The shoe box is mistakenly stored upon a shelf of shoes, and when I open it I catch a whiff of smoked hide. It is a smell that could have accumulated molecule by molecule inside of the box only if it was not opened for a very long time. As I unwrap the doll, the fugitive taste of smoke vanishes and there is the doll herself, exquisite. The perfectly cured hide of her skin has somehow retained its softness, though from the faintly smudged darknesses on her arms and skirt I see she had been loved as a toy. Her red quill lips are stitched into a calm, amused smile, and her bead eyes are set at a lively angle. Her coarse black hair was plucked from a horse's mane and each black thread sewn into her head and then divided into braids. Her dress is also made of tanned hide, decorated with bits of shell and the old antique beads called greasy yellow and ruby red whiteheart and german blue. Her waist is belted with a woven sash. Attached to it she wears a tiny scabbard that secures a tiny skinning knife. Her moccasins are sewn with flowers, and she wears jewelry. A ring of trade silver makes a bracelet on her arm. From her pierced fawnskin ears dangle minia-ture earbobs that are hawk's bells so unusually small that they could hang from the throats of warblers. She carries a thimble-size basket woven so cleverly that I laugh in pleasure. I bring the doll out at once, and show her to Sarah.

"Oh, there she is!" She takes the doll from me and handles her with familiar tenderness, smoothing the coarse hair down and ca-ressing the slender horsehair brows embroidered above the glitter-ing eyes. "My uncles used to let me play with her if I was very good."

"*She's* very good, you know. Valuable, I mean. We should have a museum curator look at her."

"Yeah?" Sarah is surprised, but not particularly pleased. I think she feels the same way I do about the doll. It is personal—the de-light of the doll's presence has nothing to do with her worth.

"Were there other things, American Indian I mean, of that era?" I ask. "Did your uncles keep them all together somewhere? In a cabinet? Trunks?"

"Oh God, yes, I'd forgotten all about it. One of the Tatros way back lived with Indians," she says. "There was a lot of old bead-work and stuff. Come on upstairs, I'll show you."

On the way up the stairs, I try to breathe slowly. There is an attic room of course—a long unfinished tar-papered hall lined with simple board shelves and stuffed with old suitcases. The major por-tion of the collected items are kept in the suitcases, Sarah tells me. There are as well some larger things wrapped in old bedspreads and horse blankets. We unveil these at once—a cradle board not as good as mine, large birch-bark winnowing baskets, a curious, bead-

worked footstool. A drum. The suitcases hold some precious ex-
amples of late-nineteenth- and early-twentieth-century bead and
cloth-appliqué work. There are moccasins, leggings, beaded ceremonial breech clouts, a vest, and two bandolier bags (in extraordinary condition, worth a great deal). There are also a number of
lesser items—small purses of the sort once sold to tourists, a band
for a headdress from which the feathers are all removed, tobacco
pouches, woven carrying straps and reed mats. We lay things out,
unwrapped, on the tops of suitcases, draped off the edges of drawers and shelves, but stop eventually. The collection goes on and on.

"Congratulations," I say. Sarah Tatro looks startled.

"Congratulations for what?"

"You can probably retire. Or at least take a long vacation. No
more early-morning wake-up calls."

"You think all this is valuable. . . ."

"Very."

Sarah drops to a trunk and stays there, puts her head in her
hands. "You mean, they were sitting on this all along?"

I don't reply and after a time she shakes her head and laughs
shortly, without humor. "They were so cheap with themselves that
they ate oatmeal for dinner. And they spread Crisco on their bread
instead of butter. The taxes on this place had gone sky-high, of
course, and they wanted to keep it. So they lived on nothing. But in
the end"—her voice lifts—"I have to say I think they enjoyed their
stinginess." And then she laughs with more ease. "They probably
enjoyed what they had here. You can see they went through things.
Checked them for mildew or bugs, I guess, rewrapped them. Set
mousetraps. Look." She shows me the date on a newspaper that
was used to cushion a lovely little sweet-grass basket. "Last year's."

"That's fortunate," I say, "the acid in the newspaper could have ruined that basket." I move closer to look at the little coiled and sewn basket, and that is when I step close to the drum.

I'm not a sentimental person and I don't believe old things hold the life of people. How can I? I see the most intimate objects proceed to other hands, indifferent to the love once bestowed. Some people believe objects absorb something of their owner's essence. I stay clear of that. And yet, when I step near the drum, I swear it sounds. One deep, low, resonant note. I stop dead still, staring at the drum. I hear it, I know I hear it, and yet Sarah Tatro does not.

"I'm getting out of here," she merely says. "Too dusty. I'll be back later on this afternoon. I've got some errands in town."

And so I am left with the original Tatro's loot. I continue to stare at the drum, what I can see since it is mostly swaddled by a faded quilt. I don't just hear things and I'm not subject to imaginative fits. There will be an explanation. Something shifting to strike the skin. A change in air pressure. The quilt isn't anything special, a simple collection of squares, yarn-tied, the sort of thing sold at church bazaars. I step over to the drum and pull the fabric entirely away. The light comes from two bare bulbs with pull chains, and casts harsh shadows. The head of the drum glares out, huge, three feet across at least. The buffalo or moose skinned to make it must have been a giant. In spite of its size there is something delicate about the drum, though, for it is intricately decorated, with a beaded belt and skirt, hung with tassels of pulled red yarn and sewn tightly all around with small tin cones, or tinklers. Four broad tabs are spaced equally around the top. Into their beaded tongues of deep indigo four white beaded figures are set. They are abstract but seem to represent a girl, a hand, a cross, a running wolf. On the face of the drum, at the very center, a stripe is painted in yellow. That is all. The figurative detail, the red-flowered skirts, the tinklers, combined with the size of the drum, give it an unusual sense of both power and sweetness.

I draw a folding chair close, sit, and jot down the details. My hand drags across the page. This is the sort of find that would usually thrill me, but I am not pleased. I put down my pen. I am uneasy, anxious. I look around. I hope that Sarah has not returned from her errands yet. I set my hand on the drum and then I feel, pulled through me like a nerve, a clear conviction. It is visceral. Not a thought but a gut instinct. I cover the drum again with the quilt and go downstairs to make sure that Sarah is really gone. When I see that the garage is empty and I've called through the house to make certain I am alone, I prop open the back door and go straight back upstairs. I bundle the quilt more tightly around the drum, and then I carry it out of the house. I set my bundle on the gravel only briefly as I lift the hatch on my car, then I slide the drum into the cargo hold and hide it by pulling over it the theft-deterring blind I always use when parking at big auctions.

I work the rest of the afternoon without thinking about what I've done. When my thoughts flicker toward the drum, I veer away from any further examination. What I've just done, or am about to do, is probably a felony and could ruin our business. The ease with which I have done it bewilders me. For a person who has not stolen so much as a candy bar in all of her life to walk coolly out of a client's house with such a valuable object might signal insanity. The beginning of a nervous breakdown. But I don't feel that way. I feel quite lucid. And I wonder whether others who suddenly commit irrational and criminal acts feel this calm acceptance of an unknown part of themselves.

*   *   *

Dusk is forming, blue and cold, by the time I arrive at home. I leave the drum in the car, wrapped in the quilt, underneath its stretched plastic curtain. I don't want it in the house yet. I have to think—not about whether what I've done was right: I have decided that I wouldn't have done it unless it was on some level *right*. And yet the explanation of this rightness swirls out of my reach. My real concerns are whether I can keep the drum hidden and whether I'll get caught. I am pretty sure that Sarah Tatro hasn't noticed the drum; in fact, she seemed indifferent to all of her uncles' objects save the doll she played with as a child. I'm also fairly certain that she is the only one who'd have any possible knowledge of her uncles' collection. And even she had forgotten it existed. I'd had to take the drum that afternoon, if I was to take it at all. Once I catalogue the objects and have them appraised, the drum will price itself out of reach of any but the wealthiest collectors, or a museum. Yet I don't want the drum. What would I do with such a thing, where would I keep it? No, I didn't take the drum for myself. I reassure myself of this again as I sit down to dinner with my mother.

"You have an odd look on your face," she says. "So, how was it?"

I take the salad bowl from her hands and begin forking leaves onto my plate.

"Well, it was there," I tell her.

"Oh!" She puts her fork down.

I've taken a mouthful of spinach leaves but suddenly I feel too tired to even chew. I slump in my chair, throw my head back, stretch my arms. "I've been crouched over the notebook all afternoon. It's a real haul. Old—I mean old *old*—Tatro, walked away with everything—dolls, beadwork, cradle boards. You name it."

"The thieving bastard!" she marvels again. "So he got away with the good stuff. He had an eye."

We sit there with our food between us. Elsie's hair, sleek and pulled back in a knot, is very white. I am always very proud when people tell me that she is beautiful. She bore me, and then my younger sister, in her thirties when she had given up on getting pregnant. I was a gift. It's very nice being told, all of your life, that you are a gift to someone. We are very happy right then, although I don't know exactly why. Perhaps it is just that our secret expectations or suspicions have been met.

"There was a drum," I say to her.

She pushes her plate away and puts her elbows on the table, leans toward me, peering at me. Her eyes are narrow and slightly upturned at the corners. The iris, dark brown, has the milky blue ring of age but her gaze is still sharp. She is waiting for me to describe the drum.

"One of the big drums," I say. Her fingers flicker on the table.

"Was it dressed?"

"What?"

"Decorated."

"Yes."

"How?"

I tell her about the figures and the cross.

"Not a cross, not Christian. That is either a star or the sign of the four directions. Was it painted?"

"There was a yellow line."

She closes her eyes, presses two fingers to the space between her eyebrows. I watch her carefully because she does this when she is trying to form a thought. I am quiet. Finally, she speaks. She talks a long time, and I can only sum up what she says: The drum is the universe. The people who take their place at each side represent the spirits who sit at the four directions. A painted drum, especially, is considered a living thing and must be fed as the spirits are fed, with tobacco and a glass of water set nearby, sometimes a plate of food. A drum is never to be placed on the ground, or left alone, and it is always to be covered with a blanket or quilt. Drums are known to cure and known to kill. They become one with their keeper. They are made for serious reasons by people who dream the details of their construction. No two are alike, but every drum is related to every other drum. They speak to one another and they give their songs to humans. I should be careful around the drum. She is bothered by its presence in the collection.

"It's more alive than a set of human bones," she finishes, then hesitates. "Of course, that is a traditional belief, not mine."

I nod with some relief, for although I am surprised by my actions this afternoon, I do not believe of course that the drum itself possesses a power beyond its symbolism and antiquity.

After my mother goes to bed, I clear a pile of my files and notebooks off a low table in the corner of my bedroom and then I bring the drum inside and balance it carefully on the table. I shove two chairs up against each side. Whenever I touch the drum, even to set it down, it makes a sound. A high, hollow note. An uncertain creak, like a question. A slight tap on its edge sets up reverberations. It is exquisitely sensitive for so powerful an instrument, and I wonder what it sounds like when struck with force, by many and in unison. I turn off the light, get into bed, and lie there in my room with the drum. I leave my windows open just a crack at night, even in the winter. I like my room chilly. The darkness crackles with March cold and from time to time, deep in the woods, a barred owl screams like a woman in pain. I imagine that I might have dreams—

pragmatic as I consider myself, it has been a long, strange day. The realization that I've stolen the drum outright surfaces and sinks. Tomorrow's Saturday and I'm glad that I have got the weekend to decide how to proceed with the estate—I'm not sure I trust myself to catalogue another thing. No matter how justified by history I feel, I tell myself that I will not evade my guilt or rationalize away my conduct.

Which is not the same as even considering that I might do the right thing and return the drum to Sarah Tatro.

All I have is other people's lives. What I do belongs to them and to my mother—her business, her legacy, her blood. Even the box of tears in my closet belongs to another woman, L.M.B. But now I've stolen the drum. And it seems to me, as I am lying in the dark of my room, that my instinctive theft signifies a matter so essential that it might be called survival. I have stepped out of rules and laws and am breathing thin, new air. My theft is but the first of many I'll accomplish—though not of objects. There are other things I need and will have to have, things I'll take. Thoughts, plans, private rages, and even joys now secret to myself.

I am usually a devoted sleeper, but tonight I'm wakeful. All night, it seems, I am listening. Thinking. So many ideas float in half-formed and then veer off.

When things are very quiet, the old house ticks. Not regularly, like a clock, but softly all through itself as the slats in the walls change temperature or the plaster tightens or the earth shifts underneath the granite slab foundation. From time to time, the little sounds that the house makes reverberate inside of the drum. My breath does, too. I hear a rising, then a falling. In and out. A greatness, a lightness. I grow heavier, then so inert my body seems without life. Between breaths, I lose feeling. And then my chest fills, a resurrection.

There is another thing that our old house does in the deep of night. I have heard it before and now I wait for it to happen. The house releases the whole day's footsteps. All day we press down minutely on the wide old floorboards, moving about on small, regular errands, from room to room. It takes hours for the boards to readjust, to squeak back up the nails, for the old fibers of the pinewood to recover their give. As they do so, they reproduce the sounds of footsteps. In the night our maze of pathways is audibly retraced. I am used to it, as is mother, but sometimes a wakeful guest is frightened. I can understand this. For now, as I rise and I stand in half-darkness in the doorway of my bedroom, I hear the distinct creak of footsteps proceeding toward me, then past me, over to my bed. It's very cold. My skin prickles. I feel the breath of my own passage, as though my dead self and living self briefly met in that doorway to sleep.

3

The Orchard

A disturbed hush has fallen upon our road. The two young people haunt it more than one would think. It is impossible to pull out onto the gravel without thinking of Davan's rattling, red car or without imagining the long, slight form of Kendra trailing black scarves as she took her moody ambles, ears plugged with music. After the Assembly of God outpouring for Davan, which left Elsie and me in a daze, we attended the strangely shuttered memorial service for Kendra, along with Krahe's sister from Vancouver, and seven or eight of Kendra's drooping friends. Since then I have been afflicted with the pity and guilt that comes over one at the death of a person disliked. I now think of good things about Kendra, and there are many—her affection for her father, her goodness to Davan, even her self-absorbed dramas now seem so innocent: the searchings of an artistic child. I begin to wonder at my own antipathy—or jealousy— and as I do I wonder again at Kurt's hostility toward Davan. These days Kurt looks stunned and confused, and I see that he's turned inward, blamed himself for a purely emotional, fatherly mishandling of things, a tampering, a fatal clumsiness. His rage at Davan was disturbing, even brutal, but it was part of his protectiveness and Kurt castigates himself for it now.

Night after night, he comes to me. He never leaves the road. There are no trips to the city. No restless absences, unexplained. Kurt's step is nearly silent, as he knows just where the stairs creak. When he pauses in the doorway to my room, my two selves stand apart and allow him to pass. Yet I am a realist. I know why he's always here. One night he says, "You're getting me through this, you know." His voice is low and ragged. I can't bear not knowing anymore.

"You had someone, before," I say.

There is silence.

"Answer me."

"Yes. Not anymore." There is a lonely pause. "Never again."

I stare at his face, all shadows in the silver dark, and the terrible, familiar wish to be nothing, to shatter to dust, moves me. His lie kills all feeling. I break along with him and go where he is. Our struggle goes on and on in the blackness. We are like feral children, with no rules. Pain and sex dull grief and we are both in grief, it seems. For me, this is old. I probably know what is happening better than he does because I've tried over and over to wreck myself on another human, and always failed. I fail now. For it seems that my sorrow is deep in my bones and I'd have to break every single one to let it out.

He falls asleep with his hand between my legs and his face in my hair. He is weeping in his dreams. I stay awake, considering. He said that he wants to marry me now, that we must always be together. But now that I know he can lie to me, what comfort can there be? His turning to me in such need is not a true statement of his feelings; there is nothing to make of it, really, except that I am near and willing to stay. After a short while, he wakes again, and turns to me and I am there. The night is very black, there is no moon, and I am glad that I've put the drum outside my room, on a table at the end of the hall.

When I wake in the morning, he is gone. I roll over, put on my robe, and go down the hall. Not until I'm brushing my teeth do I notice that my face is smeared with blood. Red-brown streaks mark the back of my hands, my arms, my body. I walk back into my room and see that the sheets are splotched and rubbed with signs. It isn't, somehow, horrifying. I conclude he's slashed himself, and it seems to me that this is what people do. Later that day, when I walk up the road to see him, and when I find him staring quietly at a certain stone he has been thinking about for years, I touch his shoulder.

"Where have you cut yourself?" I ask.

He shrugs.

"Kurt, I should look. They might be deep. You're bleeding a lot."

He raises his eyebrows and looks into my face.

"Leave it alone," he begs.

I return to my house.

As in French novels when the scheming Marquis boasts of a lover *I have made her my creature*, so I begin to understand that Kurt Krahe is making me his own. His grief is sucking me into an old persona, one I have forced myself to leave behind. Yet I must admit, and this shames me, his tearing need is a thrill to me, and I am convinced that he is mine alone. I am reduced, but I need him, too.

And as with all matters of too serious nature, there is absurdity. One morning, instead of contemplating the heft and soul of his sculpture, or driving twenty miles for his favorite dark roast coffee beans, or fixing his garage door, or sitting by his daughter's grave, he is cutting the dead grass in my yard. Davan Eyke's job once. Krahe is pushing the finicky red mower now.

I bought that mower for myself. The mower was the first birthday present I ever bought for which I would be the recipient. By which might be assessed the level of self-indulgence I commit. Who buys oneself a lawn mower for her fiftieth birthday? Shouldn't I have given myself a spa package, a new bathrobe? Shouldn't I have had someone else to give me a present, perhaps? Of course, I did get one from mother—a cameo strung on a velvet cord. Circa 1910. Italian, with exquisite detail, pink and white shell. I hung it over my bed and have never worn it. But I used my lawn mower last summer. It made me feel good, even when Davan nearly wrecked it, until now. I realize I am dismayed to see Kurt working on my lawn, though I am pleased to see that the machine is holding up well.

Kurt is cutting at a pretty good speed. He prefers the side-to-side strip pattern. I, on the other hand, am the type who cuts the lawn in ever smaller squares. He marches back and forth across the yard. But here's the thing. The grass doesn't need cutting. It hasn't even started growing yet. It's still practically winter. There is green beneath the unraked thatch, but not a shoot that reaches past the toe's tip.

I call my mother to the window. We stand together watching our road's resident artist. He is dressed out of character, like a student's preppy dad, in dull orange pants, a white golf jacket, thick white socks, and cushiony walking shoes, also white, now mud-stained.

"How did this come about?" I ask.

Elsie gives me the suspicious and assessing look that she should be directing at Krahe. It is not my fault that he's here. "I have no idea," she says. "He just appeared."

"Appeared?"

"And began to tinker with the lawn mower. Then he took it out."

I nod. I think of saying to her, Don't you know what this means? But then she would say in all innocence, Getting the grass cut? And I would have to tell her, No, cut by Krahe. Who has just lost his daughter. Who is not really cutting the grass at all, at least the living grass. He is perhaps shredding the tips of last fall's dead grass, but that is beside the point. I would have to explain.

Elsie, when a man as arrogant as Krahe, a man who believes that he is touched by genius, an artist, comes to the house of his lover and cuts her grass during his usual working hours, not to mention those hours he should be devoting to his own personal mourning, he is saying, "Look what you've done to me. Observe my devotion. My wastage of genius hours on your lawn. Here I am cutting your grass, which will grow back. While I could have been creating something out of my sorrow, for the ages."

But of course it would go further.

"And, darling," he would say, "now that I've wasted time on your lawn, I expect that you will spend your time (much different from wasting it, as I am a genius and you are not) on me. You are my creature."

I turn away from the window. My thoughts are too cynical. Perhaps I should see his action as another irrational sign of his bewilderment. I should treat him gently—as one comforts those caught in the unruly dictates of their mourning—but the drone of the mower on the other side of the house drills my thoughts and I quickly leave, jump into the car, and drive off, too fast.

*   *   *

There is a man at the isolated end of the road who exists in the firm conviction that he is an American Indian—apparently, though, he cannot decide which kind. He probably has no tribal blood whatsoever—he knows that—though his origins are complicated by the vastness of his family, who came over on the next boat after the *Mayflower*. They are originally the same family as the one whose estate I'm handling (and thieving from, I remind myself)—the Tatros. Except that the Tatros are not all related anymore. They've lived here and there in the town and on the flats for as long as the town has been here. In fact, they owned the original land grant and the town's main road was named for Colonel John Tipton Tatro. They are the Tatros of Tatro Road and Tipton Hall and Tatro Fairgrounds and, up until now, of Tatro Farm. Having sold the land grant and bought bits of property here and there, they are less prominent, and some have fallen onto the fringes, like outbred dogs. Yet they are still a force. There is always the peculiar feeling that they could spread, once again, link acreage, and take over. Probably not Squaw Man Tatro, though. That's what he's sometimes called. His name is really Everett. He's nicknamed Kit. He's got an Indian name, too, one that sounds like something from an old gunslinger movie or a Karl May novel. It might be White Owl, same as the drugstore cigars. At any rate, as I drive toward the clarity of my bank account, there beside the road is Kit Tatro, hitchhiking. He wears jeans, a vest of some poorly tanned animal hide, a salmon-colored polyester shirt, the kind that transforms human sweat to toxic gas. The fumes waft in when I roll down the window to ask his destination. There is a method to his decoration that I can't read. He is cleanly shaven and his longish gray-brown hair is clipped more tidily than usual. That indicates grooming. Yet there is the awful odor. Around his neck he wears five or six leather strings from which hang various amulets. At first glance, I see a bear's claw, a small tusk of some sort, a brown leather pouch that looks like it contains herbs, or maybe human knuckle bones. He thrusts his head a bit wildly in and says he has to visit the bank.

"Happens I'm going there. But—"

"I know. I stink." He opens the door and slides into the passenger's seat. "I've been tanning hides."

I keep the windows open and put the air on full blast. The smell seems more bearable at first when I know it isn't actually Kit, and then I think of the skins and the whole mess of scraping them down and somehow I would rather smell Tatro again. Every time I've been tempted to tell him that my mother is an actual American Indian, an Ojibwe, something about Kit Tatro has stopped me—the sight of some newly skinned creature in his yard. Or, as now, a certain look he has, or smell. At least it isn't far to town. What we call the bank is just an automated teller machine at the center store. Once the store was named Tatro's, of course. For some reason the place has recently been remodeled on the outside to resemble a general store out of the Old West. The building is low and square with a tall false front and a sign painted with fake old-timey serifed letters. So in a way, Kit Tatro fits there. A hangdog mountain man come down to the settlement for grub.

"I've been doing more research on my genealogy," he says. "I've come a cropper on the great-grandmother's side, though I still think she must have been an Iroquois. They would have hid it for the shame." He sounds a note of indignation and despair. "Always the secrecy, the hushed voices! Nobody will say what it was my great-grandfather did, who he married, what she was, who she was."

"It's so complicated," I sympathize, stopping the car, opening my door quickly. Kit gets out too, and we walk up to the cash machine together. There is a light breeze blowing. I step upwind of him. He lets me go first and studiously looks away as I tap in my PIN. The machine offers me a little stack of money; I take it, and walk over to the store to buy some cream, a six-pack of Krahe's favorite beer, a can of ginger ale, a newspaper, and a muffin.

"I think the best kind is lemon poppy seed," says Kit. He holds out a root beer to show the teen behind the cash register, pays, and we walk out the door together. A ride home is assumed. At least he's changed my focus somewhat, and I've stopped dwelling on Krahe's lawn cutting. I've always been a little curious about Kit's passion to be an Indian. It seems a lonely obsession—I never see him with other Indians or would-be Natives. And as the point is to have a tribe and belong to a specific people, I wonder what he gets out of his fantasy. But of course, he explains on the way home, his search is about making some connection. *Only connect*, he says, absurdly, and adds, *Maybe E. M. Forster was an Iroquois at heart.* Once he knows for certain where to connect, maybe everything about him will fall into place. Then again, maybe Kit Tatro irritates me because at some level I understand his longing and confusion all too well. I let him out at the turnoff to his house, and keep the windows wide open the rest of the way.

When I walk into the house, I see immediately that Elsie is serving Krahe a cup of hot chocolate. He's gotten a chill—cutting the grass! It upsets me to see that she's poured the chocolate into one of her favorite cups—exquisitely etched and hand-painted, one of an incomplete set she bought before an estate sale. She's put the cup under hot water to warm first, then dried it, her little trick, to pre-

vent a skin forming on the milk. She has given up her disapproba-
tion, or her fear of my being used, and she has decided to encourage him, I fear. A low sensation of hurt boils up in me, its source
mysterious. Why, now, has she decided to stop looking the other
way? Because she can't. I see now that the grass cutting is Kurt's
way of bringing our relationship into the open. He's doffed his
jacket. They are talking in normal, convivial tones about the town
road agent and how he has suggested inserting speed bumps on the
straight, paved section of Revival Road.

"He says he's clocked some going seventy." They both nod, together, almost in unison. Then a stiff break, a beat of silence as both
remember Davan's run and wish to veer away from unsteady
ground. I have timed my entrance perfectly. With relief, both realize
that I am standing in the kitchen entrance.

"Would you care for some hot chocolate?" says Elsie, getting up
to fetch another of her special cups from the high shelf of the cupboard.

"Sit down!" Krahe rises to give me his chair, a gesture of old-
fashioned courtesy that might touch me, as he is not at all chival-
rous, except that I feel so awkward and suspicious.

"Thanks for cutting the grass." I roughly pull a different chair
out and plop down. I find myself glaring at the cup in his hand.
"It's very thoughtful of you. And very unlike you," I add once
Elsie's back is turned. "You've got more important things to con-
cern yourself with. I've got someone else to cut the grass, anyway."

Not true, but I'm determined to quash Krahe's possible repeti-
tion of this favor, no matter what motivated it.

"Who?" says Elsie, overhearing me.

I turn, widen my eyes, and blink meaningfully at her, but she is
bending to place the chocolate before me. I am stung by this fake

demure look of hers—the downcast eyelashes hide righteous glee and it seems to me, suddenly, they are a *they*, in cahoots. Elsie has decided something. She's ahead of me. I am bewildered. And I'm also caught in my grass-cutting lie, because they know everyone I know, and I wouldn't ask a stranger, and they'll expect whomever I mention to come and cut the grass. I open my mouth not knowing what I'll blurt and out comes the name Kit Tatro. It makes sense, as I've just dropped him off, that his name should still be on my tongue. Now I'll have to rush back and persuade him to cut our lawn before either mother or Krahe find and question him.

"Oh, Squaw Man," says Krahe, dismissive. "He doesn't even cut his own lawn."

"He needs the money." True enough. I gulp down the chocolate too fast, scald my throat, and rise with a rude abruptness.

"And for your information, squaw means vagina, or rather, cunt. It is an insult."

"Oh," says Krahe. His eyes flicker as he scrambles for a light tone. "Knowing Tatro, he'd probably find that a compliment."

"An insult to *us*," I say, indicating Elsie, who turns away to show she'll have no part of this. I am the one embarrassing her. It is then that I am positive she is rejecting me, pushing me out the door toward Krahe. Perhaps she is tired of the secrecy, or the discretion, really, but wasn't it for her benefit? Perhaps she wants to set me free, thereby invalidating all we have carefully constructed, cheapening all that I've given up in order to stay with her. I don't want to be free in that way. Krahe pretends not to notice that I am standing now, breathing hard, upset, ready to escort him out. He continues the thread of a conversation that he and Elsie had seemingly left unfinished.

"Just let me know," he says, "about those trees. I'll be glad to bring my chain saw over and—"

"What trees?" I break in.

"The apple trees," says Elsie, "the orchard. Krahe thinks that with a bit of judicious pruning—"

"A great deal of severe pruning!" Krahe says with an infuriating laugh.

"—we could bring back the orchard!"

"Now while it's still cold, before the buds form. They could even bloom this spring."

"The orchard is gone." My heart flares with anger and I want to reach over and shake her, but I keep my voice even. "You know I like it ruined."

"It could be beautiful again, alive," she says. And just like that I know she has abandoned me. Leaning on the table, I knock over my cup of chocolate and must grab dish towels off the counter to mop with. Krahe actually tries to help me and suddenly, over the spilled chocolate and in the smell of dusty grass clippings, I detect the shadow of a masculine expectation. It advances across the floor like a gloaming, to where I'm mopping up the syrupy spill on hands and knees, a dusk of longing that I would have loved to enter the day before but which panics me now. I rinse a towel out beneath the faucet, wringing it too hard, glancing out the window at the rows of beautifully gnarled trees.

The kitchen feels too small, even the house too enclosed. Elsie's sudden betrayal has pierced me. I feel childishly vulnerable. I hang the towel up and smooth my hair back into its clip. "I'm going out," I say before either Elsie or the too attentive Krahe can form the next sentence. And I do go out. I've still got the car keys in my pocket. I climb swiftly into the Subaru and drive to Kit Tatro's. Though I could easily have walked there, Krahe might have taken his leave of Elsie and followed, cut me off, found me out.

*　　*　　*

I pull into Tatro's littered yard and park next to piled bones and the tatters of a painted tipi. I've seen it often, hiking by, and now I notice up close that the symbols painted on the sides with worn acrylics are finely done, very detailed. A black bear, side view, is caught in midstride. There is a white line leading from its mouth into the bear's stomach, ending in a sharp spear point. I suppose this has something to do with hunting magic, and indeed, Kit Tatro can use some. I happen to know, because he sometimes asks permission to hunt on our land, that he takes advantage of the doe season open only to those who shoot with muzzle loaders. I've lost track of his comings and goings. Sometimes he gets his doe, other years he complains of wet gunpowder or the excitement of a misfire. He's never talked of going after bear.

I get out and walk past the rusted Studebaker that I imagine Tatro has had towed here intending to restore, past a stack of mink or chicken crates, an unraveling yellow roll of crime scene tape perhaps bought at a garage sale, a little tan junked computer, a bowl of teeth, open cold frames jammed with milk cartons full of dirt out of which frail tomato seedlings urge themselves to light, hardening off. There is no sign of Kit and he doesn't answer my knock. But the solid door behind his screen door is open. The doorknob to the screen door is a screwed-on wooden spool, the old kind before thread came wound on plastic. I touch the knob. Somehow it charms me, that little thoughtfulness of saving and using the old spool. Maybe one of Kit's wives saved the spool—he's had a succession of pale and stoop-shouldered girlfriends, unhealthy-looking women all alike, sad and rickety-boned. Not one of them can I put a name to, and not one of them has stayed with him.

"Hey!" Kit rounds the corner, wiping his hands on the droopy stomach of his T-shirt. "You're back!"

"I had a thought." I want to get this over with as quickly as possible. "Would you be open to taking care of our lawn? Can we strike a deal? We need somebody to mow."

Kit Tatro gives me an ironic, awful smile (two of his teeth are gray and fanglike), and he holds out his hand in a sweep to show me that he isn't a person who mows even his own yard.

"Well, I know that," I say, "but you can use our mower."

"I dunno, I'm kind of backed up."

I want to say, Backed up skinning roadkill? But I find myself instead doing something that I wouldn't ever have thought of doing. I am desperate to seal this pact with Tatro, and most of all anxious to make certain Kurt Krahe never again has an excuse to mow our lawn.

"Did you know, by the way, that my mother's one-half Indian? That she's Ojibwe? That's why I was looking at your Native stuff." I nod slowly at the tipi and heaped bones.

Kit Tatro suddenly stands rooted, serious, silent but electrified like a person who has grabbed hold of a live-current horse fence. He darts his eyes from side to side and then his whole face twists with a weasel interest. I've somehow risen from the dead, or at least from a place of low obscurity. I'm magnetized, a super-being. I can't help feel gratified, though I can see right now I will regret this revelation.

"Gee," he marvels. "I thought you guys were, like, Korean or something." He turns his mouth down, lengthens and strokes his stubbly jaw. "Yeah. Whew. When should I start?" An unworthy thrill of gratification takes me by surprise. I've managed not only to thwart Krahe's lawn-mowing plot, but also to punish Elsie by means so obscure she'll never know what I've done. Now she'll be saddled with Kit Tatro's attempts to untangle his genealogy and join his tribe, and she'll have to endure his questions about her own knowledge and upbringing, which will disappoint him, as my mother is perfectly assimilated, cold-blooded and analytical about the reservation present, and utterly dismissive of history.

I am not inexperienced in love, I just haven't been successful at it, if you count long-term marriage as the benchmark. But the couples I used to envy have all broken apart. And marriage simply scares me. Perhaps I excuse my lack of courage in the matter by observing that those I do know who've stayed together have fused or discarded chunks of personality. Canada geese. Swans. Crows. Ravens. All creatures who mate for life. Perhaps they have an ancient genetic command woven into them that we now lack and long for in equal measure. The phone beside my bed rings. Krahe calls me at midnight, knowing I fall asleep shortly after. Sometimes he calls to say good night, and tonight I consider not picking up the telephone.

"Just called to say good night," he says, and because his voice has always moved me with its resonance and depth, and because he is on the other end of the telephone, not here with me, I feel safe enough to be somewhat more direct than I usually dare. I actually tell him not to cut the grass because it makes me uncomfortable, because I can't stand to see him doing something so mundane, and because I think it is a bad sign.

"A bad sign of what?"

"Your sorrow," I say, wary of referring to our relationship. "Going around cutting people's grass is so completely out of character that it signals, to me at least, how broken you are and how lost in your grief. Just to see you behind a lawn mower is disturbing."

But he seems pleased about that, and he laughs a little.

"You don't know me well," he says. "You don't know that I actually like cutting grass and that for me it is a sign of getting better. It represents new growth. Besides, it is not just anybody's grass. It's your grass."

"Which you are shaving to the bare earth," I say, then I soften, and drop my voice. "There wasn't any grass there to begin with, Kurt, it's too early in the spring. The grass has really not begun to grow yet."

He's very quiet. We breathe on the line. Eventually he clears his throat.

"Oh, fuck," he says, "maybe I'm in bad shape. I didn't notice that."

Then he asks me to go out to dinner with him at Sweet's Mansion, a grand house restored as a restaurant and considered quite romantic. He's never asked me out or taken me anywhere in public before and perhaps out of sheer surprise I accept the invitation.

After I hang up I unplug the phone. I have brought the drum back in and covered it with my favorite old star quilt, but I am very conscious of it and I have developed more affection for it than I should feel for an object that I intend to repatriate—for we'll find the rightful owner by inheritance, I've no doubt of that. At the furthest reaches of my doubt, I admit of possibilities. In dark hours, my mind creaks open and allows a sensation of comfort in the great drum's presence. The house is quiet, the road still, even the wind in the pines a mere shiver. It is one of those hours when the world takes a breath. When for a moment there is peace, not desolation, at the heart of things. I turn out the lights and lie on my back, bunch a fat pillow under my knees, stretch out my arms, take up the whole bed, close my eyes. I try very hard to put Krahe out of my mind, and after a while I succeed in drifting into a delicious state of half-sleep. I love to fall through that transition alone, to feel the gentle prickling of my body lifting off, the fluttering of my mind as it releases images, talk, pictures that begin to lose reference until they take on a dream irrationality. Tonight there is the brilliance of Krahe's white shoes and socks methodically striding back and forth across the dead lawn. There is my mother's earnest and disquieting betrayal. Chocolate steaming in figured cups. The drum gradually falling asleep beneath its quilt. Then, as I am tumbling toward sleep through the brain's dark, I see a tarp of battered canvas, frail seedlings, a painted bear and the white arrow at its heart.

I am much more familiar with the Sweet Mansion and its furnishings than are most who come to dine. The Greek Revival mansion was built by the New Hampshire mill owner Henry Sweet, who worked hundreds and maybe thousands of young women into early graves and created of their dead-hearted misery and the electricity generated by the millrace he owned an illuminated park for his children. The glow cast from the high plateau of Goodie Hill, the setting for the mansion and its grounds, could be seen far into Vermont and was used to guide aircraft down the Connecticut River well into the 1940s. The children kept up the property into the second half of the last century and then sold the place to a developer. Elsie handled the estate sale, which was surprisingly paltry as all of the furnishings and heirlooms had long been divided up among the many Sweet descendants. The developer speculated by building a dozen houses on five-acre lots on one end of the property, and used the proceeds to restore the mansion and open it as a restaurant, which was his dream. My familiarity with the contents of the place is the result of having scouted out and sold most of the nineteenth-century (we try not to use the word Victorian) furnishings to the owner. Almost none of them are original to the mansion, but they look as though they are because we took such care in finding good pieces from that period.

I am sitting across from Kurt, knees under a starched white cloth, in one of a set of Belter tiger-oak rococo chairs, in a corner of what was once a formal parlor. He is dressed as himself once again, a rumpled shirt of some rugged mixture of silks and cottons, a beautiful tweed jacket, jeans worn in for real, not distressed. He runs his fingers across the top of his head. His hair is longer than he usually allows it, and I notice as I always do when it is a bit too long that he has really got quite beautiful hair, thick and springy, with a wave to it. He is one of those men who'd turn heads if he let his hair grow out, become a streaked mane. Maybe he'd be insufferable, I think, maybe he'd never even look at me. Then I'd be safe.

"I can't stop thinking about Kendra today," he says. "I feel heavy."

"What do you think of when you think of Kendra?" I ask.

His face freezes to a careful mask, but after a little while he smiles and his features soften. "You know what I think of? How she traced her hand and drew a beak on her thumb and made a turkey. You know, the turkey hands they make in kindergarten at Thanksgiving. She made one for me last year as a kind of joke."

"A sweet joke."

"I know." His hand on the water glass trembles a little. He takes a drink. "What do you do with it," he says. "What do you do?"

There is nothing to say to that.

"She was lucky to have you as her father. You were a good father" is all I finally come up with.

"Do you think so?" He searches my face, his eyes bleak, his stare endless.

"Yes, I think so."

He nods. He keeps on staring at me. "Faye, I know she's gone. And I sometimes feel you slipping away, too, please don't slip away."

"I'm not."

But inside, I know I am and he knows it too, and it isn't just the lie, unless the lie stands for everything I am afraid of. I do not know why it is happening.

"You can't stand it, can you," he says after a long pause.

"Can't stand what?"

"What I'm going through. You think it's catching."

"No."

"You think you'll get sadness, grief, whatever, like a virus."

"No."

"Then what is it? I lied to you, I know I did, but I never will again. I have taken a vow in my very being that I will die first. No lies, ever."

I nod, I want to say I believe him, I want to answer, but a nameless feeling close to dread sifts up inside me and covers my heart and takes away my words, leaving a kind of shame.

"I don't know what it is," I whisper, after a time, and we sit there together in baffled silence, touching the bases of our wineglasses.

"I spent about six hours in the woods today," he says at last.

"Looking at rocks?"

"And at stumps. There's something human about them. I've decided that I hate them." Kurt frowns and shuts his eyes, cocks his head to one side as though listening to an interior voice. When he opens his eyes, they are a smoky, soft color and filled with sadness.

"You know, I think I'll have the halibut," I say, then I look down at my hands, and am overtaken by a wash of despair at my clumsiness.

The menu is slightly blurry and as I pretend to read it I am visited by the idea that even our most intimate sexual moments, when he sobs into my hair or I lose all sense of where my body stops or my pleasure and his begins, our nakedness, our imperfections bare to each other's sight, our coarse humor, our dirt, lack of shame, our easy joy, have nothing to do with aspects of ourselves that, if we let them develop, become actual and other selves. The thief in me. The murderously jealous father in him. The wish I have to make him feel better, which seems so pure, may be selfish. I understand his tedious anguish.

There is very little said about how repetitious grief is.

"Why don't you want me to prune the orchard?" asks Krahe.

A surprise darkness skims up my back. It is a prickle so unfamiliar that at first I do not recognize it as anger. And in fact, my voice emerges sounding different from how I feel. It is light, maybe girlish—a mature woman's panic.

"I told you I like it the way it is," I say, "dead and ruined."

"It could be beautiful."

"It is."

Before he can speak again, I've risen and turned away. I thread among tables and chairs, and then up a set of stairs, gliding my hand along the smooth banister. The feel of old wood calms me a little, but I still feel like running down the back stairs and out what was once the scullery door. Instead, I continue down the hall. The ladies powder room is furnished with an exquisite Egyptian Revival dressing table that I remember as having gone very reasonably at auction. There is also a fainting couch upholstered in striped golden satin. I sit down on it and then tentatively lie back, close my eyes.

Perhaps it was easier to live with the longing for Kurt, the uncer-

tainties, even to indulge the unnecessary, and maybe insulting, se-
cretive precautions. To deal with him in the everyday world of
sorrow and surprise takes the mythology out of the relationship,
but it is more than that. I feel his suffering when he is near as a
physical weight, crushing one heartbeat and the next, squeezing my
breath. The madness of sorrow emanates from him. It enters and
unfurls in me. It revives my own pain. Unsolvable. Alive. Death has
again brushed close, hurled Kendra and Davan off the bridge,
tossed Tatro down a steep ditch and allowed him to die in the earli-
est spring growth. I am part of the chain of events that began when
Davan gunned his engine on Revival Road. And the drum is part of
it, too, and my taking of it. Kurt Krahe's mowing of dead grass is
part of it, as is his pledge to prune the orchard. For death has set
changes into motion all up and down Revival Road, and there is no
telling when one event will stop bumping into the next.

Returning to the room where Krahe is waiting, I pause in the
doorway. I have taken another route back to the table and Kurt is
staring at the place where he thinks I will appear. It seems a bit un-
derhanded to watch him as he watches for me, but I do anyway. He
is not talking on his cell phone, which actually gets a signal high on
this hill. He is not even looking at the woman at the next table, who
is beautiful. He's not drinking wine or fiddling with his napkin. He
is just waiting. Waiting for me. And the way he is sitting there, unaware and waiting for me, strikes me. Perhaps this is the last
moment in my life I will be truly appreciated by a man. I stand there
and take it in.

When finally he rises, anxious, I propel myself into the room.
He doesn't say "Where were you?" and I don't make an excuse. We
sit down slowly at either side of the table and proceed to order and
then eat our food—everything is either tasteless or too rich. We

speak about small things with calm detachment. I marvel at this. You would not think we ever slept together. You would not think he pulled my hair until tears filled my eyes or that I bit him so hard I drew blood. You would not think that sometimes we have gone so far into sex that we could not get out, that sex kept driving us, hurting us. You would not think we have looked into each other's eyes, boundlessly at peace, or that we'd ever lain naked in the raining woods and laughed ourselves sick. I know he is on the brink of asking *what is this* the way people do, but I will not allow him to speak. So we talk about the rocks, the ravens, the trees, and all of the little things that happen on our road.

I'm home before eleven, like a good teen on a demure date. The light is on in the first-floor living room, where Elsie likes to sit and listen to music. She has Satie on. The master of punctuation. When I walk into the room she stiffens in her chair, casts her gaze upon me, and says, in that parental voice even grown children dread to hear, "Sit down, we have something to talk about."

"Can it wait?" It must be that she has seen the drum, and although I know it is inevitable, I really don't want to talk about it tonight.

Elsie stares at me, trying not to blink. The music has become the backdrop to a suspense movie. All jagged exclamation points. I turn it off and sit down across from her. She is wearing an old pink chenille bathrobe and elegant turquoise earrings.

"You left these in." I tap my earlobes.

"On purpose," she says.

"Oh?"

She pauses in an ominous way before she speaks. "Years ago, I nearly stole these earrings from a client."

I turn away and busy myself examining the folds and stitches of one of her more complex afghans. She continues.

"I was very tempted. I happened to have recognized the earrings from a little-known Curtis photograph. It wasn't that the earrings are so valuable, but that they'd lain close to the girl's neck, the subject, and if I had them it seemed, I felt, as though I was part of his work too."

"I took the drum for similar reasons."

"Oh, no doubt." Her voice is dry. After an empty pause, she prompts, "When are you planning to return it?"

"I'm not."

She throws her hands up, lets them fall to her knees and hang down, limp rags of dismay.

"It would look odd if I just brought it back now. No one knows it's missing."

"Nonsense. You could say you had it repaired."

"Well, I could. You're right."

"But you won't. You don't want to."

"No."

"What are you going to do with it?" she asks, and I respond before I've thought out my answer. The resolute note in my voice surprises me.

"For now, keep it. Later we'll find the rightful owner."

She shrugs and seems to think aloud. "Well, yes . . . it's Ojibwe and the fact that Tatro spent his life as an Indian agent on our home reservation probably makes your guess as to its origin, maybe even your intention, fairly reasonable." She opens her arms as though surrendering. "Good luck to you, then. Not only do I want no part of it, I'm thinking of bringing it back to the Tatros' myself. You could purchase it, you know. I bought the earrings."

"Before or after you told the family that they were in a famous photograph?"

I think I've got her, but she refuses to be embarrassed.

"Only a fool would have revealed that. Of course I got them for a good price."

It's no use, and I hate being at odds with her. Still, the idea that she would actually take it upon herself to return the drum makes me regress a little. "Don't you touch that drum!"

"You exasperate me." She closes her mouth in that tight, straight line that means we're finished arguing. This is as angry as we ever get, and we both know it won't last. Sure enough, over breakfast, Elsie tells me that she's decided, upon reflection, that the fact that the drum was stolen from our own people is a piece of sychronicity so disturbing that she now understands how I was motivated. I, on the other hand, am moved to tell her that I am sorry to have possibly compromised her also in the theft, as it is both of our business reputations at stake, and even (now that I know she won't hold me to it) that I'll consider returning the drum. But she says that she wouldn't think of returning it, that she's always wondered exactly how it was that Jewett Parker Tatro acquired his hoard, and that maybe in discovering more about this particular drum we will find that out. She's willing to help me, in fact, learn its origins.

Elsie has ideas. She is spilling over with ideas and with lists of people and with plans to see them. "I'm thinking of old Shaawano, gone now," she says, "and Mrs. String. Her first name is Chook and she's related to the old man and married to Mike String. Lots of the people have passed on, of course, the ones who would know. But to lose or be swindled out of a drum like this is no small thing."

We are sitting together over our usual spare female breakfast of coffee and whole grain toast. Sometimes we add yogurt or fruit, but I haven't grocery-shopped yet this week and we are even down to the last of the bread. Elsie has toasted the heels for herself and given me the last two regular slices. I didn't like the heels as a girl, and that little forgiving sign of her motherly attention, a tiny thoughtfulness, touches me. But I say nothing about it. I only agree that we should hire some extra people this spring or summer so we can travel as we choose. I know that the Shaawano family is of the original people who either moved south and returned, or who originally came from the south and were named for that direction. I remember Mrs. String, a round woman shaped more like a knot than a string. She is a vivid, little, lumpy-bodied lady with dark, age-freckled skin and a fluffy halo of dandelion white, permanented hair. She tends to dress in outfits of bright, flowery rayon separates that mock each other and yet somehow make their peace. I remember admiring how a skirt blazing purple iris and a burst of roses on her vest oddly complemented her poppy-dotted blouse and gave a kind of whirling effect to her, as if she were always in motion. Mrs. String's voice is extremely gentle, marked by the old sweet accent of a person who grew up speaking Ojibwe and whose English is forever rounded and shaped so that all of the words seem kindlier. Mother tells me that Mrs. String's mother would have known some of the original signers of the treaty that provided for the reservation. She probably spoke about them to her daughter. Those people were the holdouts, the ones upon whose stubbornness the land claim is based. She might have known about the ones who famously would not sign the payoff later, as well, like Old Nanapush, whose formal portrait by a government photographer around the time of his death by old age features a discreet but unmistakably obscene gesture. As she speculates, I can see that Elsie is becoming so intrigued with the hunt for the drum's origins that she really may have forgotten, already, that it is stolen property.

"Not so fast," I break into her schemings. "We should wait for a while. I don't want the drum resurfacing so closely connected with Tatro's death that it gets back to his surviving family . . . well, his niece."

Elsie agrees and goes off, muttering, to comb through her files of letters and old papers. There is more to it, though. Even then I know it. I want the drum for myself, at least for a while. I'll keep it off the ground. Already I've got a wooden tobacco box set on the windowsill beside it. I don't know much, but I've got this certainty: That for the time, at least, the drum should stay with me.

Who in all of this time mourns for Davan Eyke? His mother took no more than a few days off of work and still drives the school bus. Every time I see her grim face high in the driver's seat I imagine that she is aching for Davan, but perhaps it's also true she's yearning for a cigarette, for instance on the Monday morning I pass her on the way to the Tatros'. She is standing beside the parked and empty school bus, smoking with calm determination, stoking herself with nicotine. She lights a new cigarette from the still burning stub of the old one and gestures to me as I draw near. I stop in the road and roll down my window. It would be rude to do otherwise. "Hello," she says, and offers me a cigarette. I get out of my car to accept, though I rarely smoke. She lights it for me. I ask how she is.

"I am not so fine," she answers.

"Has your church been supportive?" I ask, because I can't think of anything else to say.

That's when she laughs, in surprise or derision. And her laughter is exactly like Davan's laughter the last time I heard him. It is the laughter of ravens. Grating, unreadable. I stare at her and nod in sudden understanding. The reeking blue smoke curls around us. We are silent. After a few moments, I feel we have entered a nameless and intense mental engagement, that Davan's mother in her sorrow has become savagely herself, and so needn't speak again. Yet she communicates perfectly. She knows. She knows that her son's death had something more to do with Krahe than the eye or facts can tell. She stands with me to try to absorb in words what it is she senses in images. But nothing comes clear.

We grind out the cigarette stubs with the ends of our shoes and then she nods and steps up into the bus. She settles into the driver's seat and looks away from me as she starts the engine. She is an oddly put together woman, with exquisite black eyes and a big white dumpling of a chin. She wears no makeup and cuts her dark hair in a boxy helmet. As she shifts the bus into gear, she lifts her face keenly forward and moves down the bumpy road. She knows all about me, as people on this road do who have known my family since my grandparents came here. Most of all, she knows what happened. She would never wonder why the orchard is forsaken, or try to fix it. I suppose she pities me in some abstract way, as they all do. But that is neither here nor there.

I get back into my car. Driving toward the Tatro place, I am stricken with a familiar and weary repulsion. Everything around me is ludicrously, suddenly, worthless. The Assembly of God sign is even blank. Mrs. Eyke's black laughter and the hard edge of her grief have invaded my thoughts, and I even feel complicit in the death of her son because of my uneasy relationship with Krahe. I am too tangled in what happened, it disturbs me. Perhaps it started on the day I tried to unwedge the Eyke car from the V of birches.

Or it started when I looked too long at Krahe, and he at me, and we knew that we were going to sleep together.

Later that day, as I am taking notes on the contents of the Tatro kitchen, I remember the orchard. It occurs to me that I must develop a more serious plan to thwart Kurt in his next helpful policy. I'm not sure our conversation at Sweet's Mansion persuaded him to leave those trees alone, and I plan to call him that night. I practice several ways to let him know, again, why his attentions aren't wanted in the orchard. I plan to tell him my reasons for leaving the place unkempt, blowzy, unproductive. I want to make sure he lets those apples rot. Fewer blossoms every year, the apples crabbed with thrips and worm-riddled. Branches down, dying, silvered in the heavy sun. I want the long grass to shield the starving mice who gnaw rings around the bases of the apple trees, girdling them, choking them off, bringing them down. But even as I'm thinking this, I am too late. My imaginary conversations and persuasions are a waste of time. For he is revving up his chain saw, macho New England accouterment. He is striding into the orchard and lopping off deadwood with furious ease. Even as I am leaving the Tatro estate, he is piling brush. As I drive home he is putting a cone of fire to the driest twigs. I see the white spiral of smoke as I turn onto Revival Road, and breathe the scent of burning apple wood.

There are weeks of dry warmth, which is bad for our wells and ponds but wonderful to see in the woods. The willows blaze in tender bud. Drifts of wild plum blossoms float among the cavern pines. The rapturous trilling of spring peepers begins, that electronic sexual whine. I keep the windows slightly open as I drive the back roads to the Tatro house, and breathe the watery air. The road's final quarter mile is now almost impassable, the bedrock sunk against gaping holes, swamp grass and overgrown ponds to either side where the peepers warble and moan at a throbbing pitch. As I bounce along I quiet the frogs, momentarily, so that I seem to be continually piercing a wall of sound.

In the orchard, the tiny cold buds are deep pink at the base, white at the tip. The apple trees with their low, thick crotches are shooting out leaves from every node of trunk and every branch behind the cuts. I sit an afternoon away in the snow-drifted grass, the sun-blasted grass, the grass thrown back in long shines of wind, the new grass rising underneath in shy waves of power. I want to remember the orchard as cold, sleeping, wrecked, and still mine, before it happens.

One hot ninety-degree May afternoon throws the switch.

Full moon, a spring midnight. Over everything like clear glass the light falls evenly, a tarnished silver. I am awakened by something stealing up on me, creeping through the window screens, over the drum. A breath of orchard sweetness sails, curls into my room, and I remember the days when the orchard bloomed this way every spring.

My little sister was alive then. Over the years I've warped my life around her memory, I think, even though sometimes now I can't picture her at all except from photographs. I cling to what I do remember of her—little incidents. The time she ripped my fairy book or squeezed the paint from my paint set, or left my clay out to dry. The times she crawled into bed with me after bad dreams—her telling me about them, her breath hot along the side of my face. She tickled spiders out of their webs and wore pink Keds with laces she colored blue with a ballpoint pen. She was a very good sister who loved me so much that she sacrificed herself for me without hesitation and for no use, no use at all. It happened out there in the orchard.

With their deadwood sawed away, the trees have come alive. Each is loaded with as many open blossoms as the live twigs can hold. I rise and walk to the window and sit there with my hand on the drum. I can see her, running in her checkered shorts, with her flag of brown hair flying. She is climbing, quick and nimble. I can just make out the dim shapes of the trees, their twisted arms that hold her. There is no wind and the odor of white blossoms is so profound that it makes steps into the air. Only old wood can bear such rapture, I think, but maybe you have to die first, like the trees, like her.

I am making eggs for breakfast the next morning when I hear the putter of the lawn mower. I've woken furious and self-berating. I dragged my heart around like an apple on a string. Dangled it, daring some man to take a bite. Now Krahe sinks his teeth into it and I'm terrified to be devoured. I jerk away and swing wildly out of reach. And now the lawn mower! I turn off the stove and charge outside, but when the mower comes into view Kit Tatro is behind it with his shirt off. Kit's bare flesh. An unforeseen drawback. His skinny chest heaves as he cuts the rise. The arrowheads and amulets on cords around his neck tangle as he strains to round the bitten stump of an old elm. His arms are ropy and sickly pale. His tender skin is an affront. I want to tell him to put his shirt back on, but don't know how I would say such a thing without hurting his feelings. He waves at me and then I have to wave back. He cuts the engine, walks toward me.

There's a couple of things he wants to ask me.

"You should ask my mother," I say quickly. "She's the one with the cultural knowledge."

"Well, this is about the grass."

"Oh."

We talk about whether to reseed some bald spots and how there are new shade-friendly varieties. For a man with a grown-over, junked-up yard, he is surprisingly critical of the quality of my lawn.

"Some of it's just quack," he states. "Around the back of the house you've been invaded by creeping charley. And there's dandelions. I don't even know where to start with those. What do you want me to do?"

"Just leave them."

He looks dubious, skeptical, pained. To divert him I change the subject.

"Do you know how to install a new lock and key set?"

"Of course."

I show him the back door to the stairway that leads to my room, and he tells me that he can drive to the hardware store for a new lock and that he'll change it as soon as he finishes the lawn. Later, while I am working upstairs, I hear the whine of his drill and the fumbling and knocking of his tools as he sets about the task. Once, twice, I nearly go down and ask him to quit, but then I look out a back window onto the trees, the bursting clouds of blossoms.

4

Jewelweed

The summer passes and I handle the sale of the Tatro collection to a Cincinnati museum, all except for the drum. I've grown very attached to having it in my bedroom; I touch or gaze upon it every time I enter. The drum exerts the most connective hold upon me, and it even starts to influence my dreams. Years ago, my sister stopped coming to me at night. I stopped dreaming of her, and I missed that because it was comforting to imagine that she lived a life parallel to mine and was not dead but merely somewhere else. I even wrote down things she said to me. She spoke in the form of poems. Now I am surprised to dream that she's learned to play the piano. Her hands move with an alert grace, and she glances up at me and nods. She has a husband, a dark man walking at a distance. She is a woman, all grown up in spite of death. Bach's Thirteenth Invention fills my dream with dark rigor, a precise contrapuntal tangle of notes. I confuse her fingers with the passionate mechanism of the spider, and I wake up sweating and cold again with loss. I lost myself along with her back there, I know it. When I touch the drum and think of her, though, I feel much stronger. I feel she has come back to help me. And so the summer, with my dreams of her that return, precious and specific, passes too quickly, as they all do here. The time of the year comes that I am always surprised to find so hard.

The orb spiders have taken up their posts in the unmowed fields of August. Just as things come ripe, the creatures always set their webs, sewn with perfect zigzag seams, across the swathes of grass, jewelweed, goldenrod, milkweed, and burdock behind the sagging barn. Last week, we were approached by a chain restaurant that specializes in false folksiness. Were we interested in selling the wide, weathered boards? Only if you'll take the orb spiders, too, Elsie said. But they just wanted the barn board, and of course she would never destroy the barn. So the spiders wait. I am careful not to disturb their quiet weavings. I watch each spider closely, admire its curved and tapered legs. They are black with hot yellow death's heads on their bellies. They are patient with the gravity of their intent. Of their means of survival they've made these elegant webs, their beauty a by-product of their purpose. Which causes me to wonder, my own purpose on so many days as humble as the spider's, what is beautiful that I make? What is elegant? What feeds the world?

Today, my art is blackberry jam. I gather my equipment. It is time. Late summer builds to a steamy and forgiving lushness in New Hampshire. There is the crushing scent of heated earth. The audible drinking of taproots of white pines. Maples sucking deep. Best, there is the threatful joy of blackberries, bushes so lush with fruit that to pick them I brave the summer's last ticks and stinging flies. We used to pick them, my sister and I, and because of the dreams I think of her with special intensity as I walk. Past the orb spider field, through the laden orchard, down a ravine, and into the boggy cutover land belonging to an absentee landlord, forty acres dense with bramble and slash. I'm heated up, sweating; my hair falls out of its tail and swings down my back. The first blackberries that I pick ring the bottom of the light old lobster pot of dented aluminum, which I've vowed to fill. As soon as the bottom of the pot is covered, a berry-picking stubbornness comes over me. I am a determined picker, lusting after the loaded branches, taking care not to knock off the berries so dense with sweetness they'll let go if the bush is roughly bumped. While picking at the edge of a clearing, I am buzzed low by a helicopter, its loud ratchet an excitement. The metal creature dips so low I can see the features of the men inside of it, and then it veers off, over a fling of young maples. I search my way through the half-dried muck of hidden ponds, skirt the edges of our neighbor's horse pasture, probe the deeper woods for an opening where sunlight has brought from the ground sweet berry bushes and burdened them with fruit. Everywhere, I find jewelweed, or touch-me-not, frail bushes of tiny, fierce, golden-mouthed flowers, spitting seeds.

As I return from my berry picking, carrying the lobster pot with both handles, I brush through the jewelweed. The light seeds bounce off me, ping off the curve of the cheap old pot. Some tear like tiny cannonballs through the webs I've tried so hard to avoid. I stop, of course, and watch the spiders. Exiting the field, I leave them to the suave calm of their thoughtful repairs. My scratches tingle and my hair's a knot of twigs. I'm slick with sweat and gritty with scrapings of bark and wood rot, and I'm peaceful. I have reached an understanding in the woods, as I always do.

Perhaps, I think as I settle the pot in the deep sink and run the water, cold from the gravity-feed well and pure as the rocks it has dropped through, my purpose in life is to pay attention and to remember. Here is my real history: a father I loved and feared, a sister I simply loved, the loss of both, then mother and I together. There were hospital stays, jobs that never quite took, loves that foundered. I always came back. The relief of returning to live with my mother got stronger every time. There was always the pleasure of constructing a secure and orderly design to our days. And our work is varied and often strange so there is always enough to think about. Of course, there is now Kurt, who in his suffering has become dangerously close. But the important thing, I think now, is to preserve what Elsie and I have made between us. Our breakfasts and dinners. Our net of small doings. Our thank-you notes. Our web. Our routine.

Which is about to be disturbed.

Three things happen in swift order.

My mother begins to sing to me. We are raided by the town police. My blackberries boil to a purple foam and then overflow the blue kettle I have transferred them to. It is a much heavier pot, sort of a large Dutch oven, sandcast and coated with thick enamel. But first, the singing, which mother often does. I don't mean that she actually serenades me. Her singing occurs when we are together in the same room pursuing mutually exclusive tasks. This afternoon, even in the heat, she is knitting an intricate afghan. After I brought the berries in, I showered so I am cool. My hair is slicked back and braided. I am washing away the detritus of the woods, swirling leaves and thrips down the drain, when Elsie starts to hum. Soon, there are words. Of course, as these are songs from my childhood, these words fill me with an awful poignancy. "Bye-bye Blackbird."

"Autumn Leaves." And yes, a few songs in Ojibwe, mainly hymns that my grandmother sang in the old language. From way back, we have been converts. As for the love songs, which she returns to, "Green Fields" and "Greensleeves" and "Silver Dagger," they have solemnly bitter endings. All the good ones do. Still, can you stop your mother from singing to you? Who would do such a thing?

I pour sugar into the berries ready to boil in the blue enameled kettle. The berries soon fill the kitchen with a fruity steam, and stain the insides of the pot blue-black. As I stand there stirring down the dark mass, the calming motion of my spoon and the sweet curls of fragrance allow me to think with indulgence about the old controversies that once surrounded the kettle I am using. This kettle was a source of enmity between my mother and my father, and so it remains for me a souvenir of their eternal contest. They argued viciously about this pot. It seems a humble thing to argue over, but for them, everything was monumental. Nothing was too small.

My father didn't like that my mother had spent so much money on it. And yet she made most of the money in the family—her business was well run even then. She even met my father through the business—he was there when she came in to assess the contents of his mother's house. They married quietly. He was fascinated with her background, I think, as though she had some mystical connection to the natural world that he lacked and loved. That was, perhaps, true enough. Their main pleasure in their first years was planting, gardening, digging wells, ponds, making patios, and setting up benches where, still, one can sit and watch the fireflies signal. I came along and surprised them, and my sister a little more than two years after. Although she was younger and followed me everywhere, her personhood was always stronger than mine. Netta had all of the sandy-haired sun in our joint personality. She burned hot. She was just my opposite. Where I was quiet, neat, untiring when it came to detail, Netta was bold and impatient; she could be careless and even cruel.

When she was still six and I had just turned nine we caught fireflies in Mason jars. We wanted lanterns, so we filled the jars with at least a dozen bugs each, then lay in the backyard across an old car blanket and played a game of memory, our favorite game that summer. We played with three decks, the cards spread facedown all around us. By dusk and by firefly light we matched the cards slowly, one to the next, concentrating fiercely on the placement of each. I think that early training is the reason I remember anything at all. The lights ebbed and burned, but at last the fireflies seemed to tire. We gathered up the decks of cards and secured them with a rubber band. I let my fireflies out and watched them waver into the cool weeds and willow bushes that bordered the yard. Then I turned to see where my sister was. Netta had smashed her fireflies onto her face and chest so that she glowed in the dark. She ran, danced, an eerie slash of heat.

Our father was an underpaid professor of philosophy, endlessly reworking his thesis on Miguel de Unamuno into a book on faith and science. He commuted thirty miles to the college town, but only three days a week. He had a way of alternating vast musings with petty concerns, announcing that *the mind is a wolf* and explaining how our illogical longing for a life after death is an animal hunger, and then stopping to castigate Elsie's blue pot. He'd light on me and my sister. *Your mother is the Renaissance and I am the Reformation,* he'd explain. *That's why you are reasonable children. Who's the most rational today? She gets the last cookie.* Both of us would reply. He would pick only one. He was very clever at setting us against each other—choosing me, then my sister, or my mother as his favorite. I remember the heat flooding into my face as he pointed out and laughed at my drooping socks or the expression on my face, and the slick black joy when he praised me at my sister's expense.

He was a striking man who cultivated a wild professorial mop of hair. Grayed prematurely, as if by the conflict of his thoughts, it flopped in long curls down either temple. When he was in a good mood, he let us brush it and arrange it and mother took pictures of him with a head full of plastic barrettes. He didn't mind looking absurd as long as he was prepared for it and was in charge of the circumstances. Caught off guard in a mistake or foolishness, he would lash out. Scream. His hair would fly around his face. On campus, no one dared touch his famous hair. I remember one trip to his office, watching from a high window as he appeared, hair first, a puffed mass that bobbed as he threw himself across the paths of the central lawn. Physically, he was a graceful man with a scholar's bowed shoulders and bloodless hands. He dressed like a forgetful monk, but he was no saint, in fact he was a liar and he was frightening—he would repeat things I said and they would be wrong. I remember that. His pants were just a bit too short, and his socks often did not match, even though my mother bought many pairs of one color to prevent this.

I've inherited the slender bones of his face, the delicate chin and severe, pale mouth, and perhaps his dark striving for explanations. But my sister had a happier love for inquiry, or would have. She was a questioner, could never get enough of things. And they looked alike, too, even though I had his features. She had his hair, only pale brown, and all of his expressions. She had his hands. She had his unmatching socks and distracted frown. She was like a whippet, and very strong. They had the same frame, Elsie said.

As I stare into the melt of blackberries, I remember my father's habit of folding his metal-rimmed eyeglasses down his nose while looking at me keenly. It was a gesture I found both sweet and stodgy. He was not a person you could feel one way about. Because like my sister, he had a cruel streak that came out in surprising ways, because he managed somehow to control my mother and sometimes exerted upon us all a disfiguring attention which set us against one another, I came to realize, even back then, that we both loved and faintly disliked him. Pop wisdom has it that the unpredictable parents hook you deepest with intermittent reinforcement; you become that rat who presses the lever a thousand times for a kind word, a gesture of love.

When he died, mother gave away everything he'd owned down to the last paper clip in his office, which has since remained an unused room except for storage. It is filled with boxes that we never open, things that we don't want to look at. The blue pot escaped the purge and reminds me of him, though.

As I am standing there stirring down the blackberries and re-membering my father, a siren, strange and alarming, goes off at the turnoff to our road. Our first instinct is to worry that our neighbors have suffered some calamity, and to stare out our window where soon, as the sound enlarges, we expect to see the squad car hurtle past. But the revolving white blue flashers and the wailing noise halt in front of our windows. I'm still stirring, mesmerized, as our town police officer, Lonny Germaine, emerges from the car, from which a magnified radio distorted voice carries. The electronic voice gives indecipherable orders and Elsie, who has stopped her singing, says, "He's drawing his pistol from the holster!"

I remove the dripping spoon from the berries and hold it over the kettle as Lonny rushes to our door, which we can see through a side window. We crane to watch him invade our house. With a mighty swing of his booted foot, Lonny kicks in our door, which gives so easily that he stumbles into the entryway, then rights himself and walks bent-kneed into the kitchen with his gun out two-handed, police fashion. Elsie gasps. "For heaven's sake, Lonny, the door wasn't locked! Put that down!"

All I can think of is that he's come for the stolen drum. I am found out. I am finally exposed. I cannot move. Lonny gapes at us and then lowers his gun. He mutters foolishly. Outside, the radio-voice squawks like some great, hungry bird. I am released from my fear.

"Lonny Germaine," I sound like a fussy schoolteacher, "would you care to explain?"

Lonny puts his gun into its hip holster, his fair cheeks suddenly mottled by embarrassment. He is a milk-white and black-haired transplanted French Canadian with round blue eyes and a pink bud of a mouth. He would perhaps have been a heartthrob in some past century, but for these times his looks are unattractively lush.

"The state police," he says.

I cry out, suddenly, like a suspect in a crime drama. "Where's your warrant?"

Lonny puts up the palms of his hands. "They said I should use extreme caution, use police procedure upon entering. They said there was a big patch—biggest ever in this part of the state—right out back of your place in a clearing in the woods. And you"—Lonny nods his head earnestly at me—"or some other lady was out there harvesting it."

"Patch of what? Who?"

"Marijuana! They saw it from the helicopter."

"Okay, I remember that helicopter."

"Yeah."

"So you decide to barge in here like some TV cop."

"Well, you never know," says Lonny, complacent and not at all defensive.

"Never know what? You've known us since you were a little boy. And you think we turned into drug lords?"

"It does pay," Lonny says. "And they saw this woman out there."

"It was me," I say, "I was picking these blackberries!" I raise my dripping spoon. "For this jam!"

Lonny, confused now, snaps the holster on his gun and walks back out to the car to reconnoiter with the squawk box. For a while, as the two of us veer between outrage and amusement, and as I keep stirring the berries, we hear the staticky burps of conversation from the open car window. Suddenly Lonny puts his siren on again and bucks off, speeds away, up the road. Apparently he's been instructed to harvest the crop, for perhaps an hour later, just as we've got used to the silence and started the rest of our day, the siren wails again. He gets so few opportunities to use it! Down the hill flies Lonny, and we jump to the window in time to see that the trunk of the police car is tied shut over a huge pile of what must be marijuana plants. As he bumps over the frost heaves in the gravel road bed, the tall fronds of the plants bob and wave, spilling out the sides of the trunk's lid.

"So then, who planted it?" I ask Elsie. "Are you holding out on me?"

"Kit Tatro planted it," she says. I'm surprised she knows this. But she goes on to say that she's noticed him popping in and out of the woods across the field.

"I thought he was hunting," I say.

"You don't keep track of the hunting seasons, do you?"

I guess not. Tatro seems so much a part of the woods around here, almost part of the scenery, that I've never questioned much about his comings and goings. With a sigh and a little *whoosh*, the blackberries boil over the pot's rim and cascade across the white enamel of the stove.

My father would have made a great thing of how Lonny burst into our kitchen. There would have been a hue and cry at the next town meeting. Delicious outrage. Letters to the Editor. There might have been a lawsuit. We just let it go. In the same way, we do not bother the spiders. I leave them alone. Father once had them sprayed to death, but they came right back. *Look and observe*, he said to us, pointing out the spiders, *the wolf spiders and the flies—one and the same—the devoured becomes the devourer.* He surrendered the field to the spiders, but continued to enforce his boundaries with nature selectively, kept birds from nesting in the eaves, but allowed cats to wander in and out of the loose rocks of the foundation. That was another thing my parents fought about. The cats. Elsie spayed. Father let them go feral.

These things may seem trivial, but they grew mighty. Great fury composed of need, duty, competition, sexual ambivalence, and pride existed between my parents. My father used his achingly snobbish sensitivities, his depressions, his startling sweetness, exactly the way trainers of horses use reins and whips in clever ways. It always astonishes me that relatively small humans can control horses weighing a ton and a half. Likewise my mother's power, which has since shown itself to be considerable, was somehow channeled by means that were nearly invisible. Some days he just seemed to wear her out with his small naggings, other days it was the big thoughts that flummoxed her and bent her to his will. In the case of the blue enamel kettle, it was not the money alone he objected to, it was that she had spent a great amount upon a pot that was just shy of being the *best* pot. There was, he knew—although pots were more in her line of expertise—a sort of pot made only in one tiny village factory somewhere in Portugal. *Not France*, he shrieked. To have spent this amount of money on a pot that wasn't quite the best that could be found was cretinous.

Cretinous was lighter fluid, the word I mean. Flames shot to the ceiling when my father said it. Other words they used in arguments had similar effects. They always used elevated words for simple insults. Neanderthalic for stupid, myopic for shortsighted, petulant for mean, and so on, as if they paged through Roget's before they fought. We learned a great deal of vocabulary from their fights. Arrogate, obfuscate, phantasmagoria, stipple, hirsute, quell, atrophy, craven, natter, gnomic, pornographic. These were not words ordinarily encountered on grade school vocabulary tests, but I, at least, began to use them in my everyday writing assignments and soon enough was treated differently, as though I was really smart.

Brush jewelweed and its seeds pop six feet. Orb weavers make a very distinctive seam down the center of their webs. The juicier the berry, the sharper its thorns. What's the difference between smart and self-protective? They are the same, I think. Only when you are secure enough not to fear immediate survival can you display creative intelligence in anything you do. For instance, once we had enough money to live comfortably, my mother proceeded to make us almost wealthy by dealing boldly in the most extraordinary rugs. She foraged for rugs in the dry, rotting attics of down-at-the-heel scions of Yankee landowners, scrounged for rugs at neighborhood yard sales, hassled over rugs that came from overseas in bales smelling of sheep fat and burnt dung. She slipped out of rummage sales with Navajo rugs woven with careful flaws to let the bad spirits out of the design. She bought the rugs and sold them and bought them again. To her, it was a dance of happy shadows, and sometimes the money was abstract, or even distracting, as was she, the buyer. It was the rug itself that chose its place in the world. She told me this with the same gravity my father used pronouncing on his book. I didn't take it the same way, though, because the notion made her happy. She believed in it the way she believed in blue.

There was a blue she worried over then, and covets even now. She still regards blue objects with ferocity, assessing and comparing their blueness to the particular hot blue she claims made queens of courtesans and fools of kings. A dye of indigo and radioactive cobalt. A blue of furious innocence within the ochre of the pattern and the cinnamon and the dried blood of the other wools. It is a blue so intense it looks as though it were made on another planet. It is the blue behind your eyelids when you press past the yellow lights. It is the O.D. blue, I tell myself, of ecstasy and death. I'll avoid it, thanks anyway. I've survived that blue and I will not look upon it anymore.

Oh yes, and my father also had blue eyes, though his were paler and a bit washed-out, with amber flecks.

"Between the eater and the eaten," said my father, absurd when drunk. "Perfect unity. I have proved it with a mathematical formula." We nodded. "I'm glad someone understands how faith eats reason and becomes a new beast. Or some two."

He liked to work in his upstairs office after dinner, and we sneaked past him, or tried to be in bed before he came down the stairs. Still, I remember him always holding hard to the stair rail, blurred and loquacious. This one night, he'd caught us and so we sat on the bottom step with him, ready to bolt. He talked to us and praised us and compared our looks and held our hands. He tried to teach us how to whistle by putting our fingers between our teeth, but couldn't do it himself and dribbled spit, which I pointed out. He kept trying to whistle in novel, boyish ways until at last he grew furious at our polite silence and we jumped up and ran.

"Get back here, you little shits!" he yelled as we leapt up the stairs. "If I really am your dad, and I'm not sure I am your father, why don't you little twats tell me to go to hell?"

"Shut up," said my mother, charging down toward him, for once forgetting that they fought with elevated diction.

The novelty of the *shut up* silenced him. We squeezed past her, thrilled we'd been called twats, which we understood. You'd think that the appalling thing he said would have upset us or caused us to lose sleep, but it didn't. Although, as I said, we loved him, not only the word but his idea excited us, for we then spent an hour whispering, imagining that he was not our father. It gave us inspiration to picture our father as, for instance, the man up the road who tapped maple trees, pounding hollow tubes into the bark, adjusting the buckets underneath with a kindly, brown hand. Or our father as the man who ran the pygmy zoo in summer, a wretched attempt at attracting tourists, of which there were none. The zoo man displayed pygmy breeds—tiny goats, dwarf rabbits, and miniature stubby-legged horses; he loved, he said, all the runts of the world. And although I was tall, his philosophy was one I appreciated. When my parents fought, they grew like giants while I shrank.

*   *   *

My father was becoming frustrated with his work, and from the upstairs bedroom he had converted into his office, I would hear him talking as he worked. Sometimes it was to argue a position along and we'd hear the muted rise and fall of certainties, though we could rarely get the words. Other times he seemed to be pleading with someone else, his voice a low wail. "Opposite ends?" I heard him cry once. "But no! Each lives by its contrary!" We melted away from the chattering sounds, usually left the house entirely, when we heard the high crackle of his voice.

Those were the times we roamed far, picked berries, waged our jewelweed wars, made investigations into the habits of the salamanders, tracked deer and coyotes, observed the spiders. One day, we returned from puttering in the woods, hoping it was all over, to find him eating a bowl of cereal in the kitchen clad in nothing but a pair of boxers made of that peculiar boxer-short material, thin cotton printed with intricate red-brown squares and diamonds. I was familiar with the melting physique of my father, the drooping muscles of his chest and arms. But I hadn't ever seen him in the boxers, legs mean and knobby, white feet tender. I turned away, but my sister turned toward him.

"Everything is elusive and in the air, but this, this is real."

The wonder in his voice caused me to look back. He was looking at Netta as he stroked a four-inch pile of neatly stacked white paper, his typescript. It didn't register to me at first that his work was finished. The way he nodded, grinning, saying *yes, yes*, alerted me to the response he was after and caused me to fear that *yes*, certainly, he had gone nuts.

The year he finished his book and developed its chapters for his lectures, the year he began to make increasingly impenetrable pronouncements, was the year that he grew a cult. The cult was like a fungus. That's how we saw it—the students in his thrall grew on him like mushrooms. In the classroom, his erratic nature became a kind of charisma. His students began to show up at our house, looking thin and fanatical in worn-out expensive clothes, their hair thickly matted or combed through with oil. Their eyes blazed through the walls. They saw everything. They slept on our floors. We stayed in our room. I developed a horror of running across them ensconced here and there in the house, smoking, muttering, surrounded by books and half-finished term papers.

He began to give them lectures in our wide, sweet kitchen. They lived on cigarettes. Saucers of butts collected. They lived on bitter black coffee and on Elsie's cooking, which they ate with famished ardor but never complimented. At first, I think, she was amused by the flotsam, and she pitied the students. Soon they bored her. And then one of them burned a neat round hole in a very old Tibetan rug and she kicked the lot of them right out the door. She rousted them from their sleeping corners and the basement couch. She chased them from the attic and the loft in the garage. She drove them back to the college and dumped them at the stone gates. They were lucky she didn't spay them like the feral cats. But then afterward, as my father, in his office, faced the lonely task of counting up his polite rejection slips from mystified editors, and rebundling his manuscript and sending it back out, she began to leave us. She took long buying trips and when she came home she was distracted, her attention had lifted from us. We could feel it. We had to call her over and over to get her to answer a question. We had to pester her and pull on the hem of her skirt or the fabric of her dress to get her to listen.

These are times a child remembers very clearly—the absence of the two of them. The clearing around my sister and me. I can remember a specific fantasy, I don't know if my sister shared it. I imagined something deliciously awful happened to one of us, and saw our parents holding hands as they sat at the bedside. Still, we were not technically abandoned, not at all, for our father never actually left the house. For days, he didn't move from his office, where he'd set himself a haven of safety, shielded himself with stacks of books, papers, files in boxes and in cabinets. Elsie utterly ignored his presence. I did not dare to go to him, nor did my sister ever part the waters of the papers that lapped up the sides of his desk. Sometimes, though, as we passed his office door we heard a dry, cold, rustling sound. It was the sound that waves make when water is frozen a few feet out from the shore, the sound of waves lapping against fresh ice. Almost a music, not a papery sound at all.

That was when my sister and I started living in the orchard—it was a fine place to be. Our trees were houses and dens, whales or seagoing boats or great flying creatures—we lived for days in the branches, brought blankets to make tents, scrounged the kitchen for lunch. Perhaps we could have stayed there day and night but we always came in by ourselves. One day around dusk, though, the first time all summer, our father came out to the orchard to fetch us. I can remember that his appearance made us suddenly angry enough to defy him and to yell down that we were going to sleep in the trees. It was a game at first, and then we became wild, taunting him, throwing down apples. He stood below glaring up at us, hands at his sides. He started to climb, but we scrambled dangerously higher. He must have decided that he'd catch us quicker if he coaxed us, then, so he put out his arms, opened his hands, spoke softly. *Come on. Come on.* We had climbed far too high by then to jump into his arms, but he didn't seem to understand this.

"You jump," I said to my sister.

"No, you jump," she said, and shook my branch.

"Okay," I said, but I really didn't mean it. I lost my balance and dove straight for my father, who stepped aside. I landed on my back just next to his legs and I remember in that endless time, windless, before I could breathe, looking up into the branches and seeing her.

I could see in my sister's face that she'd seen our father let me fall. She stared down at me with great concentration and then she stepped off the branch. Our father tried to catch her and stumbled over me. She landed next to him, I didn't see where. I think that I heard my father shriek at me *Don't you move, Faye, don't you ever move, I'll kill you myself*, and then he was running across the field with her. Again, our mother was not home, and she'd taken the car. He ran down the road to the Eykes', and I remember thinking what it would be like at the hospital, and what my father would say when they put my sister carefully on the bed in the doctor's office, and the doctor shook his head and looked helpless. I knew that my father wouldn't have to say anything to convince them all that I'd pushed her or shaken the branch or she'd taken a dare—all he'd have to do was blame it on himself too ostentatiously, but with small thoughtful pauses, and they would think he was trying to protect me, as any other father would. Somehow I knew all that was before me. I knew how my mother and my father would regard me from then on. And how I would come to regard myself.

Perhaps I even knew that his lies would squeeze his heart shut in a year, for I knew I'd lost them both, or all three of them. I knew that now I was alone. The sun gave off that sweet, endless, August glow as it sank behind the first few leaves. Eventually, of course, I disobeyed my father and moved. I didn't know where to go, so I went into the field of orb spiders. At first, as I walked in among their waiting webs, I was afraid. *The mind is a wolf.* Then the light shed down sharply golden and I began to think. Thinking saved me. Perception saved me. I saw that the spiders were just substance. Not bad, not good. We were all made of the same stuff. I saw how we spurted out of creation in different shapes. How for a time I would inhabit this shape but then I'd be the lace on my sister's shoe that had dropped off her foot onto the weeds and tamped grass, or I'd be the blue pot my parents argued about, or maybe something else. There was nothing but the endless manufacture of things out of nothing. I saw the changing and exchanging of shapes. The grass growing all around me, now, would one day be the cow, the milk, the flesh of the calf, then me.

I thought and thought in order to avoid something massive. But whenever I stopped thinking, it lay before me just the same.

The bronze sun turned across my shoulders and stung all the way down my arms. I tapped a loaded jewelweed and the seed flipped out of sight. Feral and silent as coal, the spiders ranged to all sides of me. I put out my finger and with the slightest of motions I stroked the back of a spider. I coaxed the biggest one, using a thin blade of grass, into my palm. Then I held it for a motionless time. It was a sun-warmed thing, heavy as a dirt clod, but light as a plastic toy. Poised, excited, it vibrated with cold breath, ticked swiftly in my hand. Hummed, sang, knocked away the edges of the world.

PART TWO

NORTH OF
HOOPDANCE

1

The Visitors

Bernard Shaawano

I've got a big truck, first of all, so with it comes the responsibility to haul drunks from ditches and boats hung up on shore and to make deliveries of emergency wood. Next there's the fact that I work in the hospital, which makes people think, I do not know why, that the medical profession has rubbed off on me. Like maybe I picked it up from watching how the doctors and nurses take care of people. Then there is the idea that I supposedly have so much extra time to kill, living alone as I do, that it is a favor to me to ask a favor of me. So people kindly fill up the boredom of my hours by getting me to do all sorts of boring things for them.

There is a person who asks a lot of me, a woman for whom everything goes wrong. She has tired out everyone else on this reservation. I think I am the only one who doesn't find a dire excuse of their own to get rid of her before she makes a request. So this woman, Chook she is called because of her crackling thin hair and how she always wears a hat, this Chook must think everybody on this whole reservation except me is in a state of continual emergency. People tempt fate, even, when Chook calls them up, by inventing really awful things that nobody wants to happen.

"Mary Sunday's stove blew up, so she can't drive me into town," says Chook. Or even, "Teddy Eagle has something called yellow fever that could turn into smallpox if he's not real careful."

She laughs. As she is no dummy she knows a stupid excuse when she hears one. But I just take it at face value.

"That's tough luck," I say, resigned. I wait to hear what she's got in mind for me to do. I really don't know why I always end up helping her out. She's a hard person to feel sorry for because she has more pity for herself than another person could possibly muster, but perhaps I do these things because I know in spite of everything that Chook is a good mother. Her irritating requests and desperations end up benefiting her children and the grandchildren she is raising—the oldest two grown sons, Morris and John, and the two much younger, a boy and a girl, who, unlike Chook, are always well dressed and with whom she is strict. From being around them I know they get good grades, and are not allowed to drink soda pop or watch too much television or ride around on other kids' ATVs without a helmet. Plus she is kind of hysterical about seat belts, which, really, a mother should be. Still, that doesn't make her less annoying or cause my eyes not to roll up to the ceiling when I answer the phone and it is her.

One day she calls, my day off, of course, and has a peculiar mission for me to go on. Sometimes I think she steals a look at my schedule in the back room on the hospital wall. I'm yawning. I thought for once I'd sleep in. But Chook has other uses for me.

"Bernard," she says, "have you got a pickax?"

Many of her requests begin like that. She's got most of my tools and garden equipment at her house now.

"Yeah," I say, "I still have my pickax. You haven't got that yet."

She gives a soft, sad little laugh. "When Mike died, he took all his tools with him, eh?"

Mike was her husband, whom I sometimes think died so he wouldn't get pestered by Chook anymore. He needed the peace and quiet. He went easily, no fuss. Drove himself to the emergency room and was dead of a heart attack five minutes after he got there. In the ground three days later. With all of his tools, according to Chook. I don't even want to know what she is talking about. But she tells me.

"He borrowed from everybody else, so they come here for the funeral supper and they end up taking whatever they lent my husband and more, too, I think, besides. Once that night was up I look around me and I don't see half what we used to have. But I was too broke up to say anything about it, eh? Me, I never said nothing. Just let it go."

"I've got quite a lot of business going on today, Chook, so if you—"

"Oh, Bernard? There's something I gotta ask you!"

I shut my eyes, weary already, already anticipating one of her usual requests. "Let's hear it." But instead of a ride to the bank during which I will hear the state of her meager bank account, or a plumbing disaster where I'll be confronted with a tangle of plugged pipes, she asks me something I can't register at first. She asks me to come and help her dig up her husband's body. She has to repeat it three times before I realize she's serious.

"I can't do that! I mean, I would never do that. Anyway, I think you have to get some kind of permit, or go through the church."

"No," she says, "I don't have to do that. Remember, he had himself buried on the ridge with the traditionals."

Well, I did remember that, for all it was worth; to me it didn't matter if he was buried underneath my front steps. I certainly was not going to dig him up.

"And you know what Mike had buried with him, you remember that, don't you?" Chook was going to needle at me until I did something.

"His own pickax."

"No, haha! You're funny, Bernard. No!"

"Then what was it?" She was going to tell me no matter what.

"He had the tobacco box, even the scrolls of all the songs that went along with that drum your grandfather made, the one that took the sickness out of people. Mike had that drum's belongings, you recall, because his father was on that drum and one of its keepers. Mike never thought that the drum would come back here."

"So what do you want the things for?" I said, not even then understanding.

"Because it has."

I hung the phone right up on her. I'd never done anything like that before. My hand had done it for me, refusing to have anything to do with something so alarming as the drum still existing, even much less returning. She called back.

"We got cut off!"

"Yeah." I was troubled. There was so much more to this, more than ever had been admitted to those not directly involved way back then. Many people were affected by this drum. Many people know part of the story. But I know all or most of the history of this drum. I know because my father talked once he got sober, talked like his own father had, endlessly, hoping to be redeemed by the story. And he was only one of those who could not forget. Once his mind cleared he had to contend, of course, with the shame of all he had done when he was boozed up. So he talked to try and wear down the edges of that shame. And I was the one who listened.

"So would you help me dig Mike up?"

"Chook, let me . . . let me figure out something else."

"Okay, Bernard. It's not like we have to do it today. Tomorrow maybe."

"You said the drum came back."

"The judge's got it at his house."

"Well, that's the first good thing."

"They brought it to the right person, eh?"

"Who's this 'they'?"

"Two ladies from out east. Those women had come across that drum, I don't know how. It had to do with some old man. Geraldine has been trying to get ahold of you. Me, I am getting my boy to drive me."

I knew I had to be there, right then, at the drum's return. If Chook actually got a ride from someone else, this was a big event. And I had to be there not only for my own reasons, but to neutralize her presence. I said good-bye and got ready to go over to the judge's house.

The judge lives on his uncle's old land pretty much right where Nanapush's old shack caved in one harsh winter. I don't even know if the judge ever met his uncle or if old Nanapush, of whom my father told me stories, realized that he had a nephew, anyway, drifting along through the tribal records and the off-reservation families, and those who moved to Canada, like the judge's people, who came here to powwow and felt back at home. People come and people stay. There is a strong pull. You return for one funeral after another and all of a sudden you don't leave and you are picking up where someone else left off. So with those women who traveled cross-country with the drum. My phone rings again half a minute after I hang up with Chook. I hear from the judge's wife that these women are a mother and a daughter. She says she thinks that they are connected to an old branch of the Pillagers through a girl who escaped the sicknesses here by going to that eastern school, Carlisle, where they took so many of us at one time.

The judge's house is a pleasant, modest little prefab construction, brand-new, that has a full basement garage as it sits on a little hill. From that hill, I'm told, old Nanapush used to watch all who passed and to anticipate all that would happen. The judge could look out his picture window and do the same, I suppose, but he probably sees even more than his old uncle by sitting on the courtroom bench. A little driveway curves up to the house and makes a U so that a person can easily turn around and go back out. That's a nice feature of the house. There's a lot to like about it. Geraldine, his wife, the new Mrs. Nanapush, has hung about six bird feeders outside the double glass doors on her deck and when I drive up a flock of tiny gray birds starts up, silent, and disappears. It's a good time of the year—most of the ticks gone, air cool, leaves just turning, school started but the kids still playing outside, exposed but not down with the viruses that will get them once they're inside coughing on one another all day, which will then fill the hospital—a nice time of year.

"Piindegen! Come in!" Geraldine is such a pleasant woman, wavy black hair and fair skin, her brown eyes secret and quiet, her smile a delicate curve. I always wish I'd asked her out when we were younger. Who could have known when she was gawky and her ears stuck out and she hid behind strings of hair, that she'd turn out like this?

I'm nervous as I walk into the house, and I concentrate on wiping my shoes even though they are perfectly clean. I am relieved to see that they have kept the drum covered in the middle of the room, so I don't have to look on it quite yet. I am not easy in a social setting so it is not a simple thing for me to introduce myself, and I am glad Geraldine steps in and gets me acquainted with Elsie Travers and her daughter Faye. I sit down in a chair that matches the couch. The two women are sitting on that couch. Talking requires an effort. Both of the women have long hair, the mother's in a twist and the daughter's clipped back in a tail. They are slim, and dressed in combinations of black and cream white with very plain metal jewelry—heavy chains, stoneless rings, round stud earrings. They don't go in for patterns or any sort of trim on their clothes, I see, and their shoes are very simple with no bows or tassels or fancy heels, either. The effect of them is somehow classily monklike, or undertakerish. They seem very different from people here. The younger woman speaks out like a lawyer in a hard, suspicious, accentless voice. I think her features, sharp and definite, her eyes with a Chippewa slant to them, though, are very striking or even beautiful. From one side that is, but then just ordinary from another. And the older one, too, looks different from moment to moment. First she is all excitable and anxious, then she turns right off and sits back watching everyone else like a little gray sparrow hawk ready to strike. As Geraldine says, these women who found the drum are somehow related to the Pillagers, who have mainly died out, so it is quite interesting that they've surfaced. Geraldine, especially, who is always collecting and compiling tribal history, shoots questions at them in her pleasant, friendly, interested way. If they stop talking for a minute, she fills up their tea mugs and asks them something else.

"What made you bring back the drum?"

"I kept it for a time," says the younger woman, thoughtful, "then I thought I should pass it on."

I nod as she explains about keeping tobacco near it and taking care of it. She did things just the way they are supposed to be done.

Right then Chook and her son, John, the handsome one, drive up to the house. We fall quiet, not wanting for her to miss anything important. John walks her up the steps and she enters. Chook is round as a turnip and today she is wearing a hot pink rayon top with Japanese-like patterns of black flowers. Her skirt ripples all around her like a bush, and when I bend to focus my eyes I see it's embroidered all over with tiny yellow roses and rust red twigs. She has her hair tied back in a blue headband and she is smoking a cigarette, which she puts out halfway and drops into her purse.

"They don't taste so good anymore," she says to the room of people watching her. "I think it's because of this blood-thinner medicine that they got me on. So there it is, that drum which my husband helped out with at one time."

Chook stands looking at the drum, then reaches into her big canvas purse. She takes out a package of cookies and a pair of scissors, then neatly cuts open the cellophane on the cookies. Then she pulls the plastic tray halfway out of the clear package and sets it in the center of Geraldine's coffee table, pushing aside a fresh coffee cake that Geraldine has cut in squares. I'm glad we are at Geraldine's, for to drink tea at Chook's house is almost dangerous. She scours her mugs with Comet cleanser and there is always a faint, gritty taste of the stuff. Now Geraldine pours a fresh cup of tea for Chook and she talks, addressing the two women from the east.

"That old drum, it had a reputation. You can't mess around—once you do keep that drum, you gotta keep it with respect." She looks at us all with little blinking round eyes, and nods at the cookies she brought, which happen to be the kind of deadly, sweet, pink, waffle-wafers that I am forbidden to touch by my doctor.

"Bernard here," she says, "he's the one to tell you about this drum. He knows it well, too well. When that drum passed out of their family, people forgot about them. They got no attention. But you see, that is sometimes how things heal up. Now, I think, he don't want that drum to resurrect old sorrows for him, eh?"

She looks at me with a searching expression, but I say nothing.

"We all got sorrows," Chook hunches her shoulders and holds up her bony hands. "We got sorrows or if we don't work them down, then our sorrows got us." She rattles the cookie package at me, but I resist.

"What does that have to do with the drum?" says the older of the two Pillager ladies. She is polite and yet nobody to mess with, I see. But Chook is up to dealing with her.

"Take me for instance," says Chook. "That old Mr. Bush sent John's brother here off to the Desert Storm, and he breathed something that upset his system and now it's maybe killing him. But he never yet got a medal for that. Anyway, what I'm telling you is you wear down these sorrows using what you have, what comes to hand. You talk them over, you live them through, you don't let them sit inside. See, that's what the drum was good for. Letting those sorrows out, into the open, where those songs could bear them away."

She drinks her tea, blinking all around the room.

"Drums get their power from how they are treated, though," Chook goes on. "You got to keep them protected. If someone comes in where the drum is, uses bad language, you got to put them out. As for getting the drum in the first place, if you get the right guidance you can make a drum. But otherwise a drum must be given to you. Someone must give that drum freely. You cannot buy the drum. You cannot steal the drum."

She stops right then and stares at the younger woman and says, "So you bought the drum from an old man?"

The younger woman gathers herself, sips her tea, doesn't meet anybody's eyes. "His name was Jewett Parker Tatro," she says.

Geraldine sits back on the hard chair she has brought from the kitchen. The judge, with his round cheeks and intelligent face, sits near to her. He touches his stringy little Indian mustache.

"I think that was the name of the Indian agent at one time. His name has come up on some old probate documents."

I know who this Tatro was, of course, as he figured in the shameful episodes that my father needed to confess. Tatro had gone from being an unscrupulous Indian agent, when his job was phased out, to owning a bar. The reservation, which had been dry for many years, decided to allow alcohol in order to keep liquor revenue within its borders. But the bulk of that money passed into Tatro's hands, anyway, since he was the first to open his doors, and later, made some exclusive deal with the area supplier. At any rate, Tatro was or became a collector by default—when the need is on, some people they will sell their own grandmas. Or her old moccasins or the cradle board she beaded for a grandchild or a jingle dress. At one time, the wall of Tatro's bar was full of these things—some beautiful and sacred, like the drum.

"That's all we know about it," says the younger one.

"Where it ended up," her mother adds. "Of what brought that drum into the hands of Tatro, and what it was before, who kept it and so on . . ."

She trails off. All of a sudden I can feel Chook's amused waiting. I can feel Geraldine's eyes on me and I know she knows, she's known from the beginning, why I am here. She knows enough about things generally to know where the drum came from, but she doesn't completely know its origin or kinship; she doesn't know how it is tied into my family or why my grandfather brought it into being. I look at the two women sitting in the judge's living room— so prim and intense. Their hands are folded in their laps, but I can tell they have long fingers. Their feet are tucked away from sight, but they probably have big narrow feet with long second toes. Those two don't know who they are, what it means that they are Pillagers. They don't know that they came from Simon Jack and they don't know what he did to Anaquot, my grandmother, or to my aunt whose name is never spoken, or to himself. They don't know what the drum did to him, either, what the drum knows, or what it contains. They don't know why my father sold it in spite of the many persons it healed. They don't know the whole story, but I do know it. So I tell them.

2

The Shawl

Among the Anishinaabeg on the road where I live, it is told how a woman loved a man other than her husband, and went off into the bush and bore his child. Her name was Anaquot, and like her namesake the cloud she was changeable, moody and sullen one moment, threatening, her lower lip jutting and eyes flashing, filled with storms. The next moment she would shake her hair over her face, blow it out straight in front of her, and make her children scream with laughter. For she had two children by her husband, Shaawano, one a yearning boy of five years and the other a capable daughter of nine.

When she brought the baby out of the trees late that autumn, so long ago, the girl was like a second mother, even waking in the night to clean the baby and nudge it to her mother's breast. Anaquot slept through its cries, hardly woke. It wasn't that Anaquot didn't love her baby, no it was quite the opposite—she loved it too much, the way she loved its father, not her husband. This passion ate away at her and her feelings were unbearable. If she could have thrown that love off, she would have, but the thought of the man who lived across the lake was with her always. She became a gray sky, stared monotonously at the walls, sometimes wept into her hands for hours at a time. At last, she couldn't rise to cook or keep the cabin neat, and it was too much for the girl child, who curled up each night exhausted in her brown and red plaid shawl, and slept and slept, so that the husband had to wake the girl to wake her mother, for he was afraid of Anaquot's bad temper, and it was he who roused her into anger by the sheer fact that he was himself, and not the other.

At last, even though he loved Anaquot, the husband found their life together was no good anymore. So it was he who sent word to the other man's camp. Now in those days our people lived widely scattered, along the shores and in the islands, even out in the plains. There were hardly roads yet, just trails, though we had horses and wagons and for the winter, sleds. And it was very hard when the other man's uncle came round, in his wagon fitted out with sled runners, to fetch Anaquot, for she and her husband had argued right up to the last about the children, argued fiercely until the husband finally gave in, turned his face to the wall, and did not move to see the daughter, whom he treasured, wrap herself in her plaid robe alongside the mother in the wagon bed. They left soon after, with their bundles and sacks, not even heating up the stones to warm their feet. The father had stopped his ears, so he did not hear the cry when his son understood all of a sudden that he was the one who would be left behind.

As the uncle slapped the reins and the horse lurched forward, the boy tried to jump into the wagon, but his mother pried his hands off the boards, crying gego, gego, and he fell down hard.

There was something in him that would not let her leave him, though. He jumped up and although he was wearing only light clothing, he ran behind the wagon, over the packed drifts. The horses picked up speed. His chest scorched with pain, and yet he pushed himself on. He'd never run so fast, so hard and furious, but he was determined and in that determination it was impossible for him to believe that the distance that soon increased between himself and the wagon was real. He kept running and pretended they would stop, wait for him; he kept going until his throat closed, he saw red, and in the ice of air his lungs shut. Then, he said as he fell onto the board-hard snow, he raised his head. Still watching the tiny back of the wagon and the figures of his mother and sister, something went out of him. Something failed in him. He could feel some interior something break. And at that moment, he truly did not care if he was alive or he was dead. So when he saw the gray shapes, the shadows, bound lightly from the trees to either side of the trail, far ahead, he was not afraid.

The next the boy knew, his father was shaking him, already had him wrapped in a blanket and was carrying him home. Shaawano's chest was broad and although he already spat tubercular blood that would tell the end of his story, he was still a strong man. It would take him many years to die. In those years, he would tell the boy, who had forgotten this part entirely, that at first when he talked about the shadows he thought his son was visited by manidoog. But then as the boy described the shapes, his father felt very uneasy in his mind and decided to take his gun out there. So he built up the fire in the cabin, and settled his boy near, and went back out into the snow. Perhaps the story spread all through our settlements because the father had to tell what he saw, again and again, in order to get rid of it. Perhaps like all frightful dreams, amanisowin, he had to say it to divide its power, though in this case it would not stop being real.

The tracks of the shadows were wolves, and in those times when our guns had taken all their food for furs and hides to sell, wolves were bold and had abandoned the old agreement between themselves and the first humans. For a time, until we understood and let the game increase, they hunted us. Shaawano bounded forward when he saw the tracks. He could see where the pack, desperate, had tried to slash the tendons of the horses' legs. Next, where they'd leapt for the back of the wagon, and he hurried on to where the trail gave out onto the broad empty ice of the lake. There, he saw what he saw, scattered, and the ravens only, attending to the bitter small leavings of the wolves.

For a time, the boy had no understanding of what had happened. His father kept what he knew to himself, at least that first year, and when his son asked about his sister's brown plaid shawl, torn in pieces, why it was kept in the house, his father said nothing. But he wept if the boy asked if she was cold. It was only after Shaawano was weakened by the disease that he began to tell it far too often, and always the same. How when the wolves closed in, Anaquot threw her daughter to them.

When his father said those words, the boy went still in thought. What had his sister felt? What had thrust through her heart? Had something broken in her too, the way something broke like a stick inside of him? Even then, he knew this broken place would never be mended inside him, except by some terrible means. For he kept seeing his mother put the baby down and grip his sister around the waist, her arms still strong enough. Then he saw Anaquot swing the girl lightly out over the board sides of the wagon. He saw the brown shawl with the red lines flying open. He saw the wolves, the shadows, rush together quick and avid as the wagon with the sled runners disappeared into the distance, forever, for neither he nor his father ever saw Anaquot again.

When I was little, my own father terrified us with his drinking. That was after we lost our mother, because before that, the only time I was aware they touched the ishkode wabo was on an occasional weekend when they got home late, or sometimes during berry-picking gatherings, when we went out to the bush and camped with others. Not until she died did he start the heavy sort of drinking, the continual drinking where we were left in the house for days. And then, when he came home, we jumped out the window and hid in the woods while he barged around, shouting for us. We only went back when he fell dead asleep.

There were three of us, me the oldest at ten and my little sister and brother twins of only six years. I was surprisingly good at taking care of them, I think, and because we learned to survive to-gether during those drinking years we always have been close. Their names are Doris and Raymond, and they married a brother and sister in turn. When we get together, which we do when we can, for they live in the Cities now, there come times in the talking and card playing, and maybe even in the light beer now and then, we will bring up those days. Most people understand how it was. Our story isn't that uncommon. But for us, it helps to compare our points of view.

How could I know, for instance, that Raymond saw it the time I hid my father's belt? I pulled it from around his waist while he was passed out and then buried it in the woods. I kept doing it every time after that. We laughed at how our father couldn't understand how when he went to town drinking his belt was always stolen. He even accused his shkwebii buddies of the theft. I had good reasons. Not only was he embarrassed, after, to go out with pants held up with a rope, but he couldn't snake that belt out in anger and snap the hooked buckle end in the air. He couldn't hit us with it. Of course, being resourceful, he used other things. There was a board. A willow wand. And there was himself, his hands and fists and boots and things he could throw. He'd never remember. He'd be furious and wreck us, wreck things, and then he'd talk about our mother. But it got so easy to evade him, eventually, that after a while we never suffered a bruise or scratch. We had our own places in the woods, even a little campfire for the cold nights. And we'd take money from him every chance we got, slip it from his shoe where he thought it hidden. He became, for us, a thing to be exploited, avoided, outsmarted, and used. We survived off him like a capricious and dangerous line of work. I suppose we stopped thinking of him as a human being, certainly as a father, after only a couple years.

I got tired of it. When I was thirteen years old, I got my growth earlier than some boys, and one night when Doris and Raymond and me were sitting around wishing for something besides the oatmeal and commodity powdered milk which I had stashed so he couldn't sell it, I heard him coming down the road. He never learned to shut up before he got to us. He never understood we lit out on him, I guess. So he was shouting and making noise all the way to the house, and Doris and Raymond looked at me and went for the back window. Then they stopped, because they saw I was not going. C'mon, ambe, get with it, they tried to pull me along. I shook them off and told them to get out, be quick, I was staying.

I think I can take him now, is what I said.

And I know they were scared, but their faces, oh their faces rose up toward me in this beautiful reveal all full of hope and belief. So when he came in the door, and I faced him, I was not afraid.

He was big though, he hadn't wasted from the alcohol or the long disease yet. His nose had got pushed to one side in a fight, then slammed back on the other side, so now it was straight. His teeth were half gone and he smelled the way he had to smell, being five days drunk. When he came in the door, he paused for a moment, his eyes red and swollen to tiny slits. Then he saw I was waiting for him and he smiled in a bad way. He went for me. My first punch surprised him. I had been practicing this on a hay-stuffed bag, then a padded board, toughening my fists, and I'd gotten so quick I flickered like fire. But I wasn't strong as he was, still, and he had a good twenty pounds on me. Yet, I'd do some damage, I was sure of it. I'd teach him not to mess with me. What I didn't foresee was how the fight itself would get right into me.

There is a terrible thing about fighting your father, I never knew. It came on sudden, with the second blow, a frightful kind of joy. Suddenly a power surged up from the center of me and I danced at him, light and giddy, full of a heady rightness. Here is the thing. I wanted to waste him, waste him good. I wanted to smack the living shit out of him. Kill him if I must. If he died, so be it. If I died, well, I wouldn't! A punch for Doris, a blow coming back I didn't feel. A kick for Raymond. And all the while me silent, then screaming, then silent again, in this rage of happiness that filled me with a simultaneous despair so that, I guess you could say, I stood apart from myself.

He came at me, crashed over a chair that was already broke, then threw the pieces, but they easily bounced off and I grabbed a chair leg and whacked him on the ear so his head spun. I watched, like I say, stood apart. Struck again and again. I knew what I was doing while I was doing it, but not really, not in the ordinary sense. It was like I was standing calm, against the wall with my arms folded, pitying us both. I saw the boy, the chair leg, the man fold and fall, his hands held up in begging fashion. Then I also saw that now, for a while, the bigger man had not even bothered fighting back.

Suddenly, he was my father again, as he lay there in his blood. And when I kneeled down next to him, I was his son. I reached for the closest rag, and I picked up this piece of blanket that my father always kept for some reason next to the place he slept. And as I picked it up and wiped the blood off his face, I said to him, your nose is crooked again. Then he looked at me, steady and quizzical, clear, as though he had never drunk in his life. He kept looking at me as though I was unsolved, a new thing, and I wiped his face again with that frayed piece of blanket. Well, it really was a shawl, a light kind of old-fashioned woman's blanket shawl. Once, maybe it was plaid. You could still see lines, some red, the background a faded brown. He watched intently as this rag went from his face and as my hand brought it near again. I was pretty sure, then, I'd clocked him too hard, that he'd now really lost it and there wasn't a chance. I mean, a chance of what? I suppose a chance of getting a father back. A thing I hadn't understood I wanted.

Gently though, he clasped one hand around my wrist. With the other hand he took that piece of shawl. He crumpled that and held it to the middle of his forehead. It was like he was praying, like he was having thoughts he wanted to collect in that scrap of cloth. For a while he lay like that and I, crouched over, let him be, hardly breathing. Something told me to sit there still. And then at last he said to me, in the sober new voice I would hear from then on out, did you know I had a sister once?

115

*   *   *

There was a time when the government moved everybody off the farther reaches of the reservation, onto roads, into towns, into housing. It looked good at first and then it all went sour. Shortly after, it seemed like anyone who was someone was either dead, drunk, killed, near suicide, or just had dusted themself. None of the old sorts were left, it seemed, the old kind of people. It was during that time that my mother died and my father hurt us, as I have said. But now, gradually, that term of despair has lifted somewhat and yielded up its survivors. We still have sorrows that are passed to us from early generations, those to handle besides our own, and cruelties lodged where we cannot forget. We have the need to forget. I don't know if we stopped the fever of forgetting yet. We are always walking on oblivion's edge.

I do know that some get out of it, like my brother and sister living quiet. And myself to some degree, though my wife has moved to Fargo and I miss her, and miss my children between their visits. Before my father died, he found a woman to live with him. I think he had several happy years, and during that time he talked to me. Once, when he brought up the old days, and again we went over the story, I said to him at last two things I had been thinking.

First, I told him that to keep his sister's shawl was wrong. Because we never keep the clothing of the dead, which he knew. Now's the time to burn it, I said, send it off to cloak her spirit. So he agreed.

The other thing I said to him was in the form of a question. Have you ever considered, I asked him, given how your sister was so tenderhearted and brave, that she looked at the whole situation? She saw the wolves were only hungry, she saw their need was only need. She knew you were back there, alone in the snow. She saw the baby she loved would not live without a mother, and only the uncle knew the way. She saw clearly that one person on the wagon had to offer themself, or they all would die. And in that moment of knowledge, don't you think being who she was, of the old sort of Anishinaabeg who thinks of the good of the people first, she jumped, my father, n'deydey, brother to that little girl, don't you think she lifted her shawl and flew?

3

The Wolves

My father is a Shaawano and I've grown up in the range of those wolves, though I didn't understand for a long while, of course, how it was that they related to our family. In summer that pack disappears on the far mainland where the shore is still wild and never was developed. I hardly ever hear them then. But in winter they come out onto the ice of the lake and hunt the islands. Then their howls travel through the frozen space and to hear them brings back all the tumult of my heart in younger days. I don't know why their cries do that to me; perhaps it is because I've always had that longing, that need, to pierce through my existence. I am a boundary to something else, but I don't know what. Mostly I have made my peace with never knowing, but when I hear the wolves that falls away. Unrest grips me. I have to leave my house and go out walking in the night, hungry to know what I cannot know and desperate to see what will always be hidden.

There was an old man once who wanted to be with the wolves and know their thoughts. He went out on the ice and sang to them and asked them to sink their teeth into his heart. I guess the singing kept him warm enough so he lived out there for three days and nights. On the fourth day, the wolves finally came to him, or rather, he realized that all along he had been looking straight at them and only when they were ready had they let themselves be seen. I know about this man because I sat with him in the hospital just a few years ago, and I talked to him while I was on night duty. I pulled a chair up next to his bed.

"Those wolves were curious," he said, "just like anyone would be. What in the heck's this young man—I was young then—sitting out here on the ice for? They came up to find out if I was dangerous or crazy or good to eat. Even then I was tough and stringy, so I guess they decided crazy. They sat and watched me for several hours to see if I would do anything and after a while they went away."

I asked the old man if he'd learned what he needed to learn from them, if he'd found anything out at all.

"Oh sure," he said. "I found out they think like us. They were watching me, but I was watching them, too. I was hungrier than they were. They had just eaten. They were full. One yawned. Another started playing hockey with a piece of ice."

I couldn't believe that.

"It's true," he insisted. "They play with things. They like to play with those big black birds, those ravens. Sometimes the ravens get the wolves to hunt for them. I've seen it where the ravens come back and tell the wolves where there is something to kill and eat. I thought if the raven and the wolf can get along, perhaps the man and the wolf can get along, too. But I couldn't stay out there long enough to test that out."

"Their thoughts. Did you know their thoughts," I asked. "Did you find what you were looking for?"

The old man knew I was trying to pin him down and I could tell he wasn't sure if he wanted to tell me something. He was silent, turning things over in his mind, but at last he must have decided to take a chance and tell me. There was one wolf in particular, a gray wolf, he said, who came back several times and sat before him. Suddenly that wolf was staring at him with a human's eyes in the face of a wolf. The old man did not know when it was he looked at the wolf and found he was staring back at it, but at some point he was aware that he and this particular wolf were holding each other's gazes and had been doing so for some time. The wolf was asking him a question, he realized, and he knew after some more staring what that question was. The old man stopped.

"Well, what was it?" I was impatient to know.

"Oh." His thoughts came back to me. "A standard question. He was asking me, 'Do you want to die?' But that is just wolf practice, asking that. I wanted to get past that and into something else. So I formed a question of my own in my mind and without ceasing my direct stare I spoke to the wolf, asking my own question: Wolf, I said, your people are hunted from the air and poisoned from the earth and killed on sight and you are outbred and stuffed in cages and almost wiped out. How is it that you go on living with such sorrow? How do you go on without turning around and destroying yourselves, as so many of us Anishinaabeg have done under similar circumstances?

"And the wolf answered, not in words, but with a continuation of that stare. 'We live because we live.' He did not ask questions. He did not give reasons. And I understood him then. The wolves accept the life they are given. They do not look around them and wish for a different life, or shorten their lives resenting the humans, or even fear them any more than is appropriate. They are efficient. They deal with what they encounter and then go on. Minute by minute. One day to the next. And so, my friend, I did learn what I had come there to find out. I'll tell you now: I wanted to know how not to kill myself. For that very thing was my intention and had been so for weeks, I could see no way around it. I knew what chaos and everlasting questions such a death brings down upon the living. But I was past caring about that. Since I was resigned to killing myself, you could say my life was nothing, my life was cheap. So before I went through with it, I decided I would sit with the wolves."

"You never killed yourself, obviously," I said, "but did you perhaps try?"

The old man didn't answer directly. He sat up. "Open the tie on this bare-ass dress," he said, "and look."

When I opened his shirt I saw across his back and shoulders the regular, deep, violet-brown scars of a sundancer who pulled buffalo skulls.

"That's what I did instead."

Sometimes I think that is the way to go. That old man made sense to me. I remember him always when I go out on cold nights and stand on the ice and listen to the wolves. Those wolves will tend their sick and their old; they'll bring them food. Sometimes they will even adopt a human baby as their own, I've heard, though I've never known that to be true. They are usually just hungry, as they were when Anaquot fled. The baby who was saved that day grew up and lived a long life, and as a young man I went to sit with her sometimes. Her name was Fleur Pillager. From this old Pillager lady, I learned the next part of what I'm going to tell you. She told me things in detail, as though they happened directly to her, and in a way she had experienced them, too, even though she was tiny, and helpless, and wrapped in her mother's shawl.

When a love burns too hot, it scorches everyone it touches. We old women know it is a curse to love like that. So my mother was cursed. Anaquot was numb when her lover's uncle dropped her at the turnoff to the house, and she was uncertain. The uncle gave her no directions, and seemed anxious to get rid of her, perhaps, she thought, because he needed to forget what had happened with the wolves . . . though his back had been turned. He really didn't know. He hadn't seen it happen. As for Anaquot, it was easy for her to forget. She had already forgotten. Only, the story did not forget her. When her baby peered up at her from the warmth of its fur bag, she knew the baby remembered. The knowledge was there, in the tiny black eyes sharp as bitter stars.

She stood in the snowy clearing of her lover's house with her baby, and watched the smoke curl from a small stovepipe chimney. A woman opened the door. Her face was pleasant, but worried, and she had the strong features of people on that side of the lake. In youth the women tended to be plain and as they matured their features gained a solid and attractive clarity. They grew beautiful. The woman's smile seemed kind, though there was something too knowledgeable about it. She wore a flowered dress and a neat bib apron tied over her breasts and hips. She exuded the rich smell of cooking meat, or the house did, as she simultaneously brushed her children back and signaled Anaquot to enter. Stepping gratefully into the warm cabin, Anaquot felt a hand pluck at her shoulder, as though to draw her back, to warn her, but when she glanced behind

122

her there was no one, only the empty snow of the yard where her tracks led to the house.

Had she imagined, later, another set of tracks beside hers? A set of careful, small, regular steps? It always seemed when she recalled entering the house that she had noticed she was accompanied there through the fresh snow of the empty yard. But then the drama of arrival took over. She was brought into the warmth. The woman—her man's sister or sister-cousin, she assumed—showed her own children off to Anaquot. There were three. There was a bewildered-looking boy just out of the tikinagaan and starting to walk. An older daughter whose mouth curled hard and greedy, and who stared at Anaquot's baby with the cold interest of a snake. There was a sturdy older brother just starting to get his growth, whose soft eyes reminded Anaquot of the eyes of the man she loved.

And where, anyway, was he?

Somehow, she didn't want to ask. She thought she'd pick the clues up. Maybe he'd be back that night. She looked around for his things, perhaps the beaded ogichidaa vest that she remembered, or a pair of summer makizinan, a pipe, tobacco. But she saw nothing to indicate the presence of a grown man except the rifle gleaming on the white bone antlers set in the wall. And that could have been the woman's gun. She didn't know.

"Namadabin!" The woman gestured for her to sit, and Anaquot carefully wiped her hands clean on a white cloth before she smoothed back the fur of the bag that held the baby, and looked into her face. The new one was sleeping now, her mouth tipped open in trust to show delicate, dented gums. The rose brown cheeks were plump with mother's milk, the perfectly formed head and face still wobbly on the stalklike neck. With her eyes shut in curved slant lines the baby was the picture of peace. But then the eyes opened and a little fire shot into the room. The baby was, after all, the child of an act of perfidy and thrilling joy.

What pain there had been in bearing the baby, Anaquot had welcomed. It had eclipsed her heart's agonized dissatisfactions. Now, as she tried to get her bearings in the situation, she remembered that she'd been near death when she'd bled after the birth and it hadn't mattered to her. That's how deep she'd sunk into this. That thought strengthened her. Her heart surged when she realized she'd soon see her lover and her hands traced the rim of a tin tea mug before she set her lips to it. Had his own lips touched there too? Drinking tea that morning? Was this a kind of kiss?

"Aaniin izhinikaazoyan?" she asked the woman in a pleasant voice. By any measure of hospitality, the woman should have offered her name first, but perhaps in the intrigue of seeing such a young baby she had forgotten. Even now, the woman didn't answer, as though she hadn't heard or was distracted by a child's request at the same time. She bustled, took some bannock from a cloth that had kept it warm; she gave Anaquot the bread, a bit of clear grease to dip it into, and also a small bowl of stew. Then the woman hastened to the corner to set out some blankets and make a place for Anaquot to rest with the baby. As she did this, Anaquot felt a prickling sensation along the side of her face, then at her back right between her shoulder blades, and she knew the girl child was staring at her. She turned around of course and sure enough those eyes opaque as mud slid away. Anaquot gave herself a little shake and tried not to feel the crawl of hatred that came so clearly from the girl.

"I don't need to take the girl's sleeping place," said Anaquot. "I don't need to use her blankets. I have my own."

"Save your blankets," said the girl's mother.

And a voice, a little whisper, echoed her, out of the air.

Save yourself.

The voice was just a thread of sound.

"Awegonen?" said Anaquot, looking around for the source.

The woman helped her from the chair and brought her to the corner. As Anaquot sank back into the blankets, covered herself, and began in that secret darkness to nurse her baby, she realized that she was tired, swimmingly exhausted, and the baby was still so little that the cold made it dangerously drowsy. She held it inside her shirt to warm it with her own skin, and the baby gradually relaxed. But as Anaquot drifted deeper toward unawareness, she experienced a sharp stab of lucidity. In that clear moment, she realized that she was more than tired. She was lost. The story had her by the throat. Frightened, she curled around her child as though to protect it, but sleep hurled them both to darkness and scattered them across the ice.

Her sleep was so profound that she forgot where she was and also who she was. She forgot she had a baby or was in love. She forgot her old life, her daughter, the son and husband she had left behind, and the uncle. All she could remember was the face of the woman who had greeted her at the door of this house. So she smiled when by lamplight that face appeared before her, strong and brown, the straight eyebrows concerned and her teeth gleaming in a smile. Yes, marveled Anaquot, those teeth were very white, and then she sank into a deeper obliteration and did not wake until dawn, when the people in the cabin all around her began to stir.

Although awake, she was so uncertain of her surroundings that she didn't open her eyes, but stayed hidden in the blankets with her baby pressed to her, nursing again; had it nursed all night? The hungry rhythm of its pull comforted her, made all of this seem real again. She had the distinct sensation that, outside of the blankets that covered her completely, a huge leave-taking was occurring. Many people were stumbling out, saying their good-byes in low voices so as not to wake her. Perhaps her lover had returned, she thought, with an entire hunting party. Perhaps they all had spent the night upon the floor, each curled in blankets they now carried off over their shoulders or rolled and strapped to their backs. Listening, she could see each in her mind's eye as he or she departed, and when the cabin was quiet she smiled. Her lover, she thought, had sent them all away! Soon, he would come to her. She would feel the weight of his hand on the blanket. He would slip underneath the heavy wool, the quilt, and he would curl behind her. He would bury his face in the hair flung across her shoulder. She took a deep breath. The baby stirred. Nothing happened. Slowly, she drew the blanket down, away from her face, and looked out. He wasn't there, but that same woman was. She sat in a pool of light from the window quietly sewing beads onto a swatch of velvet.

"Giwii minikwen anibishaabo ina?" The woman asked, without turning, whether Anaquot would like to drink some tea.

Anaquot crept from the blankets, still aching and tired as though she'd kept walking all night. She left the baby in the blankets and at once felt strangely light. It had been a day and a night and a morning that the baby had been in her arms. Along with her things, she had a big stack of cattail down to use when she needed to change the stuffing in its bag. Now she changed the fluff she'd pinned against the child in a scrap of bashkwegin. She put the baby back into the blanket, and burned the soiled down in the stove, which was fancy iron from the trader's store and which filled Anaquot with pride for the wealth of her lover's family. Then she poured herself a cup of tea. As she drank from the same tin cup she'd used the night before, she imagined the cup belonging to her lover. She looked around for the bag and saw that her things were neatly stacked beside the blankets she'd slept in. Her own baby's carefully beaded tikinagaan, which she'd carried with her because it was too cold to put the baby in it as they traveled, was propped against the wall. She had tied her clothing and small possessions in the skirt of her summer dress and carried the round bundle by the knot. She also had a hand drum with a white line painted across it, and a beater she had made herself with a handle of red-barked alder. She kept the drum and beater in a handwoven drawstring sack. The drum was the most precious thing she owned, and she was glad to see it among the other things, because there was something missing. She was sure of it. But her head ached and she couldn't think of just exactly what.

Anaquot carried her tea back to the blankets. Although the woman had smiled at her, she hadn't invited Anaquot to sit with her in the light of the window. As Anaquot sipped the tea, she suddenly remembered what was missing. Her daughter had brought her skirt bundle of possessions, too. Where was it? As soon as she thought of the girl, she heard a slight rustle behind her and she put down her cup of tea in order to investigate. But she saw nothing. Across the floor, the little boy who had just begun to walk was sitting in the circle of warmth by the stove, playing with a pile of pinecone dolls. Perhaps one of them had rolled into her bedding, thought Anaquot. The older boy and girl were nowhere in sight. She put her hand down and retrieved the cup, took another sip, and rocked her baby. She watched the light move across the shoulders of the other woman as she beaded the velvet. As she worked, the woman sang. Her voice was husky, sweet, pleasing. The song had a melancholy lilt. Anaquot soon found that she was drifting, her thoughts were disconnecting, her entire body was loosening. The last thing she saw was the woman, close now and blocking out the light. She saw the woman bending over her, and then Anaquot felt the woman ease the baby from the loose basket of her arms.

Anaquot was not without her own resources. In spite of her changeable nature and her weakness when it came to love, she possessed an unusual toughness of mind when it came to protecting herself. In addition, she was to find, someone had come to help her. A being had walked beside her, making tracks only she could see. Now she could feel herself plunging through sleep as into a dark lake. As she fought to swim back to the surface, someone helped pull her up. As though treading water, desperate, she managed to stay just a breath above oblivion. She opened her eyes a slit, though her eyelids seemed made of stone, and she saw the shape of the woman move across the tamped-earth floor with the baby in her arms. And then she heard the woman's song, which now had words.

This gall of the wolverine
I place beneath your tongue
To murder your mother's desire.

Anaquot lunged forward, knocking the cup aside, spilling the rest of the tea across the floor. As though noticing her clumsiness, but kindly attempting not to draw attention to it, the woman brought the baby back and nestled it in the blankets. Then she wiped the tea off the blankets and asked Anaquot if she would like to eat.

There can be nothing in the bannock, which she shares, but you must dip the stew from the pot yourself, someone whispered in Anaquot's ear. With a huge effort, she cleared her mind and rose to her feet, thanking the woman, pretending she hadn't heard the song. The baby slept soundly now, its breath quick and shallow, as infants breathe. From time to time it whined or growled a little in its sleep, but that was nothing to worry about. Anaquot ate hungrily and watched as the woman continued to bead the velvet bag. At first, Anaquot thought it was for a baby, as it laced up the middle, but the top looked like the bottom and there was no place for the baby's head to peep out on the world. *Look more closely*, said the little voice. If a baby was put inside there, Anaquot thought, it could only be sewn in for burial. As suddenly as she thought this, she imagined that she knew just exactly what the kindly-looking woman was doing. She had put the poison under the tongue of the baby so that, when it nursed, Anaquot would absorb the killing stuff through her breasts. And the poison would eventually kill the baby, too. The woman was looking forward to putting it in the ground.

I don't know why, thought Anaquot; her heart beat crazily and her brain spun but she managed to shield her knowledge from the other woman. I don't understand! As she pretended to busy herself with her child she thought hard, and harder yet, until the answer finally came in the shape of her lover's eyes. She had seen those eyes on the older boy. His own son. Which would make the woman not his sister, aunt, or cousin, but his wife.

All that had happened now laid itself out very clearly before Anaquot. The woman had intercepted the message from Anaquot's husband and found out everything. She had sent her own brother in the wagon across the ice. That was why the man she thought was her lover's uncle had been so cold to her, so guarded. The woman had chosen a time when her husband, Anaquot's love, was gone on the trapline. That way, she could kill Anaquot and the baby and have the bodies stiff outside the door when he returned with his load of furs. Closing her eyes in an effort to contain her fear and panicked anger, Anaquot saw the scene this woman planned: there was her lover returning through the snow, dragging his toboggan laden with bales of skins. How surprised was he to see that she was standing at his cabin door, holding their baby in her arms! How long did it take for him to notice, as he neared, her icy rigidity, her eyes staring blind and her mouth frozen open on a word? How many endless steps before his cry of greeting turned to a wail of horror? How long the quiet, how closed the smile, as his wife slowly opened the door?

I know that I have done a wrong thing, a bad thing, thought Anaquot. But I don't deserve to die for it! The small whispering voice, which she now thought of as a helpful spirit, answered her somewhat mockingly. *You don't deserve to die? What about your little girl?*

My little girl? thought Anaquot. Do you mean the baby in my arms?

The whispering laughter grew lighter and spoke. *No, mother, don't you remember? There was one who gave her life for you.*

All of a sudden Anaquot let what happened on the way there flood into her—the ice, the wolves, her daughter. When she remembered, her mind cracked open. She knew that she loved that daughter more than anyone in her entire life. She loved her more than her little brother or her father, more than the baby in her arms and more, even, than her lover. She loved that daughter more than she loved herself. Her mind veered off. She knew if she absorbed the knowledge directly into her heart now, it would kill her. So she sat there humbly and let her mind be taken wherever it would be allowed to go. As she sat there, the voice returned and she grasped at its words with hope.

My things are inside of your things, my bundle is safe in yours, just like when I was inside of you, mother, when you carried me safely into life.

Anaquot busied herself among the few possessions she had brought, and while the woman continued to sew the burial shroud for her baby, she untied the bundle of her skirt. Sure enough, inside her rose red skirt there was her daughter's smaller bundle of things, which she now took apart and examined.

There was the little hatchet that her father had made, a toy, but sharp and capable of chopping thin poles to make playhouses. There was a small bark box that contained three awls and three thorn-apple needles, a ball of waxed sinew, and a packet of thread. The bundle also contained a little sheaf of bird bones, bleached hollow, for making whistles, and a packet of medicines that Anaquot now remembered making up for her daughter and teaching her to use. When she saw these medicines, and held the bark packet in her hands and examined the powders and twines of roots, Anaquot realized that she had not always been such a bad mother to her older daughter. Not at all. Until her love burned out of control, destroying her perspective, she had been a careful and knowing mother. She had loved her daughter, taught her sewing skills, and provided her the medicines to cure all ills she could imagine. There was even, she saw, taking from a tiny feather pouch a bladder of oil, just enough to strengthen the baby to withstand the poison laid under its tongue. There was nothing else she could think of, however, to protect herself from its effect.

After she administered the medicine to her child, it stirred and became more eager, lifted its head, peered at her wailing to be fed. Its hunger grew uncontrollable after a while and it began to beg with small complaining noises and then to roar with despair. Anaquot could not bear it. Even though she believed the poison that the woman had given would harm her, Anaquot put the baby to her breast.

First, she knew the pleasure of solving its desperation. Next, with a deep sigh, they melted together as one. She closed her eyes and saw the two of them together, as a dot of light and then they grew and grew until they had no edges at all and were the radiant center of an infinite wheel.

This vision frightened her with its strangeness, but when she opened her eyes they were still there in the ordinary afternoon. She realized her belief about the poison might be wrong; still, she couldn't shake it from her mind. The winter sun had entered the window at a fierce angle and its red-gold light blazed across the blue cupboard in the corner, the table, the stove, the other piles of blankets and the pole bed and the chair where the woman sat counting the little boy's fingers over and over with him. Bezhig. Niizh. Niswi. Niiwin. Naanan. This counting between a woman and a child had been happening since numbers began. The blazing light intensified. It burned a hole in her heart, as neat as a bullet hole, and then, just as the woman's song meant to, it took away her desire.

She experienced her love's absence as a gradual clarity. The light faded into the trees, the room grew cold. The woman set her little boy in the corner with a rind of deer meat to chew, and then set about perfecting the fire in the stove so that her bannock would cook evenly. By the way she did this, her movements careful and spare, Anaquot saw how many thousands of times she had made food for her family. She looked past the woman, saw the milk cans full of water in the corner, knew she'd hauled it from the river or melted fresh snow. So much work and care was apparent all through the little house. The logs were neatly tamped, the quilts clean and mended. The little boy wore a shirt of thick flannel and little pants sewn of deerhide. There was a rabbit-skin blanket laid over the bed the woman was now sharing with her daughter. Those blankets took long weaving, skill, as did the reed mats on the walls and the beaded vest that Anaquot now saw was set out for mending in the last light of the day.

It was this vest, exactly, that she remembered her lover wearing. She had traced the beaded flowers and the maple leaves, the curl of the vines, as she talked to him in the shadowy overhang of rich new leaves the previous summer. Now the sight of the vest filled her with a new feeling—not of longing, but of sorrow. How hard his wife had worked, placing each bead just so, and how many hopes she had sewn into the colorful centers of the roses! Even now, the woman bent above her stitching with a singular attention that re-vealed her love for the wearer of the vest. Anaquot saw that. In fact, once Anaquot began thinking this way and noticing everything around her, all the work the woman did, all that she needed to pro-tect, Anaquot didn't blame her for the poison.

"But you don't have to poison my baby," said Anaquot, clearly, to the woman. She rose from her blankets with energy. "I'm ready to do all that needs to be done."

The woman put down her needle, folded her hands on the table, and frowned as Anaquot sat down across from her. This time, when Anaquot demanded her name, she told her that she was named for the spirit of the wolverine. Ziigwan'aage was indeed a poisoner, or rather, she was one who was entrusted with all of the most dangerous medicines and deep knowledge of them. She knew the properties of all the plants and how they interacted, especially mushrooms, the food of the dead. She knew which fish spines to strip for venom and twice a year she traveled west to trade for the milk of snakes. She had never used her medicines for a dark purpose until now, but she had reason.

"So you've awakened" was all she said.

"I have," said Anaquot, "in every way."

Ziigwan'aage waited calmly for her to go on.

"I see your love for him and for your children. I know why you brought me here. I understand it. We would not in fact be enemies were it not for him."

For the first time, the woman seemed a little shaken. Perhaps it was Anaquot's directness, or the hard confidence in her eyes, the smooth power of her movements. Or perhaps Ziigwan'aage hadn't put the thoughts together in her mind like Anaquot did. Perhaps she'd laid all the blame on Anaquot and not on her husband because she loved him so, and wanted to believe him. Whatever the reason, Ziigwan'aage now found the things that Anaquot said were compelling to her. Ziigwan'aage could think of no reason that she shouldn't continue to listen, and gestured for Anaquot to continue.

"He told me that he once had a wife, but he threw her away," said Anaquot.

Ziigwan'aage's eyes jumped to Anaquot's face and her mouth squared when she saw it was true.

"He didn't mention his children," said Anaquot. "I never heard about them."

At this, Ziigwan'aage's body stiffened. She looked away from

Anaquot and her stare scorched the air all around the two. For a long time they sat, in silence, until the light of the afternoon disappeared entirely. Then they got up at the same time and began to work, as one person, their movements smooth and spare as if they'd been sisters since they were born. Sisters who might hate each other at times, but who matched so well that the work almost did itself.

When the two older children returned from their day at school, they were cold and hungry, laughing. Banging their empty lunch pails they looked eagerly at the stove. They went silent when they saw the visiting woman at work, chopping gristle from frozen meat to add to their mother's stew. Because something in their mother's bearing had led them to believe, even before the visitor arrived, that she was a threat and not to be trusted, they were surprised to see that the two were speaking calmly and easily, working side by side.

The children knew in this way that something had changed; what it was they couldn't tell. They had no way of knowing that a great change was being effected in the two women. As Anaquot and Ziigwan'aage worked, their hearts turned slowly, suspiciously, unevenly at times, toward each other and against the man they had both loved, whose name was Simon Jack.

He had a strict mind and a somewhat foolish heart. A contradictory person, he was known for his rigid memory of ritual and detail. He was the one they called upon for the sequence of songs, the order of creation, the accounting for of spirits. He had a love of little pleasures, like gambling, and he was vain of his looks, though he wasn't even that handsome. His wife oiled and combed and cared for his long, stringy hair better than she cared for her own. He was picky about his shirts and trousers, and he wore a white shell earring. At the same time, he cared nothing for the things of this world and would spend days in the woods, fasting, humbling himself before the eternal mystery of existence. He was ten years older than his wife, and Anaquot was a few years younger than she. So he had seen enough of life to know that such love as he and Anaquot felt was sure to bring disaster. He had hoped that there would be no child of their intensity. By leaving his family for a time, living up on the trapline, making himself secret and scarce as his wife's name-sake, he thought he could weather the storm in his heart. He both hoped and feared that it would be the same with Anaquot. But when he came home, his blood still raged and it was all he could do to contain his black longings and hide the estrangement of his af-fections from his wife. She knew anyway, found out the details from other women, and sent him out again while she decided what to do with the situation.

As for Ziigwan'aage, she was by no means a simple woman either. She was born in spring, when the wolverine kits come from the den and proceed to sink their teeth into anything that moves. She grew up in the twilight time when her people, the Anishi-naabeg, were battling great waves of disease. Those were the times when the entire force of a woman's existence was focused on keep-ing her children alive. Ziigwan'aage kept her ear to the ground and took note of illnesses as they passed into the settlement. She kept her children home at the slightest hint of something dangerous and allowed no visitors. When they weakened, she made sure she had the plant medicines she needed, picked at the highest concentra-tion of their power. Every morning, she checked her children's eyes and tongues. She smelled their breath and sometimes even frowned over their stools to make certain that they were healthy enough to send out into the world. Her pharmacopoeia was the woods, and at the slightest hint of trouble—dulled gaze, white tongue, a sour heat in the lungs—she picked what she needed, rummaged in her stash for the ingredients to teas, burned a powder beneath their noses, or swabbed a tincture on their gums. There was no chink in her vigilance, no margin for error. She could not afford a distraction. So when her husband began to behave in a way she found all too familiar from other women's reports of their husbands, she decided she would cut short this nonsense. She had no time for it. She wouldn't tolerate it. Not when she had the lives of children on her hands.

Ziigwan'aage had deemed it most expeditious to get rid of the other woman, though she was still deciding whether to spare the baby and raise it as her own. But then Anaquot had startled her, and made her think. She had impressed Ziigwan'aage as a formidable opponent and, still better, as an invincible ally. Not that they'd actually decided what to do about Simon Jack. His fate was on a thread that they pulled between them, this way and that. Sometimes as they talked they laughed at his transparent ways and marveled, with deep irony, at the similarity of things he'd said to them both, promises he'd made, endearments even. They held nothing back in their dissection of his behavior; they continued on until both felt they had purged themselves of any pity or attraction. Of course, they both knew, they hadn't any illusions—not loving Simon Jack in the abstract was much easier than not loving Simon Jack in the flesh.

In this regard, Ziigwan'aage had the advantage of living in the heart of her family. Her old mother and sisters, her aunts and uncles, and of course the brother she'd relied on, lived all around her and could be reached via endless networks of trails broken through the trees. These people were, in fact, the crowd of beings Anaquot had sensed leaving very early that morning, having already stayed the night. They had congregated in order to take a look at the woman who had tried to steal Simon Jack. While Anaquot slept in the grip of the sleeping medicine, they had gloated at her capture and admired her baby, then melted off into the blue morning air, leaving so little trace of themselves that Anaquot had wondered whether they were actually spirits. She found now that they were tremendously real.

They came back that night and sat quietly or talked of their own matters. One by one they took the baby in their arms and admired her, examined her fingers, exclaimed at the depth of her eyes and the bow of her mouth. They noted the curve of her ears and texture of her hair, even unwrapped her feet to see whether her toes were of a uniform length. As they went over the baby with great care, by means that were invisible to Anaquot, she herself went from being outside of them all and looking in, to being one gathered into their edges and absorbed. With imperceptible gestures Ziigwan'aage told them that in the end she had decided to adopt Anaquot instead of kill her, so that gradually they stopped treating the woman as one soon to be dead. Even though no word was addressed to her, Anaquot knew that she and her baby were now under the protection of these people with the severe and handsome faces, with the hair that waved about their shoulders, and the restless hands. She also understood, to her deep unease, that they would keep her no matter what. She would not be allowed to go. Now Anaquot saw that every one of them had brought along some object that they were making. Even while speaking their hands polished or beaded or wove or quilled or whittled. As she picked up her own beading to concentrate upon, she understood that if she was to be accepted by the Pillagers, for that is what the people of this band called themselves, she must keep silence, imitate their actions, and closely observe and take note of all that might assist in her survival.

*   *   *

Because she had seen the wife of Simon Jack sewing that bundle from which no child could peep its head, Anaquot was still extremely careful with the information she divulged, for information is power. She did not tell her baby's name to Ziigwan'aage. Instead, she used a nickname she herself had been given by an old French trader. Fleur. So that baby was disguised before it had even spoken. Hidden by a lie. Watchful underneath. Too much had already happened to the baby, who hadn't even crawled yet or clapped her hands or eaten from a spoon. Her sister gave her life for her. Her mother ran from one husband to another man's intercepting wife. The baby was surrounded by sharp discord, jagged sorrows, and that cunning presence. Pain and truth. A spirit comes into the world and disrupts the flow of things. Changes the course of love. Takes lives. Challenges the order. So it was with this weak little baby, Anaquot saw, and she was more determined than ever to protect her. For it seemed the spirits had some great work in mind when they made the child.

As she sewed or cooked next to Simon Jack's wife, this woman with the powerful name, Anaquot deliberately kept herself humble. To combine humility with the unyielding directness that had already saved her life was to protect her by also protecting Ziigwan'aage's pride. Never, she promised herself, would she challenge Ziigwan'aage, especially in the presence of others, not ever when it came to Simon Jack. Anaquot would allow the family to snub her in subtle ways and when that happened she would pretend she hadn't noticed. At crucial moments, she would stand her ground. Although there was some mutual decision among Ziigwan'aage's people to tolerate Anaquot, she knew well that she was not among friends. Three of the women who came around were Simon Jack's sisters. Long ago they had accepted Ziigwan'aage as one of their own. There was no hope for Anaquot there. Likewise, she could detect no crack of sympathy in the attitudes of the formidable grandmothers of Ziigwan'aage's children. There were the uncles and a grandfather and even a great-grandfather, but Anaquot knew it was dangerous to align with men. Only one woman, Doosh, a blood sister to Ziigwan'aage, gave any sign of sympathy. Doosh was slow and somewhat vacant, but she treated Anaquot with neutral kindness. Anaquot made a great effort to remain calm and aware around these relatives, in addition to assorted cousins and clan members, and that was difficult even without Simon Jack to deepen the conflict and throw the whole mess into relief.

That the whole thing really was a mess and nearly out of control became clear when Simon Jack simply walked back into the house one day stinking of bait. He must have been prepared for Anaquot's presence by one of the uncles, for he didn't so much as glance at her, though when his snake-eyed daughter brought the baby over he cupped Fleur under her arms, held her at arms' length, and looked her over very carefully, for a long time, before he instructed his daughter to bring the baby back to its mother. Did something pass between the two? Some heat of recognition? Some bounce of delight? Why did Simon Jack smile so broadly? He kissed the baby before he handed her away and got down to his food. Deep in the night, when Anaquot woke to hear him stirring around (she thought) in the other part of the cabin with his wife, the picture of that smile on Simon Jack's face as he gobbled down food pierced her and she wept with degraded fury, making no sound. Then a thousand morbid sexual pictures went through her mind and she managed to calm herself and to slow the pounding of her heart only by conjuring up a strong rope in her thoughts and then, not without a mental struggle, tying up Simon Jack. When she had him tightly bound with those imaginary ropes, she hoisted him into a tree and let him dangle there. The gentle swaying of his cocoonlike shape lulled her. But the last image in her mind as blackness covered her was still Simon Jack's broad and uncontainable grin when he saw his baby. He loved Fleur, at least, and couldn't hide it, Anaquot was certain.

In the deep of her heart she was also certain of two other things: Simon Jack loved her, too. Or at least he would want to sleep with her. The way he ignored her was much too elaborate to be construed as anything other than his own weakness. In order to take advantage of a time he might slip, she must cultivate patience. The other thing was the girl cold with malice. She was a danger. Anaquot thought she'd better pursue a way of getting rid of her.

What there was about Simon Jack to attract two women to his bed was not apparent at first. The hair straggling down his back was prematurely gray, he was too lean in the chest and shoulders, also he was bandy-legged and he stooped a little when he walked so he looked much older than he was. Long thin wisps of mustache drooped to either side of his mouth, and he had a habit of glancing just above a person's head when he talked and never meeting their eyes. But that, it turned out, was part of his way with people, a mannerism that gave him a hold over them. For when all of a sudden he did fix them with an unblinking gaze, a look remote, chilling, intimate, and immoderate, they were often startled into silence and submission.

That's what had happened with Anaquot when she first met him. Simon Jack was known for many things, respected and a little feared, so the full force of his attention had been thrilling to Anaquot. She'd grown lovesick over him. It galled her now that she'd broken her marriage, abandoned her son, and allowed her older daughter to die, just so that she could be with Simon Jack. She'd thought she couldn't live her life without the force of him pouring over and all around her. But as women have found since love began, she found she could live. And determined that she would. Seeing the wife and children about whom he'd misled her, and feeling his studied indifference to her presence as an insult so complete that it severed her dependence, Anaquot found a solid place in the swirl of pain and panic in her heart. Too much, too much, she had given too much. She discovered a rock to stand on, a jutting reef.

The next day she stepped onto that rock with her baby and allowed all that was unbearable to rush around her—Ziigwan'aage's colliding outrages of love and hate, the daughter's black, interior purpose, the little requests and petitions of visitors who needed something of Simon Jack, the younger son's lively innocence, her own baby's needs. She performed patternless, absorbing, hectic, trying tasks with steady calm. She slowed her movements, allowed her whole body to become a contained absence. She was so conscious of keeping a close check on herself that she did not notice that when she did this, her effect upon others was something like Simon Jack's. Ziigwan'aage's attention unwillingly turned toward her, as did the frozen spirit of her daughter. Simon Jack tried to hide his uneasy curiosity. But the presence of a woman who did not belong where she was and yet kept herself keenly occupied, displaying no hint of uneasiness, disturbed them. Anaquot neither desired to please nor seemed anxious not to offend, yet she did both. Nobody could tell how hard that was. Anaquot considered each act and weighed each word before she uttered it. She found within herself a deep reserve. She exercised control only over herself, and was unaware that to do so can often cause others to lose theirs.

Which is why Simon Jack tried to slip beneath her blanket one night. It was a rash act and Simon Jack had desperately resisted it. Anaquot had only imagined that he might come, but when she felt his hands on her, she did not what she wanted to do, but what would save her life.

"Get away from me! Go play with yourself! Leave me alone!" she hissed, pushing at him violently, waking the baby to cry and to wake the others. Rejecting Simon Jack was one of the most difficult things she had ever done, but it had the desired result. Ziigwan'aage, who was of course awake, stared up into the freezing black air of the cabin and allowed a slow smile to creep across her face. She had been tempted to kill Anaquot ever since her husband had returned. Simon Jack crept to the coldest corner of the cabin and curled in his blanket, alone. Then he chopped wood all the next day with a hard, specific fury. Ziigwan'aage sang as she cooked. When she served the food, Anaquot ate heartily and without fear for the first time since she'd come to the cabin.

The two women never discussed what they would do to take away their man's power and divide it between the two of them. But after that night it began to happen that Simon Jack felt a little dizzy in the evenings and went to his blankets in the corner before they turned the lamps out, and fell asleep there while the women sat at the table working. They were beading something. They did not know what it was yet, what was taking shape beneath their hands. They placed each bead just so on the velvet and the beads turned into four-petaled flowers that told stories and held great meaning. These flowers lay along white vines that writhed like snakes across the velvet, and there were horns on the vines and leaves of impossible shapes springing off here and there. What they worked on had the most amazing vitality. It grew between them. And still they could not tell what it was until one day Simon Jack walked in and saw that they were making him a dance outfit, either that or an elaborate set of clothes to be buried in, but as the dance outfit was far the better option he mentioned it out loud.

"Oh yes," said one of them—they could never remember which—"you will dance in these handsome clothes. You will dance your heart out, little husband."

The last part was spoken beneath her breath, so he didn't hear it, but the other woman smiled and their needles flashed, spearing beads and affixing them. And so the outfit took its shape. The horned white vine twisted like a snake down the two front pieces and coiled itself around the back. Sometimes they ran out of thread and continued to sew with grasses or wolf sinew or even with their own hair. It was only from necessity that they did this. They did not mean to bind him to them in an evil way. They did not mean any evil at all. They were only caught in what the story did to them. The story Simon Jack had set into motion. No, if anybody was responsible for the elegant armbands and wrist guards, the leggings, or the too ornate breech clout, it was Simon Jack. And if each woman beaded the bottom of one of his makizinan the way grieving widows bead the soles of their dead husband's, it was only the fault of Simon Jack again. For it was he who played with Ziigwan'aage's toothed and closely guarded heart. He who had raked his eyes down Anaquot's breasts and kindled the heat that flowed up and licked through every sense until she couldn't think and let things happen that shouldn't ever have taken place. So although they didn't understand where the outfit was going or what would happen to Simon Jack once he put it on, they sewed. And it could even be said that they enjoyed their work and found the doing of it an act of love, though not exactly love of Simon Jack.

The two women stitched each other still closer, became true sisters. Anaquot had left her family behind and was hungry for connection. And Ziigwan'aage, though surrounded by family, was set apart because of the nature of her fierce personality and knowledge of medicines. She began to appreciate and then rely on Anaquot, who was almost as smooth and efficient a worker as she. A deer carcass vanished between them in no time, for instance, reduced to its respective parts, as did any animals trapped. The skins were quickly removed and beautifully stretched on frames. Ziigwan'aage had more time to do things, even to enjoy herself. And so did Anaquot. They went to town, brought Doosh along. Bartered bitterly and happily. Anaquot always bought a ribbon or a string of licorice for Doosh. One day they met a mission teacher in the store. He told them he was taking students to a place where they would get educated better than white people. "Your daughter is intelligent" was all Anaquot said to Ziigwan'aage. But Doosh would not let up on the idea that the girl with the cold eyes, Niibin'aage, should go.

They went home. Between them they carved up a bear killed in its winter den. Soon its thick, perfectly tanned fur coat lay before the warm stove and the baby rolled and played on it and cooed with that engaging and astonished recognition that occurs halfway through a baby's first year and makes everybody laugh. For it was spring now. Some days the snow dripped and melted and Ziigwan'aage let the children go without their daily bear-grease rubdown, and then without their heavy, scratchy, woolen underwear.

The ice on the lake was dull gray, soft, and porous looking. They were not allowed to cross it anymore on the way to school, but had to go the long way around, through the woods. Ziigwan'aage walked with them. That was another reason that she valued Anaquot's presence in the house—she could leave Anaquot with her own baby and Ziigwan'aage's youngest, and Ziigwan'aage could walk with the children to make sure nothing happened to them. Anaquot observed that if the girl went to the boarding school, she, at least, would not have to face that walk every day. Spring weather could be treacherous, and the animals were gaunt and hungry. Ziigwan'aage always carried the gun.

One day, when Ziigwan'aage returned from walking the children to school, she was hauling a dead wolf behind her on a toboggan she'd improvised from tree bark and some vines. It was the biggest wolf either of the women had ever seen. The fur was a light glossy gray and the brush of its tail longer than a grown man's arm. The creature's face was calm and almost smiling. Anaquot placed to-bacco on its throat and all four paws. It could well have been one of the wolves that killed her daughter. That pack was known here and it was mostly grays.

"How did you kill him?" she asked Ziigwan'aage.

"Around the bend, past that rock, he stood before us. So I shot him. It was a good shot."

The bullet had drilled the heart. When Anaquot saw the wound she put her fingers into the blood and before she knew what she was doing she had put her fingers into her mouth. Some old women say that by tasting wolf blood you will know the shape of things, but Anaquot had never known that to be true. The blood tasted like any other blood, but sharper. They would probably eat the wolf, because they ate everything, but the meat would have to be boiled in seven waters and seasoned heavily. As the women worked on the wolf, skinning it, Anaquot thought she heard someone singing; then later on a small voice whispered in her ear.

This is the one who ate my heart, mother.

With a strange cry, Anaquot dropped the knife. Ziigwan'aage picked it up. But Anaquot's hands were shaking and she could not continue to work.

"What is it?" asked Ziigwan'aage.

"My daughter speaks to me," said Anaquot.

Ziigwan'aage knew immediately just whom she meant, and put down her knife and sat with Anaquot.

"I knew there was someone else with you when you came here," she said. "She has been here all along."

Anaquot nodded. "But she hasn't spoken to me for almost two turns of the moon. I thought she'd left."

"I don't think she will ever leave," said Ziigwan'aage.

They both stared at the carcass of the wolf. After a while, Anaquot said, "We will make hoods and mitts for the children, fur on the inside to keep them warm." Without another word the two set to work, disposed of the wolf perfectly, and set its bones to boil on the stove. That night, they ate the creature, whose meat was bitter.

4

The Little Girl Drum

Now, let us not forget that Anaquot left behind a man grieving in the snow. The stricken husband, my grandfather, Old Shaawano. I knew the old man well because he'd keep me sometimes when my father and mother hit the bottle. When I was small, he tried to hold me close to him, and that's when he taught me all about the drum. Still, there are many things I know from sources other than my grandfather. I was friends with the old men who were close to him, and the old ladies too. I was the kind of boy and then young man who always felt old, maybe because my father's beatings made me old. I never wanted to be young because the young suffer. I always liked to listen to the old people. So it was through them that I know what it was like for my grandfather when Anaquot left him, and after he had picked up his daughter's scattered bones.

During that time, a sick uneasiness of grief afflicted Old Shaawano and sent him wandering. Whenever the need to tell the sad events panicked him, starting with an ache like cold and spreading outward until it squeezed his heart and prickled in his throat, he left the house. He left my father, just a little boy, to fend for himself. He could not be still. Weeks or days of wandering and talking might go by before he returned, exhausted, and collapsed in his cabin. Then, absurdly, he was enraged to find his son gone. But he always fell into a sickness and forgot to look for the boy, but instead lay helpless, his brain on fire. At the merest touch he felt his hair crackle. He hated for the wind to graze him as it fanned the heat all through his body and caused a bloody coughing that would not stop for days. He stayed indoors, usually in bed, and waited in sick trembling for the cup of despair to pass.

At these times, during the days when he was alone, my grandfather often heard things or saw things that he definitely knew were not there. His low, dark house was only one room with a small window on three sides. It still stands in the bush behind my house, used for chickens, so I know it well. The door on the fourth side opened out where it shouldn't have, west, where the dead go. From his cot, on good days, Shaawano could see out the door into the woods, but he usually kept the door shut to block the ghosts. Even so, some got by, squeezing underneath the sill or sliding through the cracks between the door and its casing. The ghosts were all strangers. He didn't know why that should be. He kept asking for his little girl, but none of them paid attention. Many were from the other side of the lake, and he'd made it a point to avoid people from there ever since that demon Pillager had stolen away his wife. That these unknown ghosts came, rather than his daughter or his own relatives, was a disappointment. My grandfather told me that our family, my ancestors, were clever people, while these strangers didn't seem very bright. He would have liked to see his grandparents, such generous, kind people, or his parents, who had died a few years before, disappointed that they couldn't cure his grief. He was even sure they would provide him help. Only, they never came.

The ghosts who did come to visit him were tiny skeleton children who flitted and zipped across his ceiling like spidery bats. Or they were shadowy, dull figures who seemed content to sit in the corner or slowly rock in his chipped green rocking chair. They usually did nothing but sigh and mutter, low, so he could never distinguish their words. That he could not make out their conversation or their complaints or whatever they were trying to tell him on these visits was maddening. He assumed they were judging him, blaming him, for letting his daughter die and his son run away. Their eyes raked over him. They sneered in his face. When he could stand it no longer, Shaawano would lunge from his bed and strike out right and left, in a frenzy, using whatever came to hand— knife, stick, board, belt. Driving them out usually put an end to his groaning need and he would totter, blinking, to the outhouse, and then return to sit by his door in the weak sun. He always felt so much better, once these hellish episodes subsided, that he often wondered why he dreaded them in the first place. But likewise, when he was curled in his bed, heart pumping with terror and longing, he could never remember how it felt to be at peace and so believed that his torment would last forever.

When he'd emerged, and was sitting in the sun, Shaawano would feel a remorse and calm so thrilling that tears might fill his eyes. He missed his son. There was so much that he wanted to show him! My grandfather noticed everything—the way wild raspberries had taken root in his torn and idle fishing nets and how young trees had grown through his junked wagon and the piles of his traps. Their prickling fronds, wildly spurting out the wood of the wagon box and through the jaws and knots of things that catch and kill, were a glorious signal. A chickadee pausing with a tiny worm in its beak, the blessed gurgle of a red-winged blackbird, the waves sounding on the lakeshore—anything, everything, caused Shaawano a happiness almost as unbearable as his pain. In this way, too, it was difficult to be so weakened. To wildly celebrate would have once been the appropriate response to any small light or joy. Now, standing up to the beauty, being small in it, taking one breath of sweet air after the next, often produced its own form of panic. This, he named after some time, guilt.

My grandfather said himself that he had been an evil person in his first season of random pain. He had done many things that were beyond the limits of decency. Things he dreaded bringing to mind. The worst things, of course, pierced into his brain with illuminating power. Those things were not the fighting or brawling or fucking or the stupid thefts. The scenes that came back vivid and sharp-edged were the cruel moments when he'd felt a black satisfaction, even a surge of glee in his throat, when he hurt his own son. He'd left the boy hungry and even ridiculed his grief over the loss of his mother. He had tampered with his son's spirit and now the boy was lost to him. Someone else had stepped in, taken the boy home, and barred Shaawano from visits. But the damage to the boy was done and some things cannot be undone. It was as though what happened with the wolves had set loose one long string of accidents that seemed like fate. And now the guilt. Shaawano couldn't get what he'd done out of his mind. He began to hate himself so much that the only relief he could obtain was to picture himself going back and savagely attacking the man he had been. He killed himself over and over in his mind. But when his bloody fantasies were exhausted, Shaawano was always left with Shaawano. The man who could never take back a single blow.

So there he was. He had started making pine pole furniture to get a living, and he could carve out and put together rough chairs and tables or bend more intricate pieces out of red willow. This passed his time between the great troughs and crests of his diminished life. If he prayed, it was for the numb peace that gave his hands the steadiness to work with those tools without one hand cutting off the other hand. He was, yes, tempted. Sometimes hating what his own hands had done he imagined taking the saw to them. But which hand would cut the other off? Which would die, which be saved, which would he choose? Sometimes he favored cutting off the right, for the right hand had certainly done the most damage. But then the sly hand would remain, the hand that pretended to be weaker and clumsier, but really wasn't. He would be left with the fist that sucker punched, the hand of deceit, the fingers that should have reached out to gather back his daughter when she left him lying in stubborn grief, and went out to join her mother on the wagon.

"That was it," he said one afternoon in the middle of one of his hand-hating reveries. He looked at his hands and flexed his fingers, broad palms, thick square fingers cushioned with calluses from his work, and saw them suddenly as innocent. Why should they suffer when they'd only done as Shaawano himself commanded? He thought immediately, with some relief, to put a bullet through his brain and send off the real culprit.

"That was it," he said again. The brain, the brain had commanded all of Shaawano, had told him to let his wife go off one winter day to live with Pillager. Maybe if Shaawano's brain had only willed his wife to stay, Anaquot would have, and then that wrong-hearted passion would have gone spent, she would eventually have accepted her place on this side of the lake, and his little girl, his baby sweetheart, would have grown up beside him. Instead, his daughter's graceful bones were picked clean by ravens. He had gathered them up, his tears freezing into an ice mask across his face, and put them in a place that only he knew about.

Now he dropped his chin to his chest and squeezed his head in his hands, but even as he put on the pressure until his eyes burned, he knew it wasn't really his brain but his heart that had made the decision to let Anaquot go. The heart with its pride, the heart that couldn't bear his wife's heart to have turned away. Shaawano's heart had refused to be patient and instead behaved with an impetuous, despairing fury. His heart had fought itself and lost. His heart had bested the brain with all its reasons. Yes, it was his own stubborn heart that failed. A knife would cut his heart out fine. Just fine. He would throw his offending heart to the ravens, yelling, "Here, have that too!"

And so it went with my grandfather. He put first one part of his body and then another on trial. Each was found guilty at first but then pointed to another culprit. He judged his limbs, his eyes, his ears, his bones, his blood. He weighed the evidence against each but always, in the end, could not think how to mete out proper justice and so had to admit, having gone over his whole body from hair to fingernail, that the criminal was not within him but outside of him. The culprit was made up of some force or intangible extra self he could only call his spirit.

Kill that! he urged himself then, but knew even as he cried out that he had already done so. He'd tried to poison his spirit, drowned it methodically, savagely, choked it off. Alcohol had been the tool. He thought back to when he took the first drink of his first real dirty drunk and remembered how he'd wept into the amber flame deep in the cup and how his sorrow had been answered with a spreading warmth and a forgetting.

"That was it," he said one more time. The pain in his life had started because he needed to forget. Now, with no part of himself left to blame, and in the ruin of his spirit, my grandfather remembered.

He remembered how his daughter had curled in the crook of his arm when he sat with her listening to the old people talk around the fire during berry-picking time. He never brushed away his little girl, even when she clung to his pant leg. Instead, he crouched at her level when she needed him and looked into her eyes before he picked her up. Always, when their eyes met, he felt that they exchanged a secret love. It was just between the two of them, his first-born, his daughter. Every time he lifted her to his chest, he experienced a fierce thump of emotion. He would protect her with his life! And so, how come he hadn't? Over and over now, he remembered the actual events of the day she was killed and how he had failed at each crux of the unfolding decision to prevail over Anaquot with his arguments. And then the unbearable findings. At the memories of what the wolves in their innocence had done, the blood crushed around my grandfather's heart and he had to gasp for breath. It was then, unable to unfreeze the pictures in his brain, that my grandfather fell into a weak faint and had a sort of dream.

He saw his little girl. She was alive and whole once again. She came into Shaawano's house through the western door and stood before him in the fringed, brown plaid shawl. Her eyes, so beautifully slanted and dark, shone with a fervent love that seemed to flow straight into him. The painful terror frozen in his chest turned to water. Then she spoke.

"I know where they put the trees for the drum," his daughter told him. "Many years ago they cut the logs and put them in the water down near Berry Point. A hundred years later they took them out to dry and set them up on a rock wash under a cliff. Now that wood is ready."

"Ready for what?" said Shaawano.

"For making a drum."

She stood there looking steadily at him for some time, and Shaawano knew she saw everything about him. She was wrapped in calm, reading the truth of his mean and shabby life. She nodded slowly as she discovered the sad things, the vicious, the cruelhearted and even bizarre little crimes. A look of disbelieving sorrow passed over her face, but just when my grandfather thought that she would turn away from him, she stepped closer.

"We are waiting to sing with you," she said in that gentle voice he had loved. He bent his head in grateful shame, and when he looked up she was gone.

Afterward, my grandfather lay on the rough boards of his floor, for how long he did not know. Tears leaked out of the corners of his eyes and ran down the sides of his face and puddled in his ears. His girl had visited from the other side of life, but though he wanted desperately to join her, he knew that her visit was meant expressly to give him a reason not to die yet. She had given him a task that was meant to keep him here upon the earth.

He didn't start right away. He had to let the whole of what had happened sink into his mind. He remembered what he'd heard of great cedars set aside until generations should pass. This wood was being cured in a special place, where it would grow in strength and resonance. From each generation certain men and women had been chosen to look after the wood, to visit and talk to it, to catch it up on local history and smoke the pipe with it. Those who were chosen had always been the kindest and steadiest among the people, the ones everybody trusted. They were not sodden drunks, or mean, or anguished and sick to death, like my grandfather thought he was. They had not let their children die or be eaten by wolves or any other animal. They had not slept for weeks out in the woods because nobody wanted them in their house, as had happened to Shaawano. They had never lain in fear of what their brains would tell them to do next. They had never had no one to talk to but quarrelsome spirits. So Shaawano could not help but feel it impossible that he, out of everybody else in his generation, should be the one to use the wood that his people had cared for with such devotion, through time. He could not believe that he should be the one to make the drum.

He had to talk to someone. But all the people who had cared for the wood were dead. The people who had come to sit with his grandmother and grandfather were long gone into the world of spirits with his daughter. As for the ones closer to his age, he didn't trust them. He had wandered too much and he knew things about them. He couldn't think of a single person, though he ground his teeth and gulped swamp tea until his brain steamed. Then one day as he dragged himself to his woodpile, he thought of a woman who was not all that old, and who used to drag her leg. This woman had never married anyone, not because of her frozen leg, but for other reasons. It seemed she preferred not to talk to people, though she wasn't unkind. There was something else about her, but my grandfather could not remember what it was. Then, oh yes, he recalled how she hid her face or turned away in agitation when she was spoken to and he knew what it was—she was very shy.

Too shy to ever marry anyone! That was it. Her name was Kak-ageeshikok. She was named for a very old woman who gave her name away when she grew too old to use it anymore. Kak-ageeshikok was named for the eternal sky, though she was just called Geeshik, sky. Like her name, she was always in the background of things and seemed a woman of endless patience. She lived alone. People didn't bother her because she never bothered anyone and she was poor—there was nothing to steal. Yet though she didn't talk to people, my grandfather remembered, she would always be seen just outside the circle when the old people talked. She was always in the lodge listening in silence to the teachings and absorbing all that happened. She was so forgettable, and yet she was always there. Geeshik never put herself forward. Shaawano now smiled at certain memories of her. Whenever an important person wanted to park his ass in her spot, Geeshik always gave way and moved. If there wasn't enough food to go around, it was Geeshik whose bowl, of course, went empty. Children loved her— they played all over her, Shaawano remembered, until they reached a certain age. Then they forgot about her. She wasn't even of enough substance for the bad ones to torment. Geeshik: the thought of her somehow gave him hope. Did she live yet? Was she even around?

Nobody knew at first, though she had never lived far off in a tangle of bush, but right out in the open on the east side of town, just off the main road. But her house was as forgettable as she was and blended into its surroundings in a quiet way. It was just a little whitewashed cabin with a yard of matted grass. Her door was a plain wooden plank with an antler for a handle. Nobody had seen her go in or out of that door, and nobody ever saw her walk any-where either, yet she was present at all events of any note, sitting in the background against the wall, overlooked. She existed in such an invisible way that maybe, thought my grandfather, she did not really exist at all. Maybe she had died in her house. He would have to find out. He would have to go there. But in a way he dreaded this as much as he had ever dreaded anything. He could not get a certain idea out of his mind—the notion that he'd find her in her house, dried out, motionless, curled up like a dead gray spider. Only she would be alive. Her eyes black and liquid as tadpoles. She'd come toward him rattling like an old seedpod. She'd call him. She'd speak his name.

So as he rapped on her door and rattled the antler handle, he called her name out first. Geeshik! He waited. Stunted trees grew here and there around her cabin. Wind ticked in the leaves. He knocked again. Once more, he leaned toward the wood and called her name. Geeshik! He caught a whiff, as he did so, of mildew and cinnamon. Then a soft voice, a whispering voice, said out loud, "I am coming."

And of course she was not frightful at all.

As she opened the door to let him in, for she knew him immediately, she knew his voice, my grandfather saw that she had grown into a fine-skinned, fragile, oddly young-looking woman. She was shadowy and small. Her eyes were not dark or wild, but open and blinking. He thought at once of a soft little owl. She fluttered a hand at his feet, and he slipped off his shoes. Her dirt floor was covered with skins and clean blankets. She had a real glass window. In her own house, she was bolder and more noticeable than she was in the world outside. She nodded in a surprisingly confident way and padded across the room. Her body had settled now so that the limp of her youth was only a rocking motion of her hips and back. She indicated a stump chair for him. She poured tea from a brown pottery brewing pot into a pretty white cup and set it before him. He put his hand on the cup. She sat across from him with her own cup. Then she waited. She didn't say anything. My grandfather stared at the cup so hard he memorized it. There were flowers painted on it, pink and lavender. It was a white lady's cup she'd probably got from the mission, not old or new, not big or small. It was the kind of cup a woman would keep special on a shelf and maybe never use, so he was touched she had given it to him. And the tea in it, he found when he sipped, was flavored with that cinnamon he'd smelled in the doorway. It had a very good taste and Shaawano remembered that tea wasn't always bitter and hard to swallow the way he made his. He knew now that he would have to speak first. But he understood there was no hurry. She didn't mind. From the way she treated him, my grandfather realized that he was not the only person to suddenly remember the existence of the little woman and seek her out. He understood that while he had grown up and lost his children and wife and started grieving, while he had become volatile and oblivious, she had continued to slowly and steadily remain herself. Things had changed on the reservation, but she had held her place. She was exactly who she always was. Her gift was to be unremarkable. She was a person who would always be there to answer her own door. There would always be tea in a flowered white cup. And there would be her silence, which was somehow so kind and restful that Shaawano had drunk two cups of tea, slowly and with pleasure, before he felt compelled to speak.

During that first visit, he told her everything. He went through it all from the day he first realized that his wife was pregnant with another man's child, to the waste of anger that followed when he'd driven off his son, to the dreams or visions he had experienced so recently and his questions and his hesitations, his belief that he was not worthy to make the drum. When he'd finished with all of it, the sky had gone dim through that one real window. Again, there was that comforting silence and in it he realized that Geeshik had not spoken. So at last he asked her the question he meant to ask.

"Why me?"

Geeshik sat there so quietly that he began to wonder if she'd even been listening at all. Then she rustled a little in her chair. Her voice came out a whisper, but her words were clear.

"Do just as she tells you."

"But I don't know how to do these things."

"Just do as she tells you. That's all you can do."

My grandfather looked at her with an appalled desperation. She blinked back at him, sipped her cup of tea. It was too overwhelming—the sacred old wood, the dream instructions. His father had made drums but that was a world ago. And not only that, but they were hand drums. My grandfather remembered his father splitting the ash and bending it after it had soaked, creating the circle, the hoop. He himself had helped stretch the rawhide on and shaped it, but those drums were different. One-person drums only, not the drum his daughter meant. No, the drum that was to be made of that special wood was a drum that would attract the spirits in a powerful communion that my grandfather could not, and didn't want to, think about.

"I must let this pass," he said to Geeshik, shaking his head. "I'm not the man for it."

Geeshik smiled a nodding smile. A very little smile. The sun came slanting through the window and warmed the smooth old table. Far away, someone chopped wood. The ax made a rhythmic, high, knocking sound. My grandfather closed his eyes and could see the movements of the chopper, steady and practiced and resigned. Over and over, the wood split, dropping to either side of the stump. The chopper neatly lifted each half on the ax blade and split a stove length with one downward stroke.

"That's how you'll do it," Geeshik said. "One stroke." It was as though she could see what my grandfather saw in his mind's eye. He went back over the timing of her words. It seemed that she was referring to the effortless fall of the ax and thoughtless grace of a good wood splitter. Maybe she was saying he had the same skill—in him, not evident, but ready to come out. Grandfather Shaawano made a groaning sound of bleak frustration. He lifted his hands and hung them in the air and put them down, an empty gesture. He didn't even know how to start.

"Just do everything she tells you," Geeshik said.

My grandfather thought of placing tobacco where his own father used to put his tobacco. At the side of the clearing around his cabin there was a birch tree stump. Over the years it had always worn a heap of tobacco. When my grandfather was little, his father used to hold tobacco every morning in his small hand with him and pray for a good life. When he grew older, Shaawano swiped some of the tobacco off the stump every now and then to roll his own cigarettes. But he had still had a good life, he thought now, up until he began to wreck it for himself.

"I'm not the man for it," Shaawano said, then he laughed a little, feeling foolish.

"Come back sometime," she said, standing up. A pretty clear signal that she wanted him to go.

My grandfather walked home and didn't feel any better about things. He went to sleep and when he woke he stretched and felt no better and got up anyway and set about his day. First he fixed up a little iron woodstove that he'd traded with a farmer for two bed-steads. The nickel plating was chipped and ruined, but the stove still gave him a feeling of cheer on a cool morning. His water was boiling. He poured half the water into another pot for mush and dropped two handfuls of meal in and put it back on to boil. He'd thrown the leathery swamp-tea leaves into the first, dented tin pot when he remembered about the tobacco. With an ironwood stick, he stirred the mush, then wiped his hands on the pockets of his pants and took a bag of crumbled tobacco off the shelf by his door. He brought it out into the yard. There was nothing special about the day. A little cloudy. Light breeze. Grandfather Shaawano found the birch stump, which hadn't rotted away like he imagined. He opened the bag and took some tobacco out and said to the twitch-ing leaves of a popple tree or to anyone or nobody or to the Creator, "Thank you for my existence."

He put the tobacco on the stump and waited for something to happen. A woodpecker tapped away, testingly, then paused, per-haps flew to another tree and began tapping, this time harder. The breeze was causing light waves to slap on shore. My grandfather forgot he was waiting for anything but his first taste of tea. He walked back into the house.

So it went like this, every day. The days began with putting out tobacco, then a breakfast of tea and mush. The day continued on and he cut poles or went to the sloughs for willow, and on yet some more as he worked on his chairs, and the tables, which he could now make because he'd bought a good hand plane. Late summer turned to fall and winter came and went and every day my grandfa-ther put out tobacco. He picked up the tobacco and went outside half in a dream, but once he put his tobacco down and said his words he always noticed something—mouse tracks in the snow, impossibly delicate, the deep scent of wood smoke, clouds booming over the leafless trees. These sharp moments of seeing did not fill him with the wild joy that had been so frightening when he first quit wandering. He wasn't swallowed up with fear or sadness, either, nor did he dream of the dead. If he was visited by spirits, they kept to themselves. For many hours, most of the day, he became lost in his work and forgot everything but what was before him—the feel of the tool in his hands, balance, the tension of fitting together his pieces, which he made with pegs and no nails, the critical shaving and adjusting that made his work stand level. He sold everything he made to a trader who came with a wagon to take it away, but he spent so much time on each that he never accumulated money. Sometimes he could afford oatmeal—zashi manoomin, slippery rice. He thought of tapping the stand of maple around him soon, in spring, so he could have pools of syrup in his gray bowlfuls of oatmeal. Then he found himself whittling the taps and spouts and making baskets or makakoog of birch bark with ash trim, to catch the sap. He surprised himself all the time. Where before he had talked endlessly of what he was going to do and never did it, now he only thought about things he was going to do and then found his actions carrying out his thoughts before he'd even given them words. One day in late spring, before the blackflies hatched and when the nights were still cold enough to kill off the mosquitoes, it occurred to my grandfather that he would go and see for himself whether that wood his daughter told him about in the dream was even in the place she described.

He found himself making his own lunch, first thing next morning.

These days, he bought a new substance called peanut butter and ate it instead of grease on his bannock. There was nothing in the world that tasted so good. He spread peanut butter on a slab of cold bannock, slapped another piece on top, and tucked it into his pocket. Then he began to walk, although he knew he could not get to the place he wanted to by walking. He would have to find someone with a boat to take him there, as it was far across the lake, where the people had lived in the old days, starting before the agents and missionaries, even fur traders, even rum, when life was no doubt hard and full of cruel tricks but at least the clans and families were together.

My grandfather went straight through the bush for a good while. It didn't bother him. He had a hundred ways of getting places from his house. Ever since he was a boy, he had liked walking in the bush. No one could get him lost. Even when he was drunk, he had never once started off in the wrong direction or found himself somewhere and didn't know how he got there. Most people are completely oblivious when blacked out, but my grandfather seemed to retain his sense of place even when the rest of him was howling crazy. So he knew just exactly at which cabin he would come out of the woods, and was there at the hour of the day when the fishermen who lived around there went out to set their nets.

Albert Ruse, Akiwenzi, Morton, Ningabianong—none would give him a ride in their jiimaanan or had an extra boat or canoe or old washtub for him to use. They knew what he was like, or thought they did, and assumed they would never see whatever scow they lent him in the same shape or maybe in this life. But then, just as they were all pulling away, Albert turned and yelled that he, Shaawano, was free to take and put back together an old wiigwaasi-jiimaan, his canoe made of birch bark, and to keep it if it hadn't already disintegrated out in the bush behind his house.

All right, all right, thought my grandfather, if that's the way you're going to play it, I'm your man. Up surged his old belligerence and off he tramped to Albert's house, where he located the broken hulk, hoisted it on his back, and without a word to Albert's old lady or the gaping children trudged back off into the bush, where he didn't let the damn thing down off his shoulders until he got home and eased it off into the patch of bright sun before his door.

"It's not in that rough shape," he muttered, running his hands over the perfectly bent cedar ribs that had somehow retained their old shape. Of course the jack-pine root lacing had popped in many places and the bark was split here and there. Quite a bit of work. My grandfather took an old makak and a hatchet, went off into the woods, and collected enough pitch to do a preliminary mending. From his ash pile he plucked chunks of charcoal, ground it to a powder, mixed the powder and the pitch. By the time it was too dark to see anymore, he had patched the burst seams and used sticks and baling twine to hold the sides in place. Tomorrow, he thought, stirring up a fresh batch of bannock for himself, I'll dig more jack pine, cut some bark to patch with. That night, as a tonic for his blood, he drank cedar tea, just as his old grandmother had. He felt the benefit, after he banked the fire and laid under the quilt, of his blood washing in and out cleanly around his heart. And then, just before falling asleep, he chuckled out loud as he thought of Albert, who always liked a good joke, even on himself. My grandfather saw himself paddling with deep, even strokes past the men as they played out their nets. He would nod as Albert widened his eyes, and indicate with a hand movement that Albert could kiss his ass. Or maybe not. Maybe he'd just enjoy the man's surprise and appreciation as he paddled by in the old wreck of the canoe, now beautiful and whole.

That canoe made my grandfather a little too famous, even before he'd gotten out to the far side of the lake. Albert heard about the first time he tried it out, and he came to see him, carrying his pipe. Grandfather Shaawano was daubing the seams yet again with pitch when Albert called out from the woods and then walked into the clearing. He had his son with him, a boy about fifteen years old, and when they saw the canoe they both grew excited with admiration for my grandfather's perfecting touch. The bent ash gunwales were laced again with wet jack-pine root and lashed with strips of rawhide that had shrunk as they dried, so everything was strict and tight. My grandfather had restained the two deep vermilion circles into the prow. And then the patching and the cleaning. All of this in just a week. Albert exclaimed so loudly and was so happy that Shaawano grew nervous, imagining he would demand the canoe back now. But he did no such thing. Albert had never been a drunk. He provided well for his family and was faithful to his wife. He was a very good fisherman but not clever with his hands like my grandfather. He wanted to hear all about Old Shaawano's work, every detail, to know where he had fetched the pitch and from what kind of tree and how he mixed it. My grandfather Shaawano found himself talking as he hadn't talked in a long time, about the pieces of knowledge he'd picked up from his father and his uncles, and about how one thing had made sense after the next in fixing the canoe. They talked at length and finally, at last, Albert took out his pipe. He put it together and loaded it, then lighted and smoked it and handed it to his son, who smoked and handed it on to Shaawano, who did also. He handed the pipe back to Albert, who smoked it again before he asked, "What about the drum?"

It was then that my grandfather made the connection. Albert was a cousin to Kakageeshikok.

"Geeshik told you."

"Who told me?"

That wasn't it at all. The night after he'd jokingly pointed my grandfather toward the old canoe, a young girl had come to visit Albert in a dream. She came to thank him. She said she would do good things for him. Each time she spoke, a drum sounded. The drum grew louder until he woke. It had taken Albert some time to puzzle out the meaning of the dream. That had not come clear until he finally thought of the old canoe he'd given my grandfather earlier that day. Then he was sure that my grandfather, the drum, the canoe, and the girl must have some connection. Albert went still and let the smoke dwindle from the pipe, waiting for my grandfather to fill him in.

Shaawano cleared his throat. He was choked up. His daughter was so polite! Even in the spirit world she remembered her manners with elders, and had thanked Albert for his help.

"N'dawnis," he said, nodding proudly and shaking his head. Then for the second time he told everything—the story Albert doubtless knew, about Anaquot, and the dull, long years of fury and wandering that followed, and at last, how his daughter had come to him in a dream and what she had asked of him.

"So I need the canoe to get to those old trees," he concluded. "I was out that day looking for a way to get there."

Albert started to chuckle at some private joke. He poked his son in the ribs and said, "You know, don't you?"

"What?" His son rubbed his side. "Know what, n'deydey?"

"About the old man," Albert laughed harder. "My grandfather."

"What?" said old Shaawano.

"Friend," said Albert, "you'll like to hear this. The old man, my grandfather, the one who made that canoe in his age and cared for it until he died, he was the keeper of that wood. He smoked his pipe with it." Albert lifted his pipe, which was long with a smooth okij, golden red. "This very pipe. This is the one he smoked with those everlasting trees."

By the end of the evening it was settled. Albert and my grandfather and the boy—whom Albert had sent to the mission school, but who kept running home, so that Albert was educating him in the old ways as best he could—would go out together and visit the old cedar trees. Albert would tell Geeshik what was happening. She would nod, my grandfather imagined, blink her grave, wide, owlish eyes, and smile her hidden smile. She knew everything, she knew it anyway, said Albert, she had learned all there was to know by sitting quietly and humbly in the corner.

"She knew you were going to find your way toward this," he told my grandfather. "This was the fourth generation, this is the time, and it was said that our drum would be brought to us by a little girl."

"It is an honor," said my grandfather, after a while. "Still, I would rather that my little girl was grown up and standing before me now in the fullness of her own life."

Albert put his hand on my grandfather Shaawano's shoulder and they stood together.

"Even this does not bring her back to you, I know. Still, it is something."

"Yes, it is something," said my grandfather.

The day that my grandfather, Albert, and his boy, whose nickname was Chickie, went out to visit the trees, new leaves were just unfurling. A light breeze gave no hindrance. There was warm sun, a clear sky. Best of all, no zagimeg and no biting flies. The three paddled all morning, ate their lunch of grease and bannock and tea on a flat gray rock, and continued on into the afternoon, until they reached the place where they thought the trees were. Albert had gone there with his grandfather when he was young, but his memory was a little off. My own grandfather's ideas had been formed by the dream, but they, too, were faulty. The three tramped around in the bush until it grew too dark to see, then they made a fire for the night, boiled more tea and roasted a duck that Albert had plugged on the way there. After they had eaten, they talked of small matters and then rolled up in their blankets.

As they were falling asleep, my grandfather heard a far-off pack of wolves raise their howl. For a long time the wolves spoke of all they'd seen and felt and eaten that day. Shaawano stayed awake listening. He had never blamed the wolves for what they had done. He had never gone to war with them. The wolves had only acted according to their natures, after all. Only humans can choose to change what they are, and change is treacherous. Even now, the first drink that Shaawano had taken still haunted him, as did the other first drink in his life—the first drink he had refused. In the howls of the wolves, full and gurgling, he saw that full glass, the one he had mystically pushed away, and even in the holy dark somewhere near the great old trees, he dreamed that instead of pushing the drink away he reached for it and put it to his lips, and as its fire entered him, he sighed and began to weep.

Those great trees had been struck down by lightning, it was said. They never had been touched by a whiteman's ax. In the morning the three walked out into the bush and after only minutes of walking a strange thing occurred. They burst into a clearing, or what seemed like one. As their eyes adjusted from the cool shade of the woods to a dazzling plain of light, they saw from the nakedness of ground that they had come upon an area of devastation. Trees had been snapped off like matchsticks and pulverized to splinters. Only a few of the toughest plants grew among the fragments of the trees. It was as if a giant had smashed its foot down and ground everything beneath his heel.

"What did this?" said the boy in awe.

"A whirlwind," Albert told him.

"Do you think it smashed the drum trees?" asked my grandfather.

"It might be good to smoke the pipe here," Albert said.

So they sat down in the glare of mild sun and Albert took out his grandfather's pipe. My grandfather had never kept a pipe. He wasn't the type to have been given one and he was glad now that by mistake he had never acquired one. If something had happened to a pipe of his during those bad years, he'd have that on his conscience along with everything else. It was good to smoke the pipe that Albert kept. All three soon felt their uneasiness lessen and a sense of admiring wonder take its place. Here was evidence of a casual, intentless power. It made and it destroyed. Grew trees and crushed them. Brought people to life and stood back as they made what they could of their time on earth. As my grandfather held the pipe in his hands, praying, his attention was drawn by a still patch of light behind and beyond Albert and Chickie. He looked at the patch of light for some time, as he spoke, before he made out its shape. A wolf was watching from the leaves, huge and gray. Its yellow eyes burned with an ancient calm but its tongue stuck out sideways between its teeth, as a dog's sometimes will, so that along with inscrutable menace it also looked just plain goofy. My grandfather laughed. The others turned to see what he had laughed at but the wolf was gone, only a few disturbed leaves quivered. Through these leaves my grandfather Shaawano saw where they must go.

"The trees are around the bottom of that cliff," said my grandfather, pointing as people pointed, silently kissing at an upwash of rock beyond the wolf and the crushed circle of trees. "We have to walk around the base until we stumble over them."

"Giin igo," said Albert, blowing the ash from his pipe. "I don't mind what we do."

"I'm ready," said the boy.

The three walked halfway around the base of the cliff and saw nothing. Discouraged, Grandfather Shaawano rubbed his hands across his face. When he opened his eyes and squinted straight up before him, he saw that just past a tangle of willow, higher than he'd imagined, the logs were lying on a rock shelf, a stone bed where nothing would take root. The three climbed a tumble of washed-down, split boulders and edged out along a broken path that widened to the shelf. There were the cedars, four of them lying together in a row. My grandfather sat down next to one of the great logs and leaned against the curve of the wood. He could see far across the bay into the opening of the channel and through that to an island so far, blue, and cloudy that it seemed almost a mirage. Yet it was very real and Shaawano remembered it well. He and Anaquot had run away to that island from their camp, and there they had made their daughter in the first sweetness of their love. They had wanted to be alone together, just the two of them, feeding each other berries and touching whenever they wanted, in the open, underneath a limitless sky.

Perhaps the great trees had seen their fumbling, human, all too brief happiness and taken pity. Perhaps the trees knew all along. Perhaps the trees had decided to do what they could for the childish lovers, and for their daughter. The body of a drum is a container for the spirit, just as if it were flesh and bone. And although love between a man and woman can change and fail, overreach itself, fall prey to suspicions, yet the drum lives on. The drum waits with the patience of unliving things and yet it heals with life itself.

5

The Ornamental Man

I was years away from my existence when my grandfather began the making of the drum sitting here before us in this room. As for the wife who had left him, and Ziigwan'aage, who had befriended her, they had long collaborated in the leisurely destruction of Simon Jack. During the making of the drum, my father was free to go wherever he willed. He sat with my grandfather, when he could sit still, and tried as best he could to be a son to the man who had left him in a cold house. But some things are only undone by the cruelest means. The ishkode wabo already had its hooks in my father's gut. Every so often, he left my grandfather and got drunk. Still, he saw the making of the drum, or much of it. When there was something that he could do, he helped. At the same time, on his drunks, he learned all there was to know, and then some, about the goings-on of people near and far, even those across the lake. He learned about his mother, Anaquot, and the wife of the man she'd gone to, and about his half sister, the one they called Fleur, whom he'd hated for her innocent part in the killing of his older sister. All these things he told me at one time or another, or I heard them from other people closely involved, like old Albert. For the making of this drum, as you can imagine, given the caretaking of the wood and the advent of dreams and the tragic incidents and surprising redemptions surrounding its origins, made Anishinaabeg from miles all around both hopeful and curious. They came to visit my grandfather. Soon he had more help than he could manage, and more advice than he could trust.

My grandfather packed his tools into his canoe and outfitted himself to camp alongside those trees for as long as it would take. After he got to the place and set up his camp, he examined each tree for rot, chose one, and cut away branches from the smoothest and most symmetrical part of the trunk. He carefully marked the trunk all around and used ax, saw, and wedge to remove a section that would make the body of the drum. Once he had that section, he rolled it to his camp, where he would hollow it out. He already had a pile of smooth rocks heating in a blaze and he kept that fire going, feeding it hotter and hotter until the rocks glowed red when he rolled them from the fire with a piece of ironwood. He used a pair of antlers to place each rock exactly where he wanted it—on the heart of the wood. The stone burned itself in, leaving a shallow, charred hole. Once the stone cooled he replaced it with another, and so it went, a tedious, exacting process. The time it took seemed endless, but my grandfather needed that time now, because the drum could not be made with a wholly conscious plan. Parts of its making had to be dreamed.

When my grandfather fell asleep at night he looked forward to the possibility that something of the drum's construction and character might be revealed. Wrapped snug in a woolen blanket, face covered with a light cloth, he drifted off in a state of comfort. He'd never rested so well. Spirits came to him, but not to torment; they were curious as their people, the Anishinaabeg, and wanted to know what Old Shaawano was doing and how the drum was progressing. Half-conscious, my grandfather heard murmuring and low arguments, tinkling bells and footsteps. Where before these sounds had frightened him, now he was lulled. He felt secure as a child snuggled up in the corner of the cabin while the grown-ups talk low and laugh around the stove.

When my grandfather had finished with the main body of the drum, he lashed it into his canoe and started paddling for home. His vision of how he would dress the drum was still incomplete— the colors, symbols, and type of ornament the drum required still evaded his dreams. He couldn't get a picture in his mind. But on the way back, something happened that he was to describe many times after in his life. He reached the smooth waters of the bay across which stood his cabin, just as the sun threw red light off, going down. A great cloud had come up behind him and lowered a blue shadow across the water. Just where that cloud stopped and the clear red sky began, there was a line of brilliant space. A yellow line glowed across the earth and the lake with a startling radiance. As my grandfather paddled into that dazzling moment then, he heard a little girl's voice calling from shore. From the south there was a clap of thunder. From the west a stiff breeze blew. My grandfather put his hand up to test the wind and the sun struck his hand a bright, startling red. He thought of the wolves and of the one that had watched him. He saw pictures. There they were. Little girl. Hand. Wolf. The bowl of reflecting water cut in half by the yellow strip of light would be the design on the head of the drum. All was still in the four directions. He saw the whole thing in his mind.

Chickie came up with the moose when he was out picking berries. It so happened that he was sitting on a flat rock and eating a sandwich. There were two buckets of berries at his feet, and his little sister was teasing crayfish near the water's edge, trying to get them to grasp onto a weed so she could yank them out. She was very quiet. Chickie was too. There was only the drone of big horseflies to bother him—an unusual number of big flies—and he remembered his great-aunt telling his uncle to go and fetch a gun because of the flies, for with big flies a moose must be about. Chickie had brought a gun to the berry-picking flats in case of bears. He put his sandwich in his pocket and picked up his gun. Just then, two moose broke cover. Deranged by the flies, they made a mad, shambling dash for water. Usually, moose are shy, almost paranoid. But not when chased by flies. Which is how Chickie got his animal. He got his bead on the hulking bull. After Chickie and Albert dressed the meat and dragged it home, they soaked and soured the hide to loosen the hair, scraped the hide clean, then brain-tanned it. From that hide my grandfather cut two circles for the drumheads, top and bottom. He would have lashed the skins tightly on right away, except that the night before he meant to do it his little daughter visited. She stood before him in a bell-shaped dress and said, "I'll tune the drum. Put me inside, Deydey. There, I'll be content."

My grandfather was mystified by this, and yet her visit was so precious to him that he didn't mention it to anyone else. He was stingy with these visions. He liked to save them to think about. Still, the meaning did elude him. Put me inside the drum. What did she mean by that? A small bell was often hung within a drum to sweeten its sound. Other things were put inside, too. Grandfather Shaawano had known the bones of seagulls to be used, suspended across the center of the interior. His little girl had loved ribbons. He decided that he would trim the drum's skirt with ribbons.

But that was not all of it because it seemed that she had wanted to be the drum itself. He decided at last that he would go talk to her, as best he could. He would go to the place he'd hidden her bones. So that next morning he made his fire in the little stove that vented straight up through the roof and he boiled water in the dinged-up kettle he had thrown many times against the wall in old rages, but always hammered back into shape when he came to earth. He poured water over a few leaves and balsam needles in another pot and let it steep, poured the tea into a cup. He brought the cup outside, where he could drink it looking into the woods. He was, perhaps, fortifying his spirit.

The path that the wagon had taken through the woods and then down to the lake was grown over. There was a copse of birch trees located maybe twenty feet into the woods. When several birch trees grow from one stump they form a central hollow that collects leaves and pine needles. In this place, so beautiful and calm, my grandfather had long ago placed his daughter's bones. He'd chiseled into the wood and then capped the hollow with a round flat stone so that the bones would not be disturbed. He had hoped that the birch trees might grow together and surround his daughter, might encompass her. But the hollow had stayed a hollow and the four trees still grew from the central core, though they held the stone in tightly. He put tobacco on the stone and then he sat down in the sticks, duff, and leaves. An old song came to him. He shut his eyes and sang it. Then he sang a lullaby, the one Anaquot had always sung. As my grandfather sang the lullaby, he felt his throat closing with tears, but they melted down inside him instead of flowing out and after a while he felt better. He had brought some pretty cloth and a stick of hard candy. He put those on the rock.

Grandfather Shaawano had also brought along a sandwich and a jug of water. He spilled a little water on the stone and tore off a bit of his sandwich and put it there too. He thought about the drum and about all that had happened. It seemed to him that since his daughter's first dream visit he had been driven from one question to the next question. He'd worked hard on putting the drum together, piece by piece. He'd enjoyed the exhaustion and he had needed the concentration. The life force, the restlessness, the need to move and think and accomplish things that had grown in him since he stopped wandering, were all directed into the making of the drum. It felt good now to sit in the woods doing nothing. Letting his thoughts range free. Enjoying each bite of the bannock with the salted and peppered venison grease spread inside. There were puckoons growing in the woods, mushrooms, berries. He thought he might spend the day hunting and picking them. But he heard, behind his head, which was pillowed against the birch, a small rustling and whispering. He heard the bones click. Then he turned and saw that two long, graceful, curved bones had crawled from the nest.

Well, maybe an animal had pushed them out, he thought, but he was sure he hadn't seen them before. He picked the bones up, cradled them in his hands. Then he knew what his daughter meant and why she'd visited. He knew what to do.

So that is why the drum that now sits in this room was made with the little girl's bones. They are strung inside on a piece of sinew anchored to the east and west, for the drum has its directions and should always be aligned as the judge has done. That little girl's bones gave the drum its voice. Everything else about the drum, all you see, was long considered, and the meanings debated by all of those who would learn its songs and take care of it. But the bones were my grandfather's secret. He didn't even speak of them to his son. It was me he told, long after the last time the drum was used.

I was born many years after the drum began its life, but my grandfather and eventually my father talked about it so much that it seems part of my first memories. When my mother was with my father, she made sure that whenever the drum came out for a ceremony, he was there too. My grandfather had my father sit at the drum just behind the other men, tapping a stick on his knee, learning the songs. My grandfather started taking him along with him even when it became clear that he was lost to the bottle. Even if my father was sleeping off a drunk, my grandfather kept him near the drum, hoping that the songs would do their work. I think it might have been, no I'm sure it was, those early years with the drum that protected him later on once my grandfather died and even, perhaps, protected me. Maybe those songs helped me to survive my father's drinking rage. For in the rare times he was sober he sang those songs and made me learn them too. And later, I never did search out oblivion in order to forget my father's harm. Something steadied me. Something gave me rightness in my mind. Something gave me an inside calm.

This drum was powerful. People searched it out. This drum was so kind that it cured people of every variety of ill. Because our family kept this drum, people came to us. All of the people who lived close to the drum and dreamed up its songs or helped the drum somehow—repaired it or gave it gifts or even helped the people who came to see it—we grew strong. That's what the drum is about—it gathers people in and holds them. It looks after them. But like a person, things can go wrong in spite of all the best care. And this drum had its own history and sorrow.

When I was growing up, singing that drum's songs, I heard things discussed. I listened in on the old men's gossip. Some stories went on for months, even years. There was one that the old men always returned to and found endlessly interesting to discuss. Years back, they said, a comical delusion had apparently gripped a man called Simon Jack. It had started with his sly mention of the fact that he was a two-woman man. That was not allowed in the church of course, or by law, but in the old days it had been the privilege of a clever hunter. A man who could attract, keep, and provide for two women was considered powerful, a man to envy and to follow.

Simon Jack had made this boast, but when the old men went to visit the cabin where, Simon Jack implied, the women served his every need, it was found that the opposite was true. Simon Jack was bossed, bullied, and disregarded. He was a slave to those women's ideas. He jumped when they commanded. And yet, when he talked in town, he boasted of their meekness and made out that he was feared and adored. Perhaps he really believed his own words. Those who visited Simon Jack's home reported, for instance, that he'd ordered Ziigwan'aage to make tea. She ignored him. After some time he went over to the stove and poured water into cups from a cold kettle and served it to his guests. Anaquot, where's the bannock, he cried. She slung the round loaf at his head. He picked it up, thanked her condescendingly, as though she had humbly delivered it. And so on it went. He claimed that "his women" were working on a beautiful beaded outfit for him, and although that was true, there was something about the way they beaded that made the other men uncomfortable. After all, everybody knew that Anaquot and Ziigwan'aage had been working on that outfit each winter for years. They hadn't finished it, or maybe they had, and then they had resewn it. What was going on? Were the two of them, perhaps, crazy too?

Then all of a sudden, the men heard that the outfit was completed. Simon Jack was seen in the woods from a long way off, flashing, gleaming, beaded everywhere. He was a riot of flowers and vines. Every inch of his clothing was covered. He wore a beaded vest and beaded breeches trimmed with otter fur. It was the most extraordinary clothing that anyone had ever seen, and he wore it constantly. He didn't take it off to go to sleep or for the dirtiest work. The outfit grew stiff and began to reek, but Simon Jack kept wearing it. He wore it for one whole winter on his trapline. He was still wearing it when he came out of the woods in the spring with a load of furs. By now he had become an object of pity. Although he was avoided because his odor had become spectacular, people left food out for him, on stumps, where the dogs could not reach. He had nowhere to go. Barred from his own cabin, chased from the tent that Ziigwan'aage now shared with a younger man, he took to sleeping in barnyards, wandering the ditches. He showed up anywhere people gathered, hoping he'd be fed.

And to think, said the old men, at one time he was well off. He had all he could want. A wife, children, knowledge, and powerful songs. Now, he has only the clothes he wears.

Which though stinking had held together. In spite of his clawlike, broken nails and the matted balls of hair that hung down beneath the hat, in spite of the filth crusted along the neck of his shirt and the perfectly black, glossy black, engrained dirt that became his skin, his clothing had not fallen to ruin. The fully beaded sashes and epaulets and leggings had lost not a single stitched bead. Nothing had unraveled. The colors held. The cut beads still glittered at the flowers' center. Manidoominensag, little spirit things, that is the word for beads in our language. They are more than just decorations. They have a life of their own. It was now perfectly understood that the women whom Simon Jack had bragged of dominating—the young one he'd gotten pregnant and the first wife, that spring wolverine—had known just what they were doing. They had trapped him. It was he who had donned the suit, after all, clothes that supposedly illustrated for the world his wives' meek devotion. But those were not just flowers, not just vines, not, as I said, little beads. Those little spirits were his arrogance for all to see. Filth and brilliance. They were Simon Jack inside out.

Ahau! said the old men. It happened this way. He walked into the dance circle one afternoon early in the summer, and he sat down next to my grandfather. They should watch out for the rain! He pointed his chin up to the clear sky and the men remembered, as much as his smell, thinking that it certainly was not going to rain. That much they thought they knew. Rain required clouds. But my grandfather took no issue with the pitiful being and only offered Simon Jack his open can of chewing tobacco. Simon Jack took a pinch, made a little wad of the stuff, and stuck it in his lower lip. His teeth were green fangs. His long narrow jaw snapped like a fox's. People were fascinated with his fingernails—long and twisted, gnarled like gray turtle shell. Of course, they also looked at the fancy beadwork designs that flowed all over him. He wore two bandolier bags with white backgrounds fully beaded. He folded his legs crosswise and people noted that the bottoms of his makizinan were beaded. The old men said that those makizinan were only worn by the dead. Simon Jack nodded critically at my grandfather when he rose to go sit near the drum.

"They are singing those songs backwards," he said. "They shouldn't do that."

The other men thought he was wrong, and who was he to criticize? But it turned out Simon Jack knew what he was talking about, for my grandfather was very troubled by what was happening. He knew the songs that had appeared in people's minds when the drum came into being, knew them like he knew how to breathe, but all of a sudden, when Simon Jack came into the circle, there was a shift. Grandfather Shaawano described it afterward as someone talking in his ear so he couldn't think. The men were distracted. The songs got jumbled.

All we crave is a simple order. One day and then the next day and the next after that, if we're lucky, to be the same. Grief is chaos. Death or illness throw the world out of whack. The drum's order is the world's order. To proceed with and keep that order is a gesture of desperate hope. Protect us. Save us. Let our minds remain clear of sorrow so that we can simply praise the world.

When the songs go backward, when they won't stay in place, when the men strike the drum out of time, things should stop. We should ponder the event. Later, my grandfather was to make clear what he should have done when things went haywire. But until that day he had never lost the order and thought that he could recover it by force of mind, so the men kept on playing and singing.

Simon Jack stood and danced in place, then he danced into the circle and rounded the drum. There was nothing wrong with what he did, at first. He was showing respect. Except that soon there were no pauses, no relief. One song now led straight into the next and it was as though they all were caught—drummer, singers, dancer, drum itself—in a dark outpouring of energy. The others in the circle were disturbed. They didn't know what they were hearing, or seeing, but they knew what they were feeling. One man said his breath cracked in him. Their hearts stopped, then raced. A sickness in another man's belly became an ache. Someone's legs itched, but he knew he shouldn't dance. It was enough to see Simon Jack out there, stamping and bobbing with a terrible intentness, close-stepping as if he was flattening the grass with his dead, dead makizinan. It was enough to understand that moving toward the drum at this time would be a mistake. Those in the circle didn't know what they felt or whether they were possessed; but nobody stopped the drummer and nobody stopped the dancer. It was as though they were all suspended, frozen, as though nothing about the scene was moving. Although everything was. And it was moving faster. The beat was. The men. Their high-pitched voices. And even faster and faster until—and my grandfather saw this, for he was staring at Simon Jack—he turned around, a flash of beads and fur and tails, and he began to go the wrong way. He went the spirit world way around the drum. The old men saw it happen. They saw his face go gray and his eyes roll white into his head. They knew, right then, he would not complete his circle and he did not. Halfway around, he fell dead.

After that, my grandfather put the drum away. He kept it off the ground, in its own place, of course. He took it out occasionally to visit other drums. He fed it tobacco and water and he made sure that it heard no bad talk and saw no bad sights. But even when the desperately ill or those pleading for the sick begged him to take out that drum, he never would. And as I said, he told me why, he confided in me. He said that he couldn't be sure of that drum anymore. He told me that the drum itself contained his daughter's bones. He believed that she was subject, as children are, to rages beyond their control, and that she had caused what happened in the circle. She was angry at the man who took away her mother and caused her own life to end. She had no pity on pitiful Simon Jack.

In the end, though Simon Jack had nearly ruined his life, my grandfather was the only one to take pity on him. The men carried Simon Jack from the circle to my grandfather's house and laid him out on a bed of pine boughs in the yard. There, the women who care for the dead made a fire that they would keep burning for three days to light the way for his spirit. They washed Simon Jack for burial. As they worked, the rain sprinkled directly down upon them from a clear sky, just as the dead man said it would.

I heard it whispered when I was young, then it was talked about more openly as people forgot who the Pillagers were or why so many had feared Ziigwan'aage. When they prepared Simon Jack, they found the reason he never took those clothes off. It was simple. He couldn't. The clothes were stitched directly to him. His skin had grown around the threads and beads in some places. The clothes were molded to him in others. The women clipped the clothes carefully from Simon Jack and burned them in a great fire hot enough to consume even the glass beads. They tied his body in birch bark and laid him naked in the ground. He was buried at the entrance to the main path out to the Pillager camp, where those two women would have to step over him whenever they came to town.

Generally, it is, or was, not considered right for a woman to step over anything that belongs to a man. It supposedly gives her power over him. So I don't know what the women had in mind when they put Simon Jack underground there—perhaps it was a warning or a reminder, or perhaps with the dead the old taboo is reversed. I really don't know whether Simon Jack's placement bothered Anaquot or Ziigwan'aage or whether his death made the least difference to them at all. They were to die in the appalling illness that shook our tribe apart. The child alone survived, my father's half sister, Fleur. And of course there was Niibin'aage, lost into the east by then. As for the drum, it was cared for in the best way possible, as I have said, but it was never used again. I think my grandfather had a conflict in his heart over what to do with it. Once, he told me about the secret location of a cave and he asked me to make sure he was buried there, and the drum with him. Another time he said it should be burned. He also told me that he'd written down songs with some old men and that the drum should be restored to use after forty winters.

My grandfather died unexpectedly. He died before any of these options could be made definite. After his death, when the old men came together to discuss who should take over his songs and feed his guardian spirits, and who should care for his little girl drum, things were disposed of as the old men saw fit. They gave the drum to my father. Perhaps they thought its power would heal him up, sober him. Or maybe they knew he would sell the drum, as eventually he did, to the trader Jewett Parker Tatro for rum and beer. Perhaps they knew how it would happen and they thought that the drum needed to go east, to grow up a little more before it returned. Because the forty years my grandfather spoke of are past. All those afflicted, bothered, or healed and made whole by that drum are gone. Only the songs remain.

PART THREE

THE LITTLE GIRL DRUM

1

Shawnee sat her little brother down and pried the crayon from his strong, chubby fist—it was purple, it looked to him like something good to eat, the name of the crayon was even *grape*. The feel of the word on her tongue made her mouth water and she wanted a cup of commodity grape juice so terribly: the feeling came over her with such a strong rush that she tasted the cold sweetness of the drink in her mind. Her brother, Apitchi, made a lip-trembling face and then opened his mouth to bawl but Shawnee had a trick she played on him. She reached toward his mouth quickly and tickled his tongue softly with her finger. Usually, he was so surprised that his howl turned into a laugh, but this time he was very, very hungry, truly felt deprived, and in his heart he really knew that the crayon would have been good to eat. So he let blast with a scream of rage that made Shawnee clap her hands over her ears and brought Alice from the other room, where she was curled up under the blankets.

Alice was six years old, way past the toddling age, her legs skinny and bare. All she wore was one of her mother's old sweatshirts, and it drooped off of her slender body, hanging empty past her fingers and knees. The sweatshirt said *University of Phuk U* in red block letters, and it was sweatshirt color, gray. Alice's thick black hair was cut straight off, right below her ears, and it stuck out on both sides of her head like Darth Vader's helmet in *Star Wars*. For a while, they had owned that movie, and also a small black TV that had a slot to insert a movie cassette in the bottom, and the movie would come on the screen. But then it had to get sold, and the movie went with it. Before it was sold Shawnee and Alice had watched the movie countless times. They knew it all by heart, every word. Alice rubbed the sleep from her face and watched Apitchi bawl, along with Shawnee. They both just watched him because they knew there was nothing that could be done once he started like this.

"I'm hungry," said Alice.

"No, you're not," said Shawnee, "because there's nothing."

Alice nodded and sucked on a finger. She knew that. They had already scraped every particle of oatmeal from the pot that Mama had left on the stove. They had been hungry the day before, and the day before that too. They had wiped the pot with their fingers. Alice's stomach felt so caved-in she thought maybe it was sticking to the back of her body, and the places that it stuck hurt with stabbing pains. While she was wrapped in the blankets, she had peeled some flecks of paint off the walls and chewed on them like candy.

"I'm cold," she said.

"No, you're not," said Shawnee, "because Mom said don't turn up the heat there's just enough to last until she gets home."

Alice knew that too, and so she put the blankets around her and waited to fall asleep. There was a thick old bearskin on the mattress they had dragged out onto the kitchen–living room floor, dusty and stinking a little, but the fur was the warmest place in the house. Shawnee wished that she could curl up on the bearskin with Alice until Mama came back, but Apitchi was everywhere, into everything. He knew how to climb. He would look for food until he discovered something that he thought he could eat. Shawnee was afraid he would find some kind of poison. She supposed now that it really wouldn't have hurt him to eat the crayon.

"Maybe I should have let you," she said gently to his screaming face. "Maybe you would have thought you really ate something."

Then he screamed again and she felt her hand go back with a sudden jerk. Her hand swept forward so fast she couldn't stop it from slapping him on the side of the face. The slap made a sharp crack in the air. Apitchi didn't stop bawling, he only whirled away from Shawnee and ran at the opposite wall, grabbed the one curtain that sagged off a window, pulled until it fell in a brown and white checkered heap. Then he kept running around the room, at one wall then the other, still crying. His shoes fell off. Snot covered his face and then quickly dried to a glaze. Shawnee tossed her long hair back and stood by the kitchen stove, watching him. Her eyes were lovely, dark and slanted in a face shaped like a heart.

Even though she'd already done this, Shawnee decided to look through the whole house methodically to see if there was anything to eat forgotten in some bag or box, some corner. There were two rooms, and the bathroom. She started in the bathroom. They had eaten the toothpaste already. Striped towels were balled up in a corner, and she carefully took them apart and shook them free of wrinkles. The bathroom was icy cold; the wind shot through the window, which did not close right. Sometimes the pipe that made the faucet work froze, and Mama had told her to leave the water on just enough to drip through the night. Shawnee opened the cupboard and dragged out the nearly empty bottles of shampoo, the cracked plastic toys, the broken tubes of hair mousse, her mother's plastic hair cap printed with bright yellow flowers. She put the combs and the brush aside in a heap. Way back in the cupboard there was a bottle with an inch of cherry cough syrup in the bottom. She drank most of it and then ran water in the bottle and shook it. She brought it out to the kitchen and gave it to Apitchi. He went quiet and began to drink the pinkish stuff with a greedy sob. Shawnee went back to the bathroom, dumped the trash out carefully onto the floor. She pawed through it and then jammed it back into the plastic bin.

She began to search all through the room that was part kitchen and part living room. She had looked all through that room before, but the find in the bathroom encouraged her. She opened the cupboard doors one by one. Easy to tell, of course, they were completely empty. But in a time past her remembering, someone had covered the shelves on the bottom with white paper, now yellowed and stained. When it occurred to Shawnee to lift those papers up, she found crumbs underneath or maybe they were crushed bugs but she did not care. She swept them carefully into a plastic bowl and then parceled them out into shallow coffee cups. Alice and Apitchi saw what she was doing and watched her. When the crumbs were evenly divided, each took a cup and then they went over to the blankets and carefully sat down. Quietly, intent, they wet their pointer fingers and then dipped into the crumbs. Put their fingers in their mouths. While they sucked on crumbs, Shawnee kept searching.

The refrigerator had not worked for some time and was used to store dishes and cereal and bread. There were only plates and cups in it now, a box of screws and some jar lids. Shawnee looked through the compartments and drawers anyway because her mother always hid treats so that the children wouldn't eat them all at once, or sometimes because she'd bought herself a special little something. Shawnee was counting on her mother's habit of stashing things away and forgetting where she put them. She opened pots, overturned empty cans, reached her hands into the creepy dark recesses under the sink and behind the stove. She unbent a clothes hanger and plucked at the catch on the rectangular hinged door beneath the oven until it opened. She stood on top of the counter and swept her hand carefully across the tops of the cupboards where she couldn't see. There were no closets to look inside, but there was a rack by the door that held coats and sweaters. Boots, shoes, socks, and slippers were piled all around. She pushed them aside and it was here, rummaging through pockets, that she made a spectacular find. As soon as her hand closed on the bar of candy, she froze. She didn't let the paper crackle. Alice and Apitchi were curled in the pile of blankets. Shawnee drew the bar out slowly until it nestled in her sleeve. If Apitchi had been crying again or Alice chewing on her hair, she might have kept it for herself. But when she turned, she saw that they were watching her with dull hope, so she slowly held it out.

They knew exactly when the oil ran out because it got so cold, so fast. Shawnee dressed Apitchi in everything that she could find for him to wear, and then she made Alice put on her leggings and three pairs of socks and snowsuit and packs. She got herself dressed, too, in every warm piece of clothing that she had. But it was a restless, unrelenting cold and it was late afternoon. If the bill was paid they could have used the stove, it was electric. They could have opened the oven and sat around it as they had done before. Or used the woodstove. They should have kept the woodstove. Shawnee's grandfather had been angry when they took it out. Now it was dumped behind the house and covered with snow. The hole in the wall was still there, sealed over with an aluminum pie plate. Shawnee knew the old stovepipe was propped next to the back door. She went outside and tugged it out of the snow, then dragged it into the house. It wasn't that heavy, it was a hollow of thin sheet metal. She stood on two chairs and ripped the pie plate off the wall. She had Alice steady the pipe as she fitted it into the hole. Twice it fell out of the wall before Shawnee thought to drag another chair underneath the bottom half. The pipe stayed, propped up.

Now the thing was to make a fire right underneath the stovepipe, without burning up the chair. It was an old metal chair but had a plastic seat and backrest. Cement blocks and boards made a shelf in one corner. Shawnee took four blocks and laid them out underneath the stovepipe. She took four more blocks and set them on top of those. The blocks were heavy. By the time she'd got them all set up she was warm in all her clothing, but she was also dizzy. She took a deep breath, went over to the stove, and removed the rack from the middle. There were two cookie sheets underneath the oven and she took those, too. She put the rack on the blocks and the cookie sheets over it, and said, "Now let's get some paper and some wood." Her voice surprised her. It was scratchy and cold as the air.

First she crushed up old papers and movie-star magazines. Then on top of that she put shredded cardboard and tiny sticks. She took a book of matches from where Mama kept them, a bowl on the counter out of Apitchi's reach. She lighted the crumpled paper, and when the flames were long she added more strips of cardboard and thicker twigs that had been lying outdoors on top of the snow. But the snow was too deep to get bigger pieces of wood and the old wood pile had been used up in the summer. Shawnee cracked apart an old stool and dragged over a laundry basket full of wooden blocks that a church group had given them—all different colors. When the fire was hot enough, she fed first the pieces of the stool, then a block, another block, into the flames. She thought Apitchi might cry, for they were his blocks, but though he opened his mouth in distress no cry came out. He clung tight to Alice. Some of the smoke went up the chimney pipe and some collected over them, but they could breathe all right. There were a lot of blocks, there was another chair, a lamp base, birch-bark baskets that her mother had started but hadn't yet finished to sell, other things that could be burned. Shawnee dragged all those things around them and then she got into the blankets with her brother and sister. The fire gave off enough warmth and they all fit underneath the bear robe.

2

"The dead are drinking here tonight," said Ira as she joined the man at the table. They were in a town bar where the hard-drinking people went, a tough place where everyone looked up each time a new person entered from the icy street. The drinkers didn't look away once the door shut and the blast of cold air was absorbed into the bar's steamy atmosphere—they just kept watching emptily the way the dead stare. Ira looked right back at them and narrowed her eyes.

"I don't feel like going home."

"You feel like coming with me," the man, who was not drunk, stated, "but you can't because if you do, you will have to sleep on the other side of my wife."

"Is she good-looking? Or is she ugly like you?" asked Ira, but she smiled to show she meant he was the opposite of ugly.

The people had turned away to resume their conversations, to drink or argue. Thirty or more sat scattered in the booths or at the tables, some in unzipped snowmobile suits or dressed in camouflage hunting parkas. The man sitting beside Ira had given her the only friendly look in the place, so she'd sat down next to him.

"C'mon," said Ira, smiling, "ugly like you?"

The man said with a kind of shy reluctance that his wife was beautiful, but for the scar on her lip. He passed his finger slantwise across his own mouth, and Ira remembered the woman he spoke of. Instead of mentioning her name, people often made a sign for her like that, and everybody knew who they meant.

"I'm almost beautiful, too," said Ira. "I would be except for what's in here."

She tapped her breast over the heart, casually, then she took a drink of the beer that the man had just bought for her.

"Maybe you could clean that up," the man suggested, nodding at that place Ira indicated.

"I'm trying to," said Ira. "Alcohol kills germs."

She took an abrupt swallow of her drink and tapped her face with her fingers. "I'm getting sterilized inside. You won't catch anything from me."

"Even if I did," the man said, "my wife would cure it. She knows a lot of these old-time medicines?"

His voice rose as though he was asking a question of Ira, who nodded just as if she was giving a real answer to his question. She drank her beer, had another, and then one more. Now she was just drunk enough. She didn't want to get any drunker, but she also did not want to get sober, not yet, not by any means. As she'd already said, she wasn't ready to go home. She said it again in a vaguer, softer way than before.

"I'm not ready to go home."

"Don't say that around just anybody," said the man, chiding her in a friendly way. "There's dirty men in here."

"Where, where," said Ira, looking openly at the drinkers now. Their stares seemed comical. "I want a dirty man.

"But not that one," she went on, following the chin-pointing nod of the man who was buying her drinks. "I've had him and he's no good. His wife hired someone, maybe hired your own wife, to put a medicine upon his wiinag so it droops when he thinks of anyone but her." She laughed and made a sad face as she held up her finger and then slowly curled it into her palm.

"I don't want to go home, but I don't want that, either."

"What do you want?" asked the man.

"I want something else," said Ira. "I definitely want something else."

"Maybe you want spiritual help," said the man.

Ira lowered her face and then cast her eyes up at him and shook her head back and forth.

"What are you doing in a bar, anyway?" she said. "What do you mean spiritual help? You don't go talking about spiritual things when you're drinking."

"I do," said the man. "I'm like that. Different because I know how to handle my drinking. Therefore, in a bar, I can talk of these things as though I was a regular person."

"I'll tell you what," said Ira, "you're not a regular person. You're a windigo. You're made of ice inside. You turn your drinks to slush in your belly, then you try and offer me spiritual help and you say your wife is beautiful, she has a scarred lip, she knows medicine. There's something not right about this conversation."

Ira pushed her finger around the lip of her glass, then scooped up some foam. She stuck her finger in her mouth. Looking at him curiously, she continued. "You know what I mean? Something off."

"I wouldn't worry about it," said the man. "You're a good-looking woman. You'll get laid."

"Any time I want," said Ira, tossing her hair back, fluffing it with her hand like an old-time movie star, "I look in the mirror, don't I? You should see me naked, but you never will. I'm so good-looking when I'm naked that it hurts to look at me. I have a painfully good-looking body that makes men beg like dogs. But you'll never see it."

"Another beer." The man signaled.

"Thanks," said Ira. "All the same, you'll never see it. Just think. There you'll be in the rest home. You open your mouth like a toothless old bird and they pour soup down your gullet through a funnel. You'll be thinking to yourself, *If only I'd seen her body, what she looked like under that sweater, that parka, those jeans. Maybe I could resign myself to drinking soup through a funnel.* But no. You'll always wonder."

"I don't need to see you that way, really," said the man. "I can tell. Of course, to raise children right, your looks don't matter."

"You got that right," said Ira, shifting in her chair, frowning at the black plastic ashtray, tipping it critically back and forth. "Kids, they don't care. They think you're beautiful anyway, no matter what. I should go home. That's where my kids are. They're sleeping anyway."

"You hope."

"Well, it's cold. It's very cold. They're not going out of doors."

"It is very bad, this cold."

"This dry cold."

"And it's still going down."

Now for a few moments neither did speak, as they were both caught up in their private worries and thoughts about the cold. The man knew his wife had the car and he hoped she would remember to start it in the middle of the night, otherwise the battery would go dead. In this kind of deep cold you had to run the car every four or six hours, unless you could plug it in someplace. He'd looked ahead. He had a heater for it because he really did work. Sometimes if you covered the hood up with blankets, to keep the wind off, that helped too. His wife also talked to the car, treated it like an animal and told it when it was going to be fed. Sometimes she was joking when she did that, sometimes she was serious. Sometimes she put tobacco down beside its wheels before a long, tough trip. She didn't drink. The scar was put upon her face when she was just a little girl.

"I don't know." Ira was talking again. "I should have a reason. I just don't want to go home. I don't know how I would get there anyhow, through the bush. I got a ride into town, here, before I knew it was going to keep on getting colder and colder like this."

"Maybe you should come home with me," said the man in a transparently false tone of voice, "I was bullshitting you about my wife."

"No, you weren't."

"Well, I am pretty sure that she is at her sister's with the kids and with the cold going deeper like this they will not be coming home. Do you want me to make a phone call?"

"I'm just that drunk I don't have good judgment right now. Do you have an STD?"

"What's that?"

"Oh right, your wife and her medicine. I'm just sure she fixed it," said Ira. "Where do you live anyway?"

It seemed to Ira that she knew where he lived, that she'd heard about him. Something more than that scar was familiar about his wife, too, but she couldn't put the story together.

"I live just outside town here. I work at the electric plant. I got my own house through the housing board." The man sounded dreamy now. "It's a three bedroom and it came to us already half assembled. They drove it up to the lot in two pieces, wrapped in plastic. Then they took the plastic off and set the halves down and fit them together. When we walked inside, the rooms already had their cupboards, toilets, everything. It was a miracle."

The man was solemn, remembering the day that the house arrived. Ira laughed. "Cheap miracle. A prefab. My father built our house by hand."

"All they had to do was hook up the plumbing, the electric, the gas."

"You might be contented," said Ira. "I wouldn't be. I'm looking for something else."

The young man now laughed. "How long have you said that," he asked, "how many times to a guy in a bar? I'm a little different because I can live with my habit, controlled drinking. You're getting drunk though."

"And you're helping me." Ira pointed at him and squinted along her finger. "You are an enabler. That is what I call you."

"Why do we do this, oh why do we do this," said the man, a false pathos in his voice at which the two of them laughed in a slightly overanimated way that made them both know they were attractive to each other, and that they were thinking about what might happen.

"I suppose your wife, with all of her medicines, she has a theory on why."

"Yes she does, it's an elegant theory. She's a social worker and she sees all that people do. Her theory? It's called sheer stupidity."

"You met her in a bar?"

"No, at a ceremony."

Ira slapped the table lightly.

"There you go again referring to spiritual things in a bar. You can either be a drunk or a spiritual person. Not both if you're an Indian. I'm sorry. That's the way it is."

"Who said?"

"Oh, come on," Ira looked around the bar, as though someone might be listening in, "the Shawnee prophet. You ever heard of the Shawnee prophet? That's who said."

The man looked down at his hands, at his beer, which he had drunk too quickly.

"I suppose I am no better than you."

"That's what I'm telling you," said Ira. "If you're here, you've made a choice. That choice is not to be spiritual. That choice is to be like me."

The man now turned and looked at her for a long time. He was in his early thirties and she in her late twenties. Their hair was identical, a dull and wavy black, and his was longer, tied in a ponytail with a band of black elastic. Ira's hair was springy and thick. She pushed it back behind her ears, but her ears were small and flat so the hair kept falling back in wiry tendrils around her face. She was lucky, she knew, to have the face she had. It could be worse. A round face with small, clever, up-slanting features. Someone had called her mouth passionate—not that she had big pouty zhaaginaash lips—her upper lip was straight across. But it curved in an arc as though a man had pushed against it with his teeth. Although she'd had three children, and ate cheap, starchy, greasy food, her body was still young and slender. Maybe her eyes, deep and smoky black, carried a wounded look in them. Maybe she was just confused because of the beers and the uncertainty about returning home. Her wants conflicted. She wanted this man to bring her home, but that was twenty miles, so she needed for him to have a working car and take her there. But first, she needed to buy food. She had already arranged for a delivery of fuel, but that would be tomorrow. At the same time, she wanted to stay here, suspended. Like one of those bugs trapped in plastic for a souvenir, she thought, looking at the light in the warm color of her beer. Halfway drunk forever. Not yet sloppy, but not back there, either, in the sober gray static. She supposed that she was desperate.

"Objectively speaking," she whispered, knowing the man would bend closer to hear, "I shouldn't have left them in this cold. But the only way I could get some money was if I came to town."

"How," said the man, "and where?"

"Here," she said, calmly. "I came here to sell my body to the highest bidder. The truth is my kids need some food, the house needs heating oil. My oldest, she's nine. They're okay for a little while. So listen, niiji, if you don't have the money, if you can't pay, tell me now so I quit wasting my time on you."

He stared at her with his mouth a little open.

"I'm just kidding," said Ira. "Thanks for the beers."

As she wasn't kidding at all, she got up. She stuffed her gloves in her purse. She zipped up her thin black parka and put up the pointed hood. Her face was surrounded by bristles of cheap black fur.

"Wait," said the man, "I can't just let you go like that. We should walk down to the gas station, get some food. I have this much." He took a ten-dollar bill from one pocket, fished a five from the other. "And I do not even have to see your naked gleaming body. We can get some milk and bread at the gas station. Peanut butter. If what you say is true, if your children are out there, then we get my brother to give you a ride to your place. Once there, you put your kids to bed and then deliver yourself to our lust."

Ira looked at him and raised her eyebrows, two clean black arches.

"Just a joke," said the young man.

"What's your name?" said Ira.

"John," he said.

"And your brother?"

"Morris." Then in Ojibwe. "Ma'iingan izhinikaazo. He is named for the wolf."

"Your brother shouldn't have that name," Ira said as she followed him out the door.

She watched him walk ahead of her. His hair hung long down his back and he adjusted a heavy skinning knife at his belt. He wore a heavier parka than she owned, and good leather boots. So maybe his story about the job, the house in two pieces, the wife, maybe all of that was true. She had persevered in the tribe's social service agency all day filling applications for emergency heating oil. Before she left home that morning, she'd cooked up a pot of oatmeal. She thought of her daughter, who was named for the Shawnee prophet like her cousin and great-aunt, so many in her family. Ira thought what a practical girl her Shawnee was, how she'd take the younger two and put them to bed, and then would crawl in next to them for warmth. They'd be sleeping by now, underneath all of the quilts and blankets, curled in the skin of the bear her father had shot. She would be back with the food before they woke, and the delivery truck was on its way. So she followed the man with the ma'iingan brother.

3

Shawnee stared into the fire for a while, then suddenly she was so comfortable that she went directly into a sleeping dream where everything that just happened was a dream and her mother was shaking her and saying, "Wake up, wake up," and when she did wake up she saw that the half-made baskets piled next to the makeshift fireplace were blazing. The fire had already spread over to the trash can just under the window. Shawnee blinked as the curtains burst into light. Then the fire licked here and there like a tongue. Alice woke up and the two girls tried to throw cups of water on the flames, but the water only trickled out of the tap, which was already blocked with ice. Still, the fire gave them time. They took all they could outdoors. The fire ate into the walls and then pulled itself under the roof until it found a way to push an arm of flame into the air. The children stepped back, and back again, then sank again into their blankets and huddled in the bearskin. There were blasts and balls of exploding shimmers and then the blaze attained a steady roar. It was warm in the blankets. *I shouldn't sleep*, Shawnee thought, but she found herself curling around Alice, who held Apitchi tight against her, and then she closed her eyes.

When they woke the flames were low and the sky was still dark. *Somebody must have seen it*, Shawnee thought. *If we stay here they'll find us.* So they edged closer, and closer, as the house cooled, but it was still dark outside when the house no longer gave enough warmth. They were standing in the ashes by then and were covered in black soot. Apitchi whimpered in a low, despairing, birdlike voice. Alice was silent. Her eyes were wide and glittered with black frost. They couldn't get warm. Their nearest neighbor was six miles down the road. Three miles if you cut through the woods. Although it had just snowed, the old snow was crusted hard enough to hold them, Shawnee thought. So she tied Apitchi onto her back with a long, knitted scarf. Then she walked into the woods. Her feet sank through the snow about three inches, then found the hard pack. She broke the trail. Alice followed in her steps.

At first they could see by the starlight reflected on the snow. Then, where the pines grew thick, Shawnee couldn't see at all. The children walked in a liquid black ice, knocking into trees and snapping sharp fir branches. "Alice, hold my parka," said Shawnee, but she felt her sister's grip weakening. "Hold my parka," she screamed, shaking Alice. The grip desperately tightened. Apitchi was a block on her back. She kept shifting him to keep her balance. The snow was softer underneath the pine trees and from time to time they floundered and fell, but always righted themselves at last and went on, weaker, colder. It would happen a little bit at a time this way, Shawnee thought, and finally they would not get up at all. The thought made her pedal her legs with more force and drag Alice with her and so they went on, forward, she thought. She didn't know anymore. She wasn't like some kids who stayed in the house. She went outside a lot. Played all day in the woods and never got lost. But she'd never been out in the dark and in the cold like this. She thought her feet were frozen, maybe. She couldn't feel them. Alice had good boots. She thought that maybe Apitchi was frozen dead, too. But she did not stop. The force of her own wanting to live drove through her. Something passed through her in the dark that was darkness also. She knew that she would keep walking and she'd drag her sister and her brother too. She fell asleep walking once, and then woke, pulled her sister's jacket, dragging her along. They would not get away from her. She wouldn't stop. And she kept on thinking that until the snow gave way beneath them.

4

At the lighted gas stop, Ira bought fifteen dollars worth of groceries—bread, peanut butter, milk, applesauce, macaroni. The man
paid and Ira took the bag. Walking back outside, they hunched
over, stabbed with cold.

"Gisina," he said.

"I gotta get home now," said Ira. "You take me."

"I told you I can't, we get my brother and he takes you in his
truck, remember?"

"I remember it," said Ira as they ducked along the edge of the
road, hunched against the cold. "But I think I would rather go with
you if you could take me. I don't know about your brother as I've
never met him. Your brother is a stranger to me."

"Morris, he's okay." In his voice there was something else, too,
and Ira's mind grabbed onto it.

"What," she said, "what about him?"

But they were at the house. It was very close to the gas station. The man's brother lived in town, in a house Ira had never before noticed, which in itself was odd, the never having noticed a house in a place so small that everything was seen many times. Now the brown-board one-story house stood out. It felt to Ira like the house had suddenly been put there, as in a dream. They walked through unbroken snow up to the door, which was clawed by animals and jimmied around the knob. As they stood before the door waiting for the brother to answer, Ira's throat tightened and she realized that even in the cold she was sweating lightly. The sweat was freezing in a sheen of ice on her brow. She wanted to turn and run away but John held the groceries. So she stood there, and when the door opened with a fierce shake, as it was stuck, she flinched and stepped back. Then she was pulled or propelled into a dark, close, rank den of a place. The two men went into another room and talked and made some deal, apparently, because when John returned, he gave Ira the groceries.

"I have to go, really, because my wife will be needing me."

"Please."

"I am who I said I was. I am not any different than that. I am not a bad person."

"But your brother is."

His eyes shifted away.

"Not always," he said. And then Ira was alone with the brother who bumped around in the half-dark getting dressed to go outside.

"Morris," she called out. "So chi miigwech for giving me the ride back to my kids. They shouldn't be out there alone."

"They shouldn't be out there," he agreed. His voice was gravelly, harsh maybe, but at least he said something to her. And he did seem to be getting ready to go. "I don't mind. We have to start my truck though and she's a bitch in this cold."

"Okay," said Ira, clutching the bag. She was encouraged and felt easier. She didn't look at the brother directly, but stole small glances in the dim light. He was tall and rangy, with a lean, hungry-looking face, powerful shoulders and a bony, jutting nose. She couldn't see his eyes, but when they went out the door she finally caught a glimpse, then wished she hadn't. His eyes were bugged out, big and staring, white all around the black pebble of the iris. He looked like a man scared permanently out of his wits.

"Don't mind it," he said, as he noticed how Ira went very quiet getting into the truck. "I got this sickness where I can't ever shut my eyes."

He frowned, jiggled the key softly, then bent to the wheel in concentration and tried to get the engine to turn over. "C'mon, c'mon," he said, "ninimoshe, c'mon baby." He cranked the engine and each time gave a squirt of gas; he had some method by which he slowly brought the frozen block to life, but it took a while and in that time Ira began to know something. There grew in her a feeling that her children weren't all right, they weren't asleep. Hungry, well, she knew that already. She began to think that she should have taken them along with her to town because at least they could have crashed someplace together, somebody's couch. Now their situation was not good; she could feel it in her gut, a crawling sensation that made her act desperately. Later, she regretted very much that she put her hand out, touching Morris. At the time she even knew it was wrong, because he looked at her as the engine groaned. Even though his face was dark in shadow, the whites of his eyes gleamed out, and there was something awful in his look.

"Gegaa, gegaa," he shouted, and then, at last, the motor caught with a roar and the cab shuddered. Morris whooped and pounded the wheel. He was sort of too excited, thought Ira, as though he was on some drug, but maybe it was for his eyes. He could be on some medication. Morris backed the truck from the snowy yard and said, "Which way?"

"I live out by the border at the old treaty signing."

"Way out there!" Morris marveled as they pulled into the road. "You guys are true-life bush Indians."

"My dad was. He still hunted and trapped all year but there wasn't a living in it. He has died since."

"You got a job?" Morris's eye rolled wildly at her and he grinned, his teeth big and sharp in the dashboard's reflected lights.

"I did until my dad went, then I didn't have no one to take care of my kids. So I get by, you know, I sell my beadwork and stuff. If I moved into town, I guess I could do pretty well."

"Oh, I'd say," but when he looked sideways at her, Ira thought he meant something else.

"Not that way," she stated, without laughing. Now was when she began to wish she hadn't touched him.

Morris gave a little hoot. As the heat came on, the cab of his truck began to smell like blood.

"You hunt yourself?" said Ira.

"Do I hunt *myself*?" Morris asked. "I'd like to see that."

"I mean, do you hunt, just hunt?"

Morris didn't answer, so Ira said, "You can't shut your eyes for real?"

"Yeah. They will not close. I put drops in. Take the wheel."

He quit steering and Ira slid over beside him to keep them from going in the ditch. He plucked a little squeeze bottle from his breast pocket and tipped back his head. "Ah," he screwed the top on the bottle, dropped it back in his pocket, took the wheel with one hand. He grabbed Ira with the other and hauled her close to him. "I liked that." The truck swerved.

"You got to keep both hands on the driving," she said, unhooking his arm from around her shoulders. She slid back to her side of the truck. "Look, it's iced up bad out there. Really, it's very dangerous." The road was plowed recently enough so that beneath the new and fluffy snow there was a hard, slick finish. "The conditions are definitely no good. Hey," she tried to shift the mood. "How do you sleep?"

"I never do sleep," said Morris. "That's why I'm crazy."

"You don't seem too crazy," Ira said.

"The VA sent me everywhere, all around the world, I been to Singapore. They couldn't do shit. I can't have sunlight or any light. Mostly I live inside listening to TV. Tapes. I got a million tapes. Cassette tapes. Nobody wants their cassette tapes anymore. The church gives 'em to me. People give 'em to me. I sit indoors and listen. So I know everything. All there is to know. It's all on tapes. It comes through my ears." He tapped the side of his head.

His ears look normal, Ira thought.

"My brother is the good talker. He's the one who charms the ladies. He told me all about you."

"What about your tapes? What are your tapes about?"

"Every kind of music, you would not believe. I got opera tapes which I can't make out the language, Mötley Crüe tapes, George Michael, every C-and-W tape there is or was. I got classical music tapes however I don't like to read the labels as it hurts my eyes, so I can't tell you who is who by name. There is this one guy I listen to all the time, the fucker plays like his hands are on fire. And books, every book. Everything from horror books to spiritual messages.

This one I had on before I left, I got the whole set of wisdom. Listen to this one," Morris spoke slowly and carefully. "'If anyone were to ask life over a thousand years, why are you alive? The only reply could be—I live so that I may live. Life lives from its own foundation and rises out of itself.' How about that?"

As they bounced along Morris steered the truck, slowly, carefully.

"A guy wrote that in the twelfth century A.D."

"If somebody asked me over a thousand years," Ira said, cold inside, "I would say I live because my children need me."

"Yeah," said Morris. "That's what my brother said. He told me all about how you needed money."

"I don't need it all that bad anymore," Ira said. "I only got to last until tomorrow."

"Well, I got money," said Morris. "I got quite a bit of money. On me. And I don't ever get a chance to be with a woman. I can't go in bars."

Now Ira knew why her throat clenched, why she'd been afraid. She knew why John had delivered her to his ma'iingan brother.

"If you have so much money," she said, her voice rising too high, "why don't you buy CDs?"

"Well, I have them too, and a player, of course. But I like listening to tapes for some reason. The assortment, I guess, and they're free. My house is a grab bag of tapes. Powwow tapes. Poetry tapes. The most beautiful stories in the language. Ira, listen to this," Morris's voice rose high, almost a wail. "'It isn't given to us to know those rare moments when people are wide open and the lightest touch can wither or heal.' What about that? Fitzgerald. I wish I could stop this truck," said Morris. "I wish that I could kiss you."

"No," said Ira, "I got to get back to my kids."

"Well, I think this is a rare healing moment, and a kiss"—Morris slowed the truck until it crawled—"that won't take a few seconds. A kiss is an efficacious drug. It might change my life." The truck stopped, idling. Morris turned to her and the light played up in his eyes so they flashed and burned. "Please," he said, putting the truck in park. Ira didn't move. "You want me to start the truck moving?" They sat suspended, breathing, looking at each other.

"You're pretty," said Morris. His voice was low. He was choking on his breath. "Want me to start the truck?"

"Yes," Ira said.

"C'mere then."

She slid across to him in a trance of fear, but when he did not move toward her but only sat very still, something else happened. She put her hands over his eyes. He seemed to be holding his breath now, even trembling a little. He wasn't going to hurt her, she realized. She kissed his mouth, and his foot pressed the gas pedal involuntarily, so it roared with a human sound. He laughed sheepishly and said, "I guess that tells you how I feel." His breath was surprisingly sweet and his face smelled like soap. Still, underneath that, the truck smelled of blood. He leaned back into the seat like he was fainting a little. She kissed him again. Then she took her hands off his eyes and got back on her side of the cab. He sat up, stared forward, then pressed the gas pedal slowly and shifted evenly so there was no sudden jolt. They went along in silence.

"You do love your children, don't you," he said.

"Yes," said Ira.

"But that second kiss," Morris said. "Was it maybe personal?"

Ira said nothing, just pointed out the many small drifts on the road. Morris concentrated, slowing now, very cautious. When the driving was smoother he put his hand in his pocket and pulled something out and slid it across the seat.

"You take this."

It was a wad of money.

"No," Ira said. "I didn't do nothing."

"Please keep it," Morris said, in a formal voice. "I feel dishonorable. Anyway, I got to get us to your place and return home by sunup. Morning light hurts my eyes very bad, I might need a pain pill, though I'm trying to get off those things. In the full sun I'll get sick. I maybe could go blind. Things are going bad for me. Yesterday I head-butted a mirror. Then I cut my feet bad walking in the bits. I scored my knuckles with a knife, cutting cabbage for a soup. I had to go to the emergency and get everything sewed up and there's still frozen blood all over in here; I guess I was hunting myself."

"You don't have a bandage on."

"I don't care to have one."

He put his hand in the dash light's glow and she saw black stitches running down between his fingers. His hand looked like a paw.

"You shouldn't go slamming your face at mirrors," she said.

"They give me the creeps. The Chinese believe you shouldn't ever have one facing your bed or your soul might crawl out of your body at night and slip into the mirror."

"Oh," said Ira, startled, "I sort of believe that too." Then she was watchful. "We're almost at the turnoff. Slow down." She helped him steer and they bumped down the awkwardly plowed road until they came to the place where Ira's house was. The dark was lifting only slightly and at first she couldn't see past the headlamp's arc. So she couldn't tell what had happened until the truck got close to the black and delicately smoking foundation.

5

Shawnee pulled herself out of her body and went up into the trees. At first she was frightened by the lightness, the drifting. She clung to her brother and sister and they came up with her. They were made of ash, black reeds, soot, a powder of loneliness, smoke. They held one another, but they couldn't speak or cry out. They were in blackness so deep that they did not know where it stopped or where they started. There were tiny blue flashes of light. Strings of electricity pulled snapping out of the air. They could hear things, just as they had before, though the reference between sound and object was fading. The wind rushed in the heavy branched pines. There was the hushed question of an owl. Then just the sound, and not the bird.

Jostling lightly as they moved along the branch, they made a sound like the scrape of dry twigs. Their heads were bowls. Air flowed through the hollows of their curved, black ribs. In the deep eyeholes, fragments of ice gleamed. When one of them bent the branch too far and fell, they found they could hang in the air. Awkwardly, slowly increasing their skill, they figured out how to maneuver from one tree to the next. Jerky and tentative at first, then launching themselves with increasing grace and ease, they traveled. But they kept returning to the tree, the shapes underneath. Those shapes drew them. They cocked their black skulls, and the ice in the eye sockets gleamed with raw curiosity.

Shawnee woke up in the dark. The sound of drumming would not let her sleep, although she wanted to. She had finally gotten comfortable, so comfortable. Her dream was dark and fantastic. Nothing hurt. But the drum was loud, insistent, a full noise that made her jumpy inside. She lifted her head and shook off the snow. That sound was coming from just outside of the ditch. A fast, rolling beat. It drew her staggering to her feet. On her back, nestled close in the shell of nylon and down, her brother stirred. Alice didn't move, but Shawnee lifted her anyway, dragged her by her hood and her hair. The drum grew louder, showing a way out, beating her around a tree and then a rock and over solid ground, all in the dark. Roused by the drum whenever she almost quit, Shawnee went on until she bumped flat into a wall. She moved along it and felt a window. She beat on the glass so hard with mitted and frozen fists that it shattered, and then she bawled like a little dog right outside the door.

6

Morris found the pile of blankets and stepped into the tumbled ash and debris of what had been the house. He put his arms around Ira and lifted her out. He shook her and kept talking to her until finally she could hear him. She grabbed his hand.

"Bernard's place," she said, understanding that Morris had found signs of her children. "They might of took the woods."

By the time Ira and Morris reached the house, it was light out and they saw the tribal ambulance team was already pulled up in the plowed drive. They ran, stumbling. The children were in back, wrapped in heated blankets. The EMT showed them to Ira, but when they stared at her their eyes looked frozen. She kneeled in the rescue truck, waiting for them to blink or move. When they slowly closed their eyes she grabbed for them, but they were all right, just falling asleep. The EMT told Morris to get in front because of his eye condition, then he told Ira she couldn't ride with her children, but had to follow with Bernard. There wasn't any room for her and they had to keep these children stable, he said, though really, it looked as though they'd all come through it.

"They were dressed pretty decent anyway, it saved them. I don't think they're even gonna lose their hands or feet."

"Their ears and noses look okay too. And they kept a core temp. Don't listen to Bug," said the other EMT. "Of course they're not gonna lose something. Make old Bernard crank the heat up and you follow us. We will not speed but we'll keep the light on and hit the siren if anybody gets in our way."

Morris sat in front, strapped in, with gauze packs on his eyes, dripping saline.

"Reach behind that bandage and put those drops in, Popeye," said the driver.

"Popeye?" said Ira.

"Nickname," said Morris.

Then they were off; Ira and Bernard followed along in his truck. Her head was tucked down. She was breathing in a panicked way, moaning a little with each breath. Bernard drove steadily along behind the ambulance, his tough old hands out of their gloves, gripping the wheel. He wore a plaid parka and a gray hat with padded flaps. He kept his eyes on the back of the ambulance, frowning in concentration. The wind was up, blowing the snow in snake swirls across the road. The cab of the truck finally began to warm.

"That's Chook's son, Morris," he said, jutting his chin at the ambulance. "Ma'iingan. He can't see nothing. Legally, he's blind."

"Well he drove me to the house. It's burnt down. Just ashes there."

Bernard looked over quickly at her. He hadn't known this.

"That's why your kids come through the woods."

"I went to the agency for emergency fuel, some groceries."

Bernard could smell the smoke and stale booze on his old friend's daughter. He knew she had done some partying, too. He didn't ask, or speak of it. He listened to her tell him about the people at the office and how the fuel truck would get out there later this morning and there wouldn't be a gas tank or a house to heat. She said that she could pick up a box of commodities at any time that day. She could have yesterday but didn't have a ride.

"I'll pick it up and have it at the hospital for you. They will keep your kids a few days, I bet. How come you never called me? I could have given you a ride."

"I didn't have no phone. I just went out to the road and waited and hitched in. Once I was there, I never thought of you, but I could of gone over to the hospital and caught you when you got off."

If you weren't drinking, Bernard thought, but he just shrugged.

"Well, I had a day shift for once, lucky thing. I was home because of it. And Morris, he got you out there somehow. And your kids made it, safe."

Ira's face was wet. Tears were leaking from her eyes now and her nose was running. It wasn't the pain from thawing out her hands and feet.

"I'm not a bad mom. I had a few drinks," she said. "I was gonna ... well, I did get some food off Morris's brother. Then he dropped me off with Morris. I knew there was something wrong."

"They said it was close," Bernard said. "Your kids were going hypothermic when they got to my house. Those emergency guys hooked your kids up right away to their warm IVs and got their temperatures regulated. That girl of yours, that Shawnee, she's a strong one."

"You got it," said Ira.

"Something else," said Bernard.

"What?" said Ira. Now that she was getting warm, now that the blood was swelling painfully in her hands and feet, she fought sleep. She was sinking into it, leaning against the seat-belt strap. Her head lolled down; she jolted herself upward.

"She said that she heard the drum," Bernard said. "She said the drum told her where to go. It was pitch-black in the woods. My lights were out. She found me anyway."

"So you were up at night, drumming in the dark, having your own little powwow," Ira mumbled, dropping into sleep. She began to breathe deep and light.

"No," said Bernard to himself, after a while. "No, I wasn't. That drum is still covered up in the corner, where it always sits. I was asleep when they broke my window."

7

A hospital is a world apart, running day and night by its own rules.
Ira had stayed in the hospital for only a short time when her children were born. Her father had been in the hospital a few weeks but then he died at home. She hadn't ever stayed overnight with him.
So the way things worked at the Indian Health Service hospital was new to her. The first day passed in getting the children settled, in watching them, talking to the doctors, calibrating each step of their recovery. That night, Ira fell asleep on a plastic recliner in her daughters' room. The chair was slippery and hard but reclined at a good angle. She'd certainly slept in worse places. The next morning, she woke stiff and sore, but that could have been from running through the snowy woods. Shawnee and Alice were in a double room and Alice still had the IV drip with the plastic catheter taped fast to the back of her hand. She was too weak to use the bathroom

and the nurses had fixed an overnight diaper onto her, which humiliated her. She wouldn't speak. She lay very still with her eyes shut, pretending to be unconscious. During the night, Ira had risen every time the nurses had come in to check the children. They used a finger tube to read their respiratory rates and oxygen levels. They checked pulse, temperature, and blood pressure. After she was sure that the nurses were satisfied, she had gone into Apitchi's room. He had a fever. She had dragged her pillow and blanket in and stayed with him for half the night in a chair identical to the one in her daughters' room.

Ira knew or was related to some of the nurses who had trained on special IHS scholarships and then come back home. One, her cousin Honey, had always said that she was going to be a nun, but ended up as a nurse. She was a strict Catholic. As Ira helped Honey and the other nurses tend to one and another of her children, they talked to her and got the story. No one blamed her outright. But the Indian Child Welfare was going to conduct an interview with her, no question, and then speak separately with each of her children. The head of that department had scheduled a case worker from ICW to come by the hospital.

Honey brought fresh clothes, and Ira showered in the bare tile bathroom next to Shawnee's bed. The water washed down black at first, and Ira remembered the soot and it seemed very long ago. She turned the water up as hot as she could stand it. There was a big plastic bottle of all-over body-wash shampoo fixed to the wall of the shower. She used a lot of it, and then stood under the hot dribble like a grateful dog, she thought, just like a grateful animal. The bathroom was full of steam as she dried off with a tiny, thin hand towel. She hadn't wanted to ask about getting a real bath towel. She skimmed her hair back in a ponytail and checked her purse, but she didn't put on makeup. Looking plain was good, she thought. She never could look good again. She would never leave her children for a minute.

Once she was clean, it felt like she really lived at the hospital now. She still felt fuzzy—too much had happened. She wished she had a cup of coffee. A woman came into the girls' room. She carried a briefcase and held a clipboard, and she wore a full-length down coat, mukluks, and St. James Bay woolen mitts. Looking straight at her, Ira's heart jumped. It was the wife of John, the woman with the neat white scar that cut across her lips. Her name surged into Ira's mind. "Seraphine!"

"Yes, boozhoo! We're getting a blizzard sometime today," she informed Ira. "We're really lucky it wasn't yesterday."

Ira was glad she'd said *we*; it would have been an accusation if she'd said *you*. Seraphine left the room and Ira followed her silently, numb in her thoughts. They went down the hall and entered a little office with a wall of gray shelves and cabinets, stacks of papers and boxes of tongue depressors and rubber gloves. A dead computer and a fake plant were on the desk.

"Let's just squeeze in here, it's private," said Seraphine.

There was a padded desk chair and metal folding chair. Seraphine swept her hand at them both and let Ira choose where to sit. Ira took the metal folding chair.

"Now let's go over things," Seraphine said. There was a pen chained to the top of her clipboard. A tribal ID hung from her neck on a bright pink, canvas ribbon. Her dress was stone gray with soft little sage-green flowers on it. Seraphine's face was extraordinarily beautiful, finely made, a haughty Michif face. Her skin was the pale gold color that white people broil themselves on tanning machines to achieve. John was right, thought Ira, his wife is very good-looking.

He had also said that she knew medicines, and Ira wondered if she would act all spiritual. But Seraphine was quietly matter-of-fact.

"First of all," she said, after she had confirmed Ira's basic information, "what are you now doing for a living?"

"I sew a lot. Quilts and powwow outfits. And I bead. I had a thousand-dollar men's fancy regalia burn up with my house," Ira said, remembering and missing, as she would now for years, something lost in the fire.

"That's a chancy living."

"True."

"I think I saw one of your bead yokes—I know your style."

"All my dad's things are gone now, too," Ira went on, and a strange feeling overtook her momentarily. Those things that had burned were all that her father had left behind in his life. Now there was nothing to remember him by but his grave. "Oh, no," she said.

"Excuse me?"

"Nothing." Ira touched her face.

"Tell me what happened the day before yesterday," said Seraphine. "Can you explain why your children were left alone for an extended period? I have to set this down in my report, so take it slow."

"They weren't alone," said Ira, "they were with Shawnee."

"Shawnee is a minor. The law says you can't leave your children with a minor overnight. Of course, you're under tribal jurisdiction, but the judge usually upholds the same standard."

"I didn't know it was against the law."

"Have you done this often?"

"Never, no, maybe once. This was an emergency. I went to the office to get some heating assistance and a food voucher or whatever. You can ask the personnel, Itchy Boyer, some others. I hitched in but I had trouble getting a ride back."

Seraphine made some notes on her pad of paper, then rested her clipboard on her knees.

"Look," she said, "I know all about it. John told me."

Heat flooded Ira's face. How much was told? What had John said?

"Morris gave me a ride out to my place."

"And John and you walked to Morris's place."

Ira hesitated. "Yeah."

Seraphine frowned at her paper, then shook her pen to get the ink to flood into the tip.

"Hey," said Ira suddenly. "I met John at a bar, but he was only interested in getting me to Morris's place. He gave me money for groceries."

Ira rubbed her hands together. Her skin was tender.

"Okay," Seraphine said, writing down some words. "So far your stories match." She was only joking, and she smiled as she wrote, but Ira felt her throat go dry and scratchy. If Seraphine wrote up a bad report on her, what? Could they take her children? Her breath snagged in her chest. Seraphine kept talking. "So you met John at a bar and he gave you money for groceries and then left you over at Morris's house."

Ira nodded. The red cotton placket-front blouse she was wearing, the too large bra, the baggy black pants, and the hospital slippers made her feel poor and beggarly. But I am poor and beggarly, she thought. Everything I have is burnt. She remembered Shawnee's school pictures. Her breath caught. And now this woman is going to ask me if I had sex to get the money. But I can honestly tell her that I did not, though I would have, but would have doesn't matter. And Morris can tell her, too.

"Morris knows," Ira blurted.

"Morris knows what?"

"I'm really tired," said Ira, wiping her hand across her face. "Can I go back to my kids? I lost my daughter's school pictures in the fire."

"I just have a few more questions."

Ira leaned across the desk, put her head on her fist. "Okay."

But Seraphine didn't ask about why John gave her money or why Morris gave her a ride. She was more interested in where Ira thought she might stay while she applied for emergency housing and got on the waiting list for permanent housing.

"I don't know yet," said Ira.

"Well, you've got to find somewhere," said Seraphine. "We can put you and your children in the women's shelter for a month, maybe, starting in a couple of weeks, but before that we'd have to put them in foster care and you, I don't know . . ." She touched the scar on her lips.

"I'll find a place," Ira said. "Bernard maybe. He might let us stay with him. I don't know. It's pretty far out there."

"That's a problem." Seraphine nodded. "You with no transportation. I'm going to ask your daughters some questions now. I need to find out how the fire started."

And do you need to check my story out, Ira wondered, see if they saw me getting high on drugs or I beat them up or fucked Morris on the living room rug while they were eating breakfast, not that we have a rug anymore, or a living room, and the whole thing that started it was there was only breakfast, only oatmeal.

"Okay," said Ira. "You go talk to them."

Ira went back to Apitchi's room. He was hot, limp, in a very deep sleep. He didn't stir when Ira kissed his forehead. Ira peered closely at him. Then she pushed the nurse's call button and went out the door.

"There's something wrong with him," she said to a nurse. "Come in here. Please. You've got to get the doctor to look at him. There's something wrong."

"We've got a chest X ray ordered," said the nurse, brushing past her, "and we'll probably get him on IV antibiotics. The doctor was here while you were gone and they think he maybe has pneumonia. It's probably pneumonia," the nurse said, as though that was reassuring. "Do you want to help me," she said, seeing that Ira looked stunned, eyes filling with tears, "do you want to help me get him ready for the X ray?"

Ira nodded and tucked his blanket in around his feet.

"We can wheel him out," the nurse said.

Ira kept her hand on Apitchi's head as they made their way down the hall. His hair was rough, thick, and matted. They had given him a sponge bath but there was still soot behind his ears, she saw, and a black line at his hairline, and soot in the corners of his nose. He didn't smell like ash, though, she thought, bending over to kiss him again as the elevator took them down. He smelled like a little boy. He was named Apitchi for the robin that made its nest just over the door and raised its babies the summer she was pregnant. Alice was named for her mother and Shawnee for the prophet. Ira's father had been religious, he had named them with spirit names, too, and he had brought Ira back from the Cities when her husband left her. He had helped her obtain a legal divorce and he had given them all of his veteran's pension money and his social security.

They went down to the X-ray room. Ira had to stand behind a

lead shield. Apitchi was shrinking, she thought, into his sleep. But the nurse assured her that she'd seen plenty of children with pneumonia and every one of them had gotten well.

Once Apitchi was settled back in his room and got his antibiotics, Ira thought she'd better go back and see the girls. Shawnee was sitting up in bed when Ira entered the room. Her hands were wound in soft clubs of gauze and she was trying to work the remote control on the television. The TV was suspended between the girls, opposite them on the wall.

"Here," said Ira, taking the remote control, "what do you want?"

Shawnee looked fixedly at the screen and shrugged.

"Alice?" Ira was carefully pressing channels.

Alice frowned at the television. They let their mother flip through the channels, twice over. Finally Alice raised her arm, the one without the IV. "I want that one."

"Okay." Ira put down the remote control and sat next to Shawnee, but Shawnee said, "Mom, could you get off the bed? I need to lay down." Ira got up and helped arrange the covers over her. Shawnee's feet were bandaged, too.

"How do they feel?" said Ira.

"Bad," said Shawnee.

"Can I do anything?"

Shawnee stared briefly at her mother, then looked away. It seemed to Shawnee that she had been on a long trip, that she had gone somewhere far away and her mother was left behind. Her mother was back in a place where nothing had happened to Shawnee, but in truth everything had happened. She had been to the edge of life. Apitchi and Alice had gone there too. Shawnee had dragged her brother and her sister back. She hadn't allowed them to die. Or herself, either. Now that she was back on this earth, she was lonely. She wanted someone to say to her, *Shawnee, you saved them.* Not to look at her with eyes that said, *You burnt the house down.*

Ira put her hand out to stroke Shawnee's hair, but Shawnee jerked her head away from her mother's touch without taking her eyes from the television screen. Ira sat down and put her hands in her lap and pretended to watch a man coaxing an alligator from its underwater den. She was wondering if Seraphine had told her children something that set their minds against her, or if they were mad at all, but maybe just surprised to be in a hospital. She thought that she should talk to Shawnee and Alice about what had happened. *I should find out, I should know, I am their mother*, she thought. But at the same time she dreaded knowing any details because all of it, every bit, was her fault. She had put her children in that danger, she had left them, and knowing more about what they had suffered could only make her feel worse. It reflected her failure to protect them. Also, she had a bad instinct. It was growing in her. Ira was afraid that at some point, when she was very tired maybe, she would say to Shawnee, *How the fuck could you have burnt down the house? Our only place to live? All we own? Gone? How the fuck?* Ira was so afraid of blurting this out that she got up suddenly, and left the room.

She sat with Apitchi until his fever let go, his skin cooled a little, and he no longer frowned in his sleep. When she returned to the girls, a nurse was giving them extra milk, juice, pudding, crackers, and they were eating every bit. It was still an hour before the lunch trays would come. Ira was hungry. Yesterday there had been an extra tray sent to the floor and one of the nurses had brought it to her. So she'd had an entire dinner—turkey, gravy, beans, mashed potatoes, even a coffee. She had eaten every scrap on that tray. But there had not been an extra breakfast this morning. Ira was hoping there would be an extra tray at lunch again, and she did not want to leave the floor in case she might miss it. But she also wanted to find out how Morris was.

Ira went searching down the hall on the adult ward. But she was too shy to actually look into the rooms. Quick, casual glances through each door did not reveal Morris, so she asked about him and a nurse took her all the way to the end of the hall. The room was dark, the curtains drawn, and Morris's eyes were covered, as Ira had thought they would be.

"You have a lady visitor," the nurse said.

"Seraphine?" said Morris.

"No, Ira."

"Boozhoo!" Morris put out his hand. "How are your kids? Come in here. Siddown. There's crackers." He didn't grope, but put his hand precisely on the table pushed up next to him. He lightly touched a stack of cellophane-wrapped saltines. "Would you like some?"

Ira took a package, opened it, and ate both saltines. They melted on her tongue.

"Have more," said Morris.

"No, I gotta get back. My kids' lunch trays are coming. My kids are doing good. Apitchi's got pneumonia, except."

"They can treat pneumonia, it's safer to get pneumonia than a lot of things."

"Yeah," said Ira. "I was scared though. How about you?"

"Me," said Morris, touching his hair, which was bunched up over the bandages, "I think I have finally done it. Maybe I'll go blind now, all the way blind. One of my cornea's all scratched up, the other got ulcerated. They just told me. Anyway, the suspense will be over."

"You won't be able to drive," said Ira.

"Well, I wasn't supposed to, really, I should have told you. I'm sorry about that."

"You tried," Ira said. "If you hadn't gone in the woods after my kids and the snow got so bright, maybe your eyes wouldn't have quit on you."

"It was gonna happen," Morris said. He patted the covering on his eyes, adjusted the bandages. "So, your kids okay, really?"

"The girls won't talk to me yet."

Morris nodded, as if that made sense. "Give them time to come out of it," he said. "There's water, too, in that pitcher. The nurse just put new ice in."

"They taking good care of you?"

"Yes," said Morris. "Morphine. They know me from before."

"You been in for your eyes then?"

"Other things, too," said Morris. "Where you supposed to live now?"

"I don't know yet. Bernard, maybe. I never asked him though."

"Your mom's dead."

"Long time ago."

"And I heard about it when your dad died. He was a spiritual man, I knew him."

"My dad knew how to give names. They gave him the ceremony. It was because he had dreams. He couldn't stop his dreams. They kept coming at him. It turned out he was meant to do certain things that would put his dreams to use."

She stopped. "Ma'iingan," she said. "He gave that name to you."

"Your dad said that was the only time he ever gave that name out."

"That name meant a lot to him because wolves saved his life, once, I guess."

"Amen," said Morris. "My name saved me, too."

"How?" said Ira.

"That's for another visit," Morris said. "I got to hook you in somehow."

Ira went quiet because she didn't know what to say to that. She didn't know whether she wanted to be hooked in or left on her own. "Anyway," she said, "Popeye?"

"Yeah, too bad about that."

"You don't like your nickname?"

They both laughed.

"Well, I must go," said Ira. "Bye." She leaned over and put her hand in Morris's open hand. He held her hand a minute. Just held her fingers with his fingers. Then he carefully let go.

Had she missed the lunch trays? Ira was so hungry that she was beginning to feel all wobbly down the center. She walked quickly back to her children and first checked on Apitchi, then went to Shawnee and Alice's room. There was no sign of lunch yet. She lowered herself into a chair. She noticed a little box of Sugar Pops on the table next to Shawnee's bed, and she wanted to say, "Are you going to eat those?" But she thought that Shawnee might give her that stare that she had given her before.

"What are you watching?" she asked.

"Powerpuffs."

"It's stupid," Shawnee said.

"No, they're good!" said Alice.

I'd better call up Bernard, thought Ira. Or maybe go look for him when he comes on his shift. She heard the rumble of the lunch cart coming down the corridor and her stomach pinched hard. An aide brought two trays in, each with a piece of skinless chicken, a spoonful of rice with some vegetables mixed in, a salad with pale pink tomatoes, and green Jell-O. There was a carton of milk and a few sticks of celery and carrots. Ira cut up Alice's meat. The girls ate everything. When they were done, Ira put their trays back outside, on the cart.

"I'm going to see Apitchi now," she told Shawnee and Alice. On the way out she asked a nurse if there was an extra tray. The nurse said no. Ira said that if anybody didn't eat their tray could she have it, and the nurse looked closely at her.

"You got money for the cafeteria?"

"No," said Ira. "I'm here with my children."

"I'll make sure they order a supper tray for you," the nurse said. "In the meantime, come over here." She took Ira to a small closet kitchen. From the little refrigerator, she took two cartons of chocolate milk, two yogurts, and a bowl of peaches covered with plastic wrap. She balanced a handful of wrapped crackers on top of the plastic wrapped bowl. "Those peaches are from just yesterday," she said.

Ira took the food to Apitchi's room. He was still sleeping, his arms tucked close. He huddled in the sheets. Ira arranged the food on the windowsill and then she sat down next to Apitchi's bed. Slowly, she reached over, selected a carton of milk, and sipped it. The chocolate milk was rich, cold, and she felt it trickle all the way down to her stomach. Next, she ate the yogurts—first the blueberry then strawberry—taking little precise scoops with a plastic spoon.

She put her head back on the chair and rested for a while. She ate the peaches and the crackers. Then she drank the last milk. When Apitchi woke, he looked anxiously all around the room and let his gaze rest, at last, on his mother's face. I don't know what I will do if he hates me too, Ira thought, but when he realized it was she, he burst into tears and tried to hold his arms out. Ira went to him gratefully. His arm was strapped to a board along with the IV and his other hand was taped to a little paddle so he couldn't reach over and pull out the needle. Ira carefully positioned him against her so that she could read a picture book to him. She read it six times, the same book, until it made her sleepy. She leaned back in the bed with Apitchi and felt his heart beating right over her heart.

When she woke from her light sleep with Apitchi, it was late afternoon. All of her children were still asleep. She went to Morris's room and stood in the entrance. He was looking at her with his lids half shut. His bandages had fallen off. She said hello, and he seemed to acknowledge her by gazing at her peacefully, but when his expression did not change, she realized from his deep breathing that he was actually asleep with his eyes open. This sight startled and made her want to turn away, but she was held by the strangeness of exchanging this calm regard with a person who was unconscious and maybe even dreaming.

"It's Ira," she said, when he stirred. "If you want to keep sleeping, I'll go."

"No, I'm not tired." He sat up and fixed the bandages back over his eyes. "Just bored. They're gonna bring my tape player and my tapes in later."

"Maybe I could read to you," said Ira. "I just finished reading to my little boy."

"What did you read him?"

"Green Eggs and Ham."

"I've heard that one," said Morris.

"Well, I could get you another," said Ira. "Probably they have a bunch of books somewhere."

"Okay," said Morris, "if you find a good one, you read it to me. It's a deal."

"I'll check downstairs later."

Ira stood awkwardly in the doorway, not sure whether to sit down or to leave.

"Look," said Morris. "I gotta say, I'm sorry. It's about what I was thinking, what I implied, when I stopped the truck on the road."

Ira dragged a chair next to the bed, sat down. She put her elbows on her knees, her head in her hands. Now that the bandages were on he couldn't see, so what did it matter. She had wondered if he was going to mention that moment.

"You were lonely, and me, I was desperate," she said at last. "And it's true, I was after some money. If somebody had offered me money to fuck them, I would have done it earlier, but then your brother gave me money for some groceries, so I wasn't that desperate anymore."

"He screwed me, then!"

She laughed a little. "We should let it go, I mean, because the kids are gonna be alive and they could have . . . whatever. But they're okay. Your sister-in-law visited me."

"Seraphine. War wounds."

"She was in the army? Which one?"

"The one that was conducted on us where they took our children prisoner."

"She went to boarding school then."

"Yes. And now as I have scratched up my corneas to the point of ulceration, I truly see through a glass darkly, as in Corinthians."

"That's the Bible," said Ira.

"Yes, the New Testament, which is on twenty-four double sided tapes."

"So you lay in the dark and you listen to the Bible."

"That Old Testament, especially, rated R for sex and violence. Don't let your kids near that book."

Ira laughed. "Wow."

"You're impressed?"

"I'm kind of scared of you."

"Why, because my eyes bug out? Most cases like mine do not persist, but I even had surgery and they still popped out again, and the treatments haven't worked. The doctors say I'm just stubborn. The whole thing stems out of my thyroid gland, and I know it got fucked up in Kuwait. They're going to paralyze my eyelids with Botox and see if they drop."

"You're kidding."

"I'll be young forever. I'll have young eyes."

Ira looked down at her hands.

"I don't know what I'd do. I feel for you."

"I'd rather you just feel me," said Morris. "Up."

"Sad."

"I know it, I'm so out of practice."

"Yes, you are. But that's a plus in my mind."

"Good." Morris paused. "Are you used to your house being gone yet?"

"I am trying to get used to remembering that I have no house, nothing, just what I have on me."

"Which is?"

Ira began to rummage in her purse. "A comb, a compact, a stick of gum, an extra diaper, some bills, food vouchers, old mascara, a bunch of toilet paper, photographs, which now I'm very glad I always carry, and lots of lint balls."

"That's in your purse."

"Right. Oh, and I also have a beadwork clip and a bag of earrings I was hoping to sell. Here," she handed him the clip, which was a sunburst design picked out in extra-small fancy cutbeads. "This is an example of my work. You can feel how I made it anyway."

"Nice."

"Yeah, I'm real careful. I do good, tight, work, me."

Morris held the clip, running his fingers over it. "Can I keep it?"

Ira hesitated, "Well, I'd like to give it to you. But I could maybe get forty for it. I was gonna show the nurses."

"I've got fifty."

"Trying to give me money again." Ira pushed the clip back at Morris. "Just take it. Keep it. I want you to have it."

"No," said Morris. He tried to give it back, but Ira had left the room. So he lay back with the beaded sunburst in the palm of his hand, running his fingers across the perfect, smooth, curved rows of beads.

"We're none of us perfect," said Honey. Ira's cousin was round, cute, and full of satisfaction about her house and children and hardworking husband. She had it all. She was sitting in the girls' room on the plastic recliner. Ira came in and sat on the end of Alice's bed and wondered if Honey had found them a place to stay.

"You blame your mom," said Honey to Shawnee. "But you shouldn't. Your mother is a human being. She has her faults, as do all of us."

Shawnee had been staring at the blank TV. Now she looked at Honey. She saw her so clearly. She saw her thin brown hair with the floss cut so it curled around her ears. She saw the heaviness in her face and neck, her strong little black eyes. She saw how Honey liked to visit them because they made her feel so much better about her own children and her situation in this life. She wondered if Honey went to school or just practiced until she got the job of nurse. Anyway, even if she'd learned all there was to know, she didn't know her mother or have the right to tell Shawnee to blame or not to blame her. And her mother was a human being, that was true, anybody could see that. This woman had not been to the edge of life.

"I'm not stupid," said Shawnee to her mother's cousin.

After that, although Honey tried to talk to her, held her hands out, Shawnee did a thing she discovered she could do with her mind. She clicked the woman's mute button. She had just learned about the mute button on the television's remote control. So it was comical—nothing she said came through—just her mouth moving, her eyebrows wiggling up and down, her finger pointing, waving, her arms finally flapping at Shawnee's mother, who went out the door with Honey and came back alone and said, "So much for that."

"What?" said Shawnee.

"She hasn't got a place for us." Ira laughed suddenly. "You told her, I guess," she said. "We're not stupid. You got that right, baby girl."

Ira sat back down on Alice's bed.

"That woman came," Shawnee said, "and Alice asked her how she got that scar on her face."

"Oh, you shouldn't have asked that, Alice."

"But it was interesting," said Shawnee.

"It was?" Ira could not help it, she was curious and still could not remember.

"A matron," said Shawnee. "What's that?"

"Oh, that's in boarding school," Ira said. "I'm not going to send you kids to boarding school."

"That's good," Shawnee said.

"Bernard came," said Alice.

"He said to tell you he has our food. He'll bring it to wherever we go," said Shawnee. Then stopped. Bernard had patted her shoulder and told her that she was a strong little girl, a good sister. Her mother had tried to touch her only that one time, since the fire. Shawnee almost wanted to force her mother to get angry with her just to get it over with, but at the same time she hoped her mother would say that Shawnee had saved her brother and sister, that she had dragged them through the snow, that she had refused to let them fly away as black skeletons.

"Where do we go now?" Alice asked.

Ira leaned over and put her arms around Alice. As she held her, rocking, she looked over at Shawnee, and that was when Shawnee thought her mother was going to say, in a mean and low voice, maybe, *How could you have burnt down the house?* But Ira didn't say it, she just kept rocking Alice, and looking at Shawnee, and looking back down at Alice. After a while her mother's face seemed to open up like a flower. She smiled and a softness flowed from her and wrapped around Shawnee and held her.

Apitchi was burbling weakly, coming out of his long still sleep. This time he didn't know his mother, he could get no comfort from her and each breath wheezed and rasped in his chest. Ira sat with him, holding him. She thought he seemed to be losing weight. Even as they sat there, he was growing less substantial in her arms. She put him down and he was motionless, hot, his skin dry and burning. Ira got a washcloth and rinsed it in cold water, squeezed it out, and began washing Apitchi down with it. With every few strokes of the cloth against his skin, the cold was gone. She had to rinse it again. She kept on rinsing and wiping and then suddenly his eyes, which had been wide open, went glassy and blank and stared sideways. His arms and legs moved in climbing motions. He grinned terribly, his baby teeth clamped tight, and he shuddered. Ira pressed the nurse call button, yelled for help, tried to hold his arms still but he was twisting, snaking along the bed. She clamped herself over him. His mouth was open and he was choking on blood and foam. She turned him over and at last the nurse came, and then more nurses and two doctors, until people filled the room. Ira stepped back into the corner, frozen to the wall. All she could see of Apitchi was his foot, still jerking, then his foot went still.

They kept working on him, calling for things she didn't know the names of. Nobody noticed her. He couldn't be dead, she thought, as long as there was so much activity. She fixed on the bustling of the nurses. The low-key, businesslike voices of the doctors reassured her. If the doctors were giving orders there was hope. At last, one of them said, "His mother?" A nurse said Ira's name and beckoned to her. The doctor turned from the bed and took Ira's hand, an act that made her gasp with fear.

"Ira," the doctor said, quiet behind the mask, "your son is very sick. But we think we have him stabilized."

Now the nurses were moving away from the bed and the other

doctor went out of the room. Ira could see Apitchi in the bed. He seemed to have shrunk yet again, he looked like a tiny monkey. He was far, far away. Ira could tell he wasn't in his body.

"We've got a problem," the doctor said, taking off her rubber gloves and removing her mask. "This seizure is probably related to the fever, but it could have some other source. Normally, I'd have your little boy helicoptered out, but we've got bad weather out there. We're going to have to keep him here until the blizzard clears up. You're staying nights, aren't you?"

Ira nodded. She reached forward and held Apitchi's foot. His foot was still fat and round. His foot still fit into her hand.

"I'm sleeping in the chair."

"Let's get a roll-away in here," the doctor said to the nurse.

"Now you"—the doctor touched Ira's shoulder—"you're going to have to keep your strength up. Your little boy is going to need you."

"What about my other two, my daughters?"

"They're going to be fine, but I'd like to keep them another day or two."

"That's good," said Ira, "because I don't know where we're going next."

"I hear your house burned down," the doctor said. "I'm sorry." Ira said thank you.

"Do you have someone you can stay with?"

"I should go ask Bernard."

"Okay," said the doctor. "For now, let's just take care of your little boy."

A hospital aide brought in a roll-away cot and shoved it against the wall. The doctor stayed and went over Apitchi's pulse and tem-

perature again, then she left and later on the nurse left too. Alone
with Apitchi, Ira didn't dare take her eyes off of him. But finally she
had to use the bathroom and when she came out he was still all
right, he even looked a little better, maybe. So she unlocked the
steel hook on the side of the cot and laid out the bed. Then she lay
down on it. The bed was so comfortable that she fell asleep for perhaps an hour. When she woke, old Bernard was sitting in a chair on
the other side of Apitchi's bed.

"Oh, hey," she said. "You're here."

"I came to work early," said Bernard. "Zero visibility out there. I
barely did make it. I heard this little one is sick."

"Pneumonia," said Ira. "But he had a seizure and they don't
know why. Maybe the fever."

"Poor little guy," said Bernard. "A seizure."

"Scared the living hell out of me," said Ira, sitting up and staring
at Apitchi. "Now they have him on a medicine for that, too."

"What about you," said Bernard. "Did you eat?"

"I forgot about supper. I slept."

"They left a tray here," Bernard said, collecting it off a table
behind the curtain. "Must have seen you were sleeping."

Bernard brought the tray around the side of the bed and Ira put
it on her knees. She'd lost her hunger, but she thought that she
should eat, in case.

"Probably got cold," said Bernard. "Should I go and leave you
to eat?"

"No, no," said Ira. "Stay here and talk to me. Can I interest you
in a piece of"—she lifted the plastic dome, wet with condensed
steam—"gray stuff? There's chocolate pudding, too."

"I'll keep you company," Bernard said. "I bring me a lunch

every night, but sometimes I eat those good old hospital cafeteria leftovers, too. They bring 'em around to me."

Ira found that, although she felt no hunger, she was eating everything with quick efficiency. She hoped that somebody had helped Alice cut her meat into little pieces. Perhaps they were asleep now, her daughters; it was late.

"Can I ask you something?" Ira was nervous. "You can say no."

"All right. What is it?"

Ira stirred her pudding around and around. "Well, I've got to ask you, I mean, can we come stay with you? Until we figure out our housing?"

"Okay," said Bernard.

Ira looked up in relief, she smiled. "Really?"

"I got room," Bernard said.

"Oh, thank you." Ira put her hands on either side of her tray. She nodded. Tears suddenly stung in her throat. "Chi miigwech, Bernard."

"I got room," he said again.

"I can cook," said Ira. "I'll cook for you."

Bernard waved his hand aside and they both sat in the quiet looking at Apitchi, watching the glowing numbers of his oxygen and the graph of his heartbeat on the monitor. Ira finished up the food on her tray and set the tray on the broad windowsill.

"I sat with your dad in the nights," said Bernard, "when he was sick in this here hospital. We used to talk."

"I didn't know that. I mean, of course I knew you two were friends, and that, but I never knew you stayed with him in the hospital."

"Oh yes, he told me things I never knew. I learned things about him, when he was here in the hospital."

"I guess people talk," said Ira, watching Apitchi's face, "at night. It can be a lonely place. I wish I could've stayed with him. I was taking care of the kids."

"He sure loved these little ones," said Bernard.

"I know he did," Ira said. "Shawnee remembers him best. What kind of stories did he tell you?"

"About the wolves," Bernard said.

"He gave that name to Morris," said Ira. "Why was that?"

"Morris was going in the army. He needed that name for protection."

"Okay," said Ira.

"I think I have to tell you something," said Bernard.

"Go ahead."

"I was sleeping when your daughter heard that drum. I never struck that drum. That drum is no ordinary drum. It is very old and originates generations back. I have been looking after this drum, waiting for it to tell me what to do. Every day I put out my tobacco, and I ask for direction. Sometimes I hear the songs. The drum talked to your daughter."

Ira sat very still, her hand on Apitchi's ankle. "I don't know what that means," she said.

"I think it means that this drum is now ready to be put to use," said Bernard. "I was going to wait and say this. But being as your boy here is sick, I think we must act."

Ira looked into Bernard's eyes, round and direct as a bird's. "It can't hurt," she said.

"Tonight I'm going to bring the drum up, then," said Bernard. "I have it sitting downstairs in my office. And I am going to get Morris to help me with the songs."

"Morris knows them?"

"Some. His mother bothered me to work with him. See, this here drum went traveling for a time. Most of the songs got scattered."

"What will the nurses say?"

"Oh," said Bernard, "they'll be all right. It's not the first time they had to contend with their own medicine. There's a hospital policy on traditional healing. We can't burn any sage, but the drum we can pound as long as we keep it low and everyone is awake. We'll do it in the morning."

Bernard left the room and went downstairs. While he was gone, Ira checked on Shawnee and Alice. They were asleep, breathing calmly, and when she slipped from their room she saw Bernard getting off the elevator. He carried the drum in a canvas case, by a strap, and he also carried a cloth case that looked as though it held a short pair of skis, but she knew it held the legs that kept the drum off the floor. She followed Bernard into the room. He took the drum from its case, then put the drum on the recliner, and pushed it against the wall.

"There's room, isn't there?"

"Sure," Ira said, "there's room."

Bernard left the case standing in the corner, and he went out the door. The night nurse came in and checked everything about Apitchi. Then she left. Ira smoothed out the covers on the cot again, and climbed in with her clothes on. The drum was behind her head, just above. Immediately, she slept.

The nurse tucked the digital thermometer underneath Shawnee's arm and she swam up from her dream to half-wakefulness. She heard the *whoosh* of the pump on the blood pressure cuff, and heard it again as the nurse stood over Alice. An hour ago, Shawnee's hands had throbbed and itched, but now that the medicine the nurse had given her had kicked in, she was comfortable. The nurse went out of the room, but Shawnee did not return entirely to sleep. The door was open a crack and she could hear the nurses talking at their big round station in the middle of the ward. It was comforting talk. A low babble. Heat flowed softly through the louvered vent alongside the window. Her mother was down the hall with Apitchi, and she had come through the woods. They were all safe. Since they'd been in the hospital, every time Shawnee closed her eyes she was back at the house as it burned, or dragging Alice, or floundering through the snow with Apitchi on her back. Now when she slept, she dreamed the whole thing over again, and several hours later she woke cold. She did not know where she was at first. Her vision was clouded, her eyes weak, and she felt the snow reaching up around her waist. But then she heard the beating of the drum, as she had back in the woods. Once she heard it she slowly allowed herself to return to consciousness. She pushed the sheet down, tossed off the pillow that had fallen over her eyes. As the room and its safety surrounded her, she was flooded by a startling and almost painful happiness.

Morris knew that he had fallen hard in love with Ira while they were back there in the cab of the truck. Did she know that her voice was lovely? So precise and yet hesitant? Could she even imagine how the give of her lips and the soft, hot little cave of her mouth, behind her lips and teeth, affected Morris? His fall was so dramatic and sudden that he'd actually trembled when she said her name in his room. They had taken him off morphine and he hadn't cared. That's how distracted he was. He thought of everything about her, everything he'd learned. The power and determination as she trudged through the snow, her devotion and her failure, her dignity which had not yet allowed her to ask to move in with him, though he hoped that she would ask. He had to know her. He had to understand the simplicity and even placement of the beads in her beadwork. It took patience and years of practice to bead that well. Yet she was impulsive, too. She made tiny mistakes, one here, one there. Some mistakes had bigger outcomes than they deserved. He felt so much pity for Ira that he wanted to take some of her trouble on. He missed her. He felt the print of her body against his when he'd dragged her across the seat. The aching print. There was the knowledge that his eyes were all fucked up and would not get better and he was addicted to painkillers. Not an ideal father figure. But there were positives. He did get a disability check and Bernard had come to talk to him about the songs belonging to the drum. His father had left those drum songs to him—taken the scrolls into the earth, but taught some of the songs to Morris first. The old man who had spoken to the wolves had both named him and taught him a few more songs. Then Bernard had taken over. Those songs had helped Morris, even kept him sane. He was sane now. He wanted her. He wanted to get his shit together and be clean. He wanted to construct a life that she could tolerate.

"Thank you for bringing my next wife," he said to his brother on the phone. "I love her and can never thank you enough."

"I got no claim on her," said his brother, who was very surprised.

"You sure as hell don't," said Morris.

"She's got kids," said John.

"Don't I know it. And don't give me any of that shit about getting herself laid for food. I want to know something. Why I saw men die for oil in this country where a woman has to sell herself for bread and peanut butter."

"Macaroni too," said John.

"The hell with you. I want to know why I lost my eyes for that. It should not be."

"Okay now," said John, "don't go off on that track."

"I'm going to have her," said Morris.

"You're not ordering a Happy Meal," said John. "She's no Happy at all that I could tell. But then again, she can talk straight at you."

"I'm going to do more," said Morris.

"And what is that?"

"I'm going to help her raise her kids. I'm going to give her all my money. I'm going to teach them everything I know."

"Well, good luck to you then, brother."

Morris hung up the phone, quiet with ecstasy. In his mind Ira drove the truck and they put the kids in the jump seats right behind. Tipi canvas and poles and their suitcases of regalia corded down in the truck bed. Him on the passenger's side. They were going to the big arbor powwows in Montana where the drum entered you straight up from the earth. Yes, it will be a beautiful, new life, thought Morris. I'm just going to lay here and pile on the details. I'll play my own tape in my head. Let's see, first I'll buy her a soft fleecy tight-fitting sweater through which I will feel her breasts with my hands. And food, we'll have food. Maybe all kinds of waffles in a restaurant. Juneberries. We'll pick from a roadside bush. The only thing is, I've seen her face for the last time, maybe. Probably. This made Morris weep. His eyes felt deliciously soothed, but the tears stung his raw cheeks.

Bernard checked the gauges on the boilers and went down his twenty-item checklist. He made sure his crew was keeping the emergency room entrance free and clear of drifting snow. He helped clean a hospital room, using proper infection-control procedures. He ordered lightbulbs and did a small repair on the intercom system. Then he sat down in his office, drank a cup of strong tea, and thought he'd go up next and check on the drum. What had happened surprised him, but at the same time he had expected something like it. Ever since his children had grown up and moved to Fargo and his wife had followed, he had wondered why he couldn't make himself move away to be near them. Though they visited often, he missed out on his grandchildren growing up. And he missed out on living with his wife, although it seemed like they got along better now. Still, he hadn't known why he stayed on the old allotment except that the city was too loud, too fast and cramped for space. There were only sidewalks to walk on, no paths. Perhaps, he thought, someone needed to keep up the old house. There was his hospital job, but he could have quit that. He was over retirement age anyway.

No, the reason he stayed had not come clear until it was piercingly apparent. He'd stayed for the drum. He had the most intimate knowledge of it, knew the sequence of all the songs, could bring together those who possessed those songs he'd forgotten. He alone could fit the scraps together. And he had, as best he could, in these past few months. His waiting was over now and he and Morris would sing the healing songs, softly enough, after the doctors did their rounds. Seraphine would come. He thought of Seraphine and of the strange thing about her scar.

Seraphine had been raised in a traditional way by her grandparents and she spoke little English. But then her grandparents died and Seraphine was sent to boarding school. Bernard recalled that life well, for he had been there, too, in his own day. Sometimes all of the children in the rows of beds cried at night and it was the saddest sound Bernard had ever heard. It was forbidden to speak what the teachers called Indian; sometimes those words seemed to inflame a special wrath from the teachers and the matrons who took care of the children. One day, Seraphine forgot or rebelled and began to speak her own language and would not stop. The matron was showing girls how to mend cushioned chairs. In her hand there was a thick needle for sewing together upholstery. She turned and struck Seraphine. The needle ripped across the girl's face, and although the doctor who sewed the wound together was sensitive and careful, the scar of speaking her language remained across her lips all of her life.

Bernard thought about Seraphine as a little girl and about the wolves who had talked to Ira's father and about the curved bones in the drum. He thought about Shawnee and her stark little heart-shaped face. And about those women who had brought the drum here from the east. Everything now fit. The little girl had come home and she had saved a girl, a relative, a sister. Bernard promised the drum that he would teach Shawnee everything he could, before she went away. She and her brother and sister would not be with him long, not if Morris had anything to say about it. But then, who knew? Who could tell what Ira was thinking?

Ira was staring at Apitchi. She couldn't sleep. She had got up to watch him. It was impossible to tell whether he was better or worse or just the same. His arm seemed even thinner than a few hours ago, and as she stroked it she felt his slim bones and tried not to let her throat shut with fear. *You'll be all right, you'll be all right*, she prayed. She closed her eyes and tried to send her spirit out of her body into his body, she tried to make her spirit fight everything that hurt him, she tried to make him well. She opened her eyes, tears fell on her hands, and she thought, *Any moment I'll start raving at the mouth. I'll start making those God bargains people do. I'll scream my fucking head off and I'll beat myself up.* But she did nothing, only sat there for a long time more, holding his arm.

She was no Christian, certainly no Catholic, but she wasn't of her father's conviction, either. An odd thing came into her mind suddenly. She realized that her father's ceremonial pipe, a sacred pipe, had survived the fire. It was the only thing besides what they were wearing, and the blankets on the ground outside the house, now under the snow. The pipe had survived exactly because she was so careless with these old beliefs. Her father had told her that when he died she should put his pipe in the woods, in a hidden place, and go and get it when she needed it. There were plenty of times since then she might have needed it, but the truth was she had forgotten all about her father's pipe. Well, she'd go out there now and she'd find it, hidden in a hollow log under rocks in a place halfway to Bernard's.

"I don't know about these things," she said out loud. "I don't know." This business about the drum sounding. This man with the eyes not closing. What, had Morris seen too much? Join the club. Was it the war maybe? Was it looking at himself in the mirror? But he had a kind face as long as he closed his eyes. Even, he would be called good-looking. Basically. Without the eyes, again. I'm starting to like him. Ira grabbed her hair. I hate looking at my face now. I don't know. And I don't know either about myself as a mother. No good, maybe. I know I love them. I know I give up things for them. I don't have men. I don't have lots of things. But why did I go in that bar on this one night of all fucking nights instead of going home? How did all of this get set into motion? Was it the oatmeal?

The last pan of fucking slop? How come I didn't walk to Bernard's then, and borrow some food and catch a ride in and out with a trustworthy person? Was it because I never thought of it, or was it because I wanted—just for a moment, or one night, just an evening, really—to get away from my kids?

She had put her hands on her head again and tugged at and messed up her hair. After a while she smoothed it down and wiped her face. Stupid drama. She whispered to Apitchi, "I am going to take care of you real good when you get well." She put her hand on his chest and felt his ribs go up and down. The regularity of his breath calmed her and she sat for a long time with him like that, just letting her hand rise and fall.

The sun blared down, slats of blinding white through the hospital blinds, the intense brilliance after a storm. Ira woke. Apitchi woke. The girls woke. Morris. Even Bernard, who got a nap in, woke. It was that disorienting day that always occurs after a storm, when there is no school so kids come in to work with parents, or the parents stay home and change shifts around. All routine is shot to hell, yet everything that needs to run, does run. The roads are not yet plowed out. Houses are covered. Or the ashes of houses. Snow blankets the whole reservation. The trees glitter. The open fields are long swoops of white. The reeds sticking out of the sloughs are spears of glowing frost. Under the whiteness the world looks perfectly arranged. Things look settled and planned and accounted for. The business of building and digging and tearing up the earth is halted. And yet, you will see that the roads that matter, the ones most necessary, are cleared between people. Just one lane at first. The plows push away the snow with a cheerful energy. By the end of the day there will again be a pattern of trails.

In the service bathroom, Bernard washed his face and combed back his hair. He smoothed his shirt down his arms and adjusted his belt, then brushed his teeth and stuck his toothbrush in his shirt pocket. He got some tea and talked to a few people, telling them that he was going to use the drum. He went back to the office area and punched his time card out. As he walked up the back stairs he sang low, under his breath, the first song that the little girl had taught to Old Shaawano. But he prayed his own prayer, and as he climbed toward the drum, he begged the guardians from the earth's four directions, and the one from beneath, and the one from above, to draw close and listen.

PART FOUR

REVIVAL ROAD

The Chain

Faye Travers

Over the entryway of our local general store, the head of an eastern coyote is mounted, teeth set and bared in pink, plastic gums, yellow glass eyes fierce and wide. It pains me to look at the poor, snarling mask, such a misrepresentation of coyote nature. The two I've seen gave penetrating stares and were calm. They veered from my presence and disappeared into the cut over undergrowth. One of them carried a limp, brown mouse. People generally believe that our east coast coyotes are crossed with dogs, but that is not true. They have actually crossed with the Canadian gray wolf, and in the process have grown large or fallen mysteriously silent. Like many who have adapted to survive in the eastern seaboard states, coyotes have become reserved and self-contained. They almost never raise yipping howls of joy over a kill, nor do they cry out when returning to their dens. They know better. There is no closed season and no hunting limit on their lives.

Still, some nights when they feel secure in their presence, and are overjoyed and thrilled, or just need to talk, they pour looping yodels for hours from the cliffs in the game park and from that end of the road where Kit Tatro lives. Elsie hears them first, wavering above the Bach, and punches the pause button on the CD player's remote control. If the howl persists we go outside to sit on the back porch and listen. In mid-September, as the nights and mornings are growing crisp and cool and the deer are retreating from the roads and orchards into the densest brush they can find, it seems to us that the music of the coydogs, as they are mistakenly called, is the music of all the broken and hunted creatures who survive and persist and will not be eliminated. For there they are, along with the ravens, destroyed and returned.

One night, almost a year and a half after changing the back door locks, we are sitting in wicker armchairs on the back screen porch, listening. Between coyote intervals, Elsie and I hear steps crunch down the cinders of the driveway and slap softly along the flagstone walk that rounds the corner of the house. Neither of us speaks a word, though I am astounded and disbelieving. We both know who it is, and also where he is headed. In addition, it is then that I know for certain that mother knew all about those visits to me in the night. Surely she would utter some startled challenge otherwise. There is a half moon out but the porch is in complete shadow, and Elsie and I are invisible. Kurt walks up the steps, the screen door whines softly open. He enters the porch and steps toward the door with the changed lock. The instant I realize that he is going to try the door I feel a pang of sympathy for him and scrape my foot on the painted floorboards. He freezes.

"Sit down, please sit down," I say. "Elsie and I are listening to the coyotes before we turn in."

He gropes for a chair, lowers himself into it right next to me. Krahe has quick social reflexes. Without revealing a trace of embarrassment and without acknowledging the awkwardness of the situation, he begins a polite conversation. Elsie answers his questions about her health in more detail than he probably wishes, but she is being game about the whole thing.

I have seen Kurt from time to time at a distance and even said hello to him once at the general store, beneath the snarling glass-eyed head. After I changed the lock, I stopped answering Kurt's calls. To find that he has, perhaps, been intermittently trying the back door is disturbing to me, and also touching. He sits so close in the dark, perhaps without knowing exactly my position, that the warmth his body sheds drifts along my skin.

"What have you been doing?" It is a light conversational question asked in a tone of voice that makes it into a deep and unanswerable query. What *have* I been doing?

"Lately?" I suppose my voice is wary.

"In general."

"We have a lot to do," I say, although things have actually been slow.

"People die."

"It's not only death," says Elsie. "Sometimes people want to downsize, dramatically. Or they move into assisted living."

"Assisted living. *Beistehendsleben*. That sounds better."

"I'm turning in," Elsie says, and then she gets up and walks into the house. I try to rise, too, but Kurt puts his hand on my arm (he knows exactly where I am) and says, "Don't go."

I am a nondescript-looking person, dark hair, dark eyes, fair skin. A face that is neither flashy nor plain. Medium build, medium height. My size is always medium, my pants length regular. I favor neutral colors. Medium heels. There is really nothing memorable or interesting or odd or certainly beautiful about me. So when Krahe touches me and I feel very suddenly that I am all of these things— odd, beautiful, interesting, drawn in color—it is very difficult. I sit back, his hard-palmed hand still on my arm. I am not capable of moving away. He speaks to me.

"I don't understand it," he says.

Outside in the dense black thicket of weeds and scrub that surrounds the mowed portion of the yard, a few hold-out fireflies pulse. Sometimes the wind takes them, scattering their lights. Beyond the tall grass the orchard weeps fruit. The branches of the old trees are loaded with tough little apples that the bears like. I've seen one on a dark afternoon, browsing there. Maybe there's one now.

"Do bears come out at night?" I ask him. I can't think of what to say, and he doesn't answer. "Because I think there might be one in the orchard."

"We never talked. You never answered your phone. You walked away from me."

"I still don't want to talk. There isn't anything to say."

"Of course there is, there is a lot to say. Why did you do it?"

"I had to do it."

"Listen, I have not gone to a woman since you locked your door on me. I have been waiting; I work with stone. I know how to wait, but tonight I couldn't help myself."

His voice is so raw I put my hands over my eyes. I am silent, paging through my thoughts like a diary, knowing that anything I say will be wrong. Or worse than wrong. I am so afraid that my hand shakes and I know my voice would quiver if I spoke out loud. The last crickets in the grass are seething and sighing, and I listen to them, clinging to my silence with desperation now, waiting for him to leave. He stirs and stretches his arm out and touches mine. I close my eyes and a kind of brilliance is wheeling there, a green, blazing circle. We sit together for a long time, not talking, not saying anything. At last, Kurt tells me things I've heard before. Other men have said these things to me. It is almost a relief to hear them. His voice floats up in the dark, disembodied, talking and talking: I am cold. I am strange. I have abandoned him. I have hurt him. I begin answering by rote, apologizing, but not explaining. We fill a crack with words that freezes and becomes a rift that keeps widening until a gulf filled with words plunges down between us. After that we just kept throwing our words into the pit. I know there must be better ways, forms of communication that work, ways that women manage to stay with men and men with women. But what are they, what can they be, other than words? The words collect between us until the coyotes start up. Then we fall quiet, sit there together, and he holds my hand. It seems to me that we are closer, listening to that unknown language pouring out of unknown heart, than we were when we tried to exchange our words. And maybe even closer still after the coyotes are finished, when he does not try to sleep with me, but leaves. And closest of all when I go inside, close the door behind me, bolt it, and walk up the stairs alone.

I sleep so heavily that I forget where I am in the morning and for a few seconds I am oddly suspended. I could be anywhere, dead or still dreaming. But when I open my eyes I have the feeling that I've just returned from an unknown journey. My vision's sharper and there is a newness to my familiar windows, the green pine tips outside, the thin light of autumn. My room is painted a pale cream color and for a few minutes I watch the light move through the tree branches outside and pool across the wall with its formal bookshelves stacked with year after year of journals, notebooks, diaries. Something about last night, despite the waste of words and my fear, has caused this surprised and secret calm.

Sipping thick coffee downstairs, I watch my mother carefully as she slices and chews the same dry toast she makes for herself every morning. This will be our routine every day until she dies, but she won't take me with her, as in my childish wish. No, I'll be left on this earth to make what I can of my own days.

"Let's sell the business," I say to her.

She turns to me; her delicately slanted eyes have a dark shine to them, a wary challenge. Of course she has always known what she can expect from me, and she has counted on that.

"And do what?" she asks.

"Let's be wholesale importers and go traveling. We'll have a house on Grandma's land and I'll write. The history of the drum. Everything Bernard told us. Or poems. Poems to Netta. We can do anything."

She ignores the fact I've mentioned Netta. Pretends not to hear.

"On what money?"

"Let's sell the house, too."

"No, we can't, we can't do that." She shakes her head, staring at me as one does in the first shock of panic or betrayal. She tries to right herself. "You're talking wild stuff!" Her mouth sags a little to one side and I see, with the most wrenching tenderness, how old she really has become. It never was my sister's loss, or the loss of my father, that bound me to this place. It was my loyalty to my mother and the determination that she should not live a life of grief alone. But I see now that she has done that anyway—for what has my presence been to her but a reflecting mirror? I have matched the gentleness and precision of her life with mine. We've really been one person, she and I. But we must go deeper now, and perhaps apart. We must see what each of us is made of, what differing stories. I have always been afraid of talking to my mother on this level, of breaking through the comforting web of our safe behavior. We have knitted it daily and well.

"Where were you that day?" I ask.

"What day?" She doesn't look at me. She pretends this is a normal question.

"The day she stepped out of the tree."

"Jumped?"

"No, she stepped off a high branch. Daddy let me drop. She saw him let me fall. Maybe she thought I was dead. I don't know. She just stepped off. The car was gone. You were off somewhere. Where?"

Now she looks straight at me with the crust of toast in her fingers, and sees that I am going to wait until she answers me. She swallows her bit of bread.

"She stepped from the branch," she says.

She nods and shuts her eyes as though looking into herself, and I know she has always seen another picture and believed another story: which one exactly doesn't matter—it is just that it had to do with forgiving me, which she has done every single day. And I fear that she cannot stop forgiving me even now. But then she opens her eyes, and with the air of having made a decision, she speaks.

"I was with someone."

"You had an affair?" I ask this stupidly, for now I'm the surprised one.

She nods and says quietly, "I was not home very much at all. Don't you remember?"

I'm quiet and at a loss for a moment, then I ask, suddenly shy, "Did you love him?"

"Of course." She is looking down at her hands. "Inordinately, foolishly," she whispers, then looks up at me. "But that is the way people should be loved."

We stare endlessly into each other's eyes, which is a very hard thing to do with your mother. It is scarily intimate to gaze into the source of your life. But I know what freedom she is offering to me now. I am in that moment so truly alone that my breath goes out of me, and I feel a bit light-headed. I have to close my eyes and then I have a strange sensation. First, I feel her flowering above me, a leafed-out tree filling the sky with darkness, growing best at the expense of what's beneath. Her guilt has been greater, deeper, and so black I've lived in its shadow. But suddenly, the sun is shining directly on me; I feel it. The brightness and steadiness and softness of light warms my skin and fills the room. When I open my eyes she is still there, but she isn't forgiving me anymore. No, it is I who am forgiving her.

As a result of having his marijuana crop, the main source of his winter income, destroyed last summer, Tatro has finally discovered what kind of Indian he is. He has done this not by tracking his bloodline back through dusty genealogies, but by consulting a shaman. Broke, he decided to start over. Find a new path. My sly revenge has backfired, as most revenges do. Elsie actually likes him to bend her ear, she finds him entertaining. So it is my own fault that I learn, contrary to any expectation I might have formed, that there are a number of practicing shamans right here in New Hampshire. A sort of underground network surrounds each shaman— people who know people who know people . . . that sort of thing. Through these contacts a person who needs to consult a shaman can trace his or her way to the center of the web.

Later on that day, Elsie is talking to Kit, who has stopped by on his way out to hunt, though I'm sure it isn't even bow or muzzle-loading season yet. Maybe he is putting his marijuana crop to bed or preparing a new spot for next year. I try to edge past them, but Elsie won't have it.

"Excuse me, I've got to—"

"Stay here," says Elsie. "Kit's telling me something very interesting."

"So they don't advertise," she goes on.

"Oh, some do. There are little newspapers that go in for that sort of thing." He is very serious. "But of course the really good ones don't need to, they are known by reputation."

"Their powers, I suppose."

He nods and tells us that the shaman he consulted gave him a blanket and a water bottle and then put him out in his backyard to fast for four days. The shaman made a circle around him and told him to stay in it. Then the shaman went back into his house and lived his ordinary life while Kit sat in the circle through a sunny afternoon, a cold night, a light drizzle in the morning, and so on. Four days of it. From time to time the shaman came out of the house and burned sweet grass or sage and fanned the smoke onto Tatro. During the four days, Kit was supposed to have a vision that would give him his financial bearings and tell him about his own tribal origins. But he didn't really have a vision, it turned out. He ended his fast dizzy, sick, calm, but utterly miserable because he'd found no answers except, perhaps, that he should visit an employment agency. It was on the way home that it happened, though, like a thunderclap.

Driving the two-lane highway, Kit passed a sleek RV, only to find there were a line of them before him, all the same, going no more than 50 mph. Irritated and anxious to get home, he passed another RV and crept up behind the next one. Kit wasn't the sort to putz along in the group and he was determined to travel at his own speed. He made it around six before he realized that they were all the same make—Winnebago. But that didn't faze him. No, he said, he had to be hit on the head by the spirits to see it. As he passed another RV on a slight uphill, a red Jeep Cherokee came barreling at him out of nowhere. As Kit swerved, his first terrified thought was *I should have stayed with the Winnebagos*. Even as he wrenched back into the right-hand lane, he braced himself, sure he'd smash into one of them. But to his surprise a space had opened. The Winnebagos had seen his plight and parted to take him in. All of this happened in a second or two, the miss and entry each only cleared by inches. As Tatro floated on, driving, half out of his body, the terror left him and in its place there grew a singular joy. He was safe, he was at ease, taken in, accepted. He belonged.

We all gave that a long beat of silence.

"So you think you're a Winnebago?" I ask.

Kit Tatro puts his hands up, and Elsie smiles and won't speak.

"We prefer to be called Ho-chunks," he says.

"There was a Cherokee. Why couldn't you have been a Cherokee?"

"Remember, the Cherokee nearly killed me. I figure that we might have been traditional enemies."

I hope he's kidding when he says that, but he doesn't seem to have a sense of humor about this.

"So your vision consists of a brand name. You are a brand name?" I can't help myself.

Kit puts his hands up again as if to say, Don't ask me. "I'm doing research now. I'll tell you all about it if you like."

Then Kit Tatro walks off into the woods just behind our house. He is carrying with him not a musket, this time, but his bow with the arrows fitted into a graceful outrigger-type rack. He is dressed not in the usual hunter orange or camouflage, but in a radiant buck-skin jacket and black jeans. He is carefully shaved and the long hair he has been growing out all year tosses across his shoulders. Actually, he does not seem to have been tending a marijuana crop. And one wouldn't like to see him gut a deer in that jacket without an apron—the unmarked leather is spotless and soft as caramel. He nods to me as he crosses the edge of our yard. As he disappears, striding along in his boots, hair flowing behind him, he looks less like the forlorn wannabe I am used to seeing. He has more presence somehow, more attitude, a new gravity. It really seems like he is someone.

*   *   *

Dear Faye and Elsie,

I have been meaning to write to you for a long time now. Please accept my apology on this delay. Things have been very busy with the drum ever since last winter. At that time an incident occurred.

*A family of four—three children and their mother—
have lived near me. Last winter, while the mother was
gone, the house burned down with the children getting
out in time. It was a subzero night and the oldest girl,
named Shawnee, decided to take her little brother and
sister through the woods to my house. There is a shallow
ravine that fills up with snow just before you get to my
yard. All three plunged down into it. They very well
might have froze. Shawnee said that she was having a
dream, and the others had blacked out and given up,
when she heard the sound of a drum. As she describes it,
the sound drew her up. It got louder and louder until
she reached my house with her brother and sister. All of
this time, I was asleep. The drum was with me as it
always is. I heard nothing. To my ear, the drum was
silent.*

*I wanted to tell you this as a way of thanking you.
The drum is in regular use now, and you are always
welcome wherever the drum is.*

*My father was the one who sold the drum to the old
Indian agent, Jewett Tatro, shortly before he moved
back east along with his collection. Selling that drum
was one of the things my father most regretted having
done in his life. When he spoke about it, he would hang
his head and stare at the floor for a long time. It was as
if he was looking right through the floor. You couldn't
talk to him at those times.*

*With the drum back, there is a good feeling here.
People have come together around it. I am surprised.
That young girl Shawnee has moved back with her*

*mother to a house built on the site of the old one. Our
housing authority did come through there pretty good.*

Sincerely,

Bernard Shaawano

*   *   *

So who can say where we'll find our rescue?

Still, this is not a story about the kind of revivals that occurred so long ago at the end of our road. For to suddenly say, *I believe, I am convinced,* even *saved,* and to throw myself into Native traditions as Kit Tatro wishes so sincerely to do, is not in my character. Salvation seems a complicated process with many wobbling steps, and I am skeptical and slow to act. We will travel back home to be part of what Bernard calls feasting the drum, and we also will learn the songs that belong to it. But I'm sure that in spite of my impulsive suggestions to Elsie, it will take us years of prudent thinking and financial juggling to actually change the circumstances of our life. Yet change they will. Even now, nothing is the same as it was before I reached out of my untested rectitude and stole the drum.

Then, too, sometimes things happen all at once.

I walk often in the woods in the early fall, before the hunters arrive from Concord and the suburbs of Boston and proceed to blast away at dogs and cows. Every year there is a goodly take of tame creatures. And people. Housewives are blown from their backyards when hanging out laundry. Flame orange is in. Nobody wears white mittens or caps. Hunters react to the flash of white, sure they've glimpsed a deer's flag, a panicked stot. And so I go out walking before the carnage begins. The day is fine. There is a snowmobile path that passes just behind the new development and then up

269

across the small tabletop pastures, a stand of birch, and into rocky pine and hemlock terrain. The trail goes straight up in places at such an angle that I can't imagine how the snowmobilers make the climb. In others, it winds among great boulders, some big as houses, and when I walk this part the pine duff and loamy dirt exude a crushed and woody fragrance at my heels.

As always, I am grateful for the stuff of life, the detritus. Things don't know that they're ruined; they glory in it, they fall cheerfully apart or decay flamboyantly. Look at the woods. I gather and closely examine things—a pale leaf, a *Russula*, staghorn moss, and fairy cups. I wonder at their nature, to be so passive and contained. I glimpse the white point of an antler twenty or thirty feet off the trail among rocks and I veer immediately off to pick it from the leaves. But it is not an antler.

I see right away it is actually a rib pulled up from its cage, and as I brush away the leaves I see that the rest of the skeleton is more or less intact and that our friends, the ravens, have neatened up the scene by picking clean the bones. They gather now, interested, laughing in the high hemlocks. I turn over patches of gray fur, strings of white. Around the bones of the neck and mossy scarp of hide, a collar pulled up tight beneath the skull. On the ring of the buckle, a stout clasp is still attached to a chain that must have been pulled taut between two boulders but has gone slack and drapes along the ground. I follow the chain to the rocks and see it is still wedged fast—a short stick that passed through the final link has locked it tight. Maybe if her collar had been leather, I think, there would have been some give. She might have managed over time to slip it over her ears. But it was a tough nylon thing with a heavy buckle and prong, and probably too tight to begin with. So she died here, at the end of it. The blue eye and the brown. The hungry smile.

Coming down off the trail, I am lost in my own thoughts and unprepared when a bear chugs across the path just before it gives out on the gravel road. I am so distracted that I keep walking toward the bear. I only stop when it rears, stands on hind legs, and stares at me, sensitive nose pressed into the air, weak eyes searching. I have never been this close to a wild bear before, but I am not frightened. There is no menace in its stance; it is not even very curious. The bear seems to know who or what I am. The bear is not impressed. I admire his size, blackness, health, gloss, the picture he makes before he vanishes. And he really does disappear. He turns and I see him take one stride before he's swallowed up. That is the only uncanny part—how he's there and then he's not. I am left in a swirl of small woods noises. A squirrel jumps from one branch to another. A chickadee scolds. A twig scrapes somewhere. And then a plane goes over. I keep walking. As I do, I think of the orchard and its ripe apples, heavy loads, and am sure the bear has been there. When I finish my woods loop and come back to the house, then, I walk back to the orchard, wondering if the bear has left a sign, scratch marks on the trees, scat, a footprint.

Nobody has been there to pick the apples except, perhaps, the bear. Wizened, gnarled, hollowed by yellow jackets to crisp husks, the apples lie in windfalls and still burden the trees, even though I see Kurt did a good job. He took out the interior shoots that a tree will grow against itself. He left the lateral branches so the fruit would be easier to pick. Still, I look with surprise and satisfaction on the mess. This is what has become of all those supernal blossoms. These judicious pruning cuts have healed over but the apples were too much. Already there's more damage and dead-wood to be left as it is—I'm quite sure the orchard will not have a savior like Kurt to contend with again. I step toward my sister's tree and see right away that her branch has cracked off under the weight of apples. It has crashed down against the tree, connected only by a few straps of bark. A hard tug and it would lie completely severed in the long, fine, pallor of orchard grass. I sit down with my back against the tree, pull my knees to my chest, and close my eyes. The weak sun flows down on me. Apples are burnishing to cider all around me in soft heaps. I hear them dropping off the trees, and suddenly I wonder what they taste like. I wonder if they're any good. I think that I might eat one.

As I walk through the door of the house, brushing sticks from my hair, the telephone rings. I hesitate, but then rush to pick it up. It is Kurt. Someone has broken into his studio, the renovated barn behind his house. That person has used all of the power equipment that Krahe keeps in the barn to demolish *Number Twenty-one* and all else that he has worked on or produced in the past year, certainly since Kendra's death. Many things that were stored alongside the new projects are also damaged. I have no idea why this particular act of vandalism frees the two of us, but hearing Krahe's agitation and reading his call as a sort of plea, I drive up to the barn to exam-ine the disaster with him. By then, the police have left and there is nothing but splintered wood, shattered rock. All of the broken stuff and the pieces so massive they could only be nicked are scrawled with loops of spray paint. The paint is an intense blue, that blue my mother loves, and in its twizzling energy it is like an obscure but brilliant form of writing. Some new language is at work. The blue is everywhere.

"Who do you think did it?"

He touches my shoulder. Although it has been over a year since Davan's mother and I met on the road, I see her right away. Mrs. Eyke's eyes are pressed like coal into the soft whiteness of her face, and she smiles, but I say nothing.

Kurt is walking around with his hands on his head, groaning, but here's the peculiar thing. He seems more excited than horrified by the trashed scene. He seems more thrilled than bereft. His face is glowing with intensity and his hands fly off his head in big gestures as he talks of the destruction. *Frohlockendzerstorung.* The word invents itself. A nameless wildness bubbles up inside of me and I want to shout. Kurt and I walk across a short piece of field to his house to have some coffee, and as we walk we link arms eagerly, naturally, as if no time had passed, as if there had been no other accidents or grief in the world, but only this one retribution from an unseen hand, which seemed to wreck with more joy than malice, the way a child does, wondering at the breakage and startled to laughter by the noise.

That night I stay with Kurt at his house, and I actually call Elsie to tell her that I won't be coming back until morning. Her voice is careful, perhaps a little sad, but mostly she sounds relieved.

"Good night, dear," she says.

There are other things that she could say to me, things I will never hear. I doubt that many mothers say these things to their daughters. Maybe it would be like telling your daughter the truth about the pain of childbirth. They try to protect us, even when we're middle-aged. So I must supply the words for myself:

Life will break you. Nobody can protect you from that, and living alone won't either, for solitude will also break you with its yearning. You have to love. You have to feel. It is the reason you are here on earth. You are here to risk your heart. You are here to be swallowed up. And when it happens that you are broken, or betrayed, or left, or hurt, or death brushes near, let yourself sit by an apple tree and listen to the apples falling all around you in heaps, wasting their sweetness. Tell yourself that you tasted as many as you could.

I work part of the next afternoon and am driving home early, having sold an Aesthetic Movement rosewood cabinet with lovely Japanese lacquer panels. The piece sat for two years in our shop and Elsie implied several times that it was a mistaken auction purchase on my part and would have to be priced too high to sell to any but the leaf peepers, who would need to hire a delivery service. So I'm happy to sell it—with a cash down payment, no less. I am carrying nearly sixteen thousand dollars in hundred-dollar bills and I am planning how Elsie and I might use this piece of luck. The Eykes' church sign tells me today that God Saves, but I am going to do something less predictable and safe, later. Right now I've decided that this is the day I will visit my sister's grave. This is a thing I do every fall just about this time. It is sort of like putting her to bed for the winter. I'll rake away the leaves to find her grave is littered with twigs or ribbons or bits broken off Styrofoam crosses and summer flower arrangements blown over from other graves. I have brought a plastic trash bag and a short clawlike trowel that clanks in the backseat as I turn down the bumpy cemetery road.

Our child cemetery was established during the flu epidemic of

1918, when Stiles and Stokes suffered a grievous number of losses. Even on the brightest days, the air seems a little darker here. The stone lambs that were popular in the early part of the twentieth century are now weathered into soft lumps. There is a headstone that reads "What wild hopes lie here," and one grave with a small statue of a dog curled at the bottom, as at the foot of that child's bed. There are cherubs of gentle marble and quiet little markers engraved with the outlines of small hands. Six great maples shed pink light and I'm caught up in their cold glow. The pines planted as seedlings here and there are now black-green and tall. I park beneath a group of three that sigh and mumble as I pass among them. My sister's stone marker is very distinctive. It's a carved angel that our mother bought from a church about to be demolished and had engraved with the date and name. Perhaps because the angel was not meant as a memorial in the first place, there is something stealthily alive about her—wings that flare instead of droop, an alert and outwardly directed expression, a hand clutched to her breast not as a gesture of reverence or sorrow, but, I think, breathless delight.

As I am raking away the papery orange and yellow leaves, I turn up a tooth, sharp and vulpine; it gleams ivory white when I polish it on my sweater. I think of Kendra—the tooth would have made a nice earring and she would have worn it with style. I head for the part of the cemetery where she is buried. Kendra's stone is a white marble sculpture. I've never seen it, and when I do I catch my breath. Kurt has made for her the simplest emotional form, a concave circle of Carrara white, both perfect and shadowed. He has never made anything that really moved me before, and I stand there with nothing to say or think at all. After a while, I set the tooth on the stone and walk back to my sister's place.

The scent of warmed earth, the mold of dead leaves, the angle of sun on my shoulders suddenly floods me with a sharp happiness and I look up to see that the ravens are crossing and circling. Silent, they pass beyond a fringe of pines. When I was small, I imagined that my sister and I would meet after death in the form of birds. I turn back to the earth and keep scratching at the ground, throwing the faded petals of plastic flowers and shatters of plastic into my trash bag. It is a long time before I finish.

On the way back to my car, I pass the space in the pines that gives out on a cliff. There must be an air bank rising and falling because the ravens are playing there. I watch as they throw themselves off a branch into the invisible stream. Over and over, they tumble into the air and fly upside down. They twist themselves upright and soar off, sink, then shoot up again over the lip of rock. Say they have eaten and are made of the insects and creatures that have lived off the dead in the raven's graveyard—then aren't they the spirits of the people, the children, the girls who sacrificed themselves, buried here? And isn't their delight a form of the consciousness we share above and below the ground and in between, where I stand, right here? As I think this, one raven veers toward me, zipping straight at my face, but I do not flinch as its wings brush through my hair. I call out my sister's name in the wildness of the moment. Then I turn and watch the raven swerve rapidly over the tops of the pines, until she plummets down the cliff again, laughs, and disappears.

AUTHOR'S NOTE

What happened to the girl in the beginning of "The Shawl" is based on the experience of an elderly man who told this to Toba-sonakwut. I thank him for trusting me with the story. There are other very similar folk tales; one appears in Willa Cather's *My Ántonia*. So I can only conclude that all stories exist in continuum and that this actually happened. Yet I also think that the story runs counter to real facts about the shyness and politic avoidance that wolves show to humans. I've tried to stay true to both. As in all of my books, no sacred knowledge is revealed. I check carefully to make certain everything I use is written down already. Thomas Vennum's *The Ojibwe Dance Drum: Its History and Construction* was particularly helpful to me. I want to thank my editor, Terry Karten, for her clear eye; Trent Duffy, for his close work; and Gail Caldwell, for deepening my vision of this book.